Red sky at night . . .

The landscape had turned red, the setting sun casting a crimson pall over the flat swamp canals and the few trees that straggled out on the distant hammocks. Red . . . it was the color that seemed to fill his lungs as he gasped against the humid air, struggling to breathe. It was the color of the saw grass, the color of the single egret that perched in a distant tree.

Rat-a-tat. Bullets flew by him again.

Then he felt a pain, sharp and piercing, sting his temple. Instinctively he reached up to touch his head, then stared at his fingers.

Red . . . it was the color of the night. It was the color of blood—his blood, seeping over his fingers.

Then the red landscape was completely lost in ebony darkness.

Dear Reader,

Once again, we're bringing you a month of books that have us excited and, we think, will excite you, too. First up is the final book in Lucy Hamilton's Dodd Memorial Hospital Trilogy, *Heartbeats*. Nurse Vanessa Rice and Detective Clay Williams made their debuts in the first book of the trilogy, and two less-likely lovers could hardly be found. But in this book they learn that differences can be exciting as they fight for a future together.

Another special book is Lee Magner's *Mustang Man*. Lee has published a number of romances in the past, but we think she's really come into her own with her first novel for Silhouette Books. *Mustang Man* combines adventure, suspense and, of course, a strong dose of high-voltage romance to come up with a reading experience you won't soon forget.

Dallas Schulze is back with *Donovan's Promise*, a deeply emotional look at a once-married couple who are destined to get back together again, and Heather Graham Pozzessere visits her home state of Florida in *Angel of Mercy*, an Everglades adventure with a romance that sizzles.

Next month, as a special treat, look for *From Glowing Embers*, the first of a new miniseries from popular author Emilie Richards. Of course, Emilie will be in good company next month and in the months to come, when you can expect to see books from new discoveries like Andrea Parnell and old favorites like Parris Afton Bonds, Kathleen Eagle and Nora Roberts, to name only a few. As always, when you're looking for romance, you can count on Silhouette Intimate Moments.

Leslie J. Wainger
Senior Editor

Heather Graham Pozzessere

Angel of Mercy

Silhouette Intimate Moments

Published by Silhouette Books New York

America's Publisher of Contemporary Romance

To Cherry Adair Tatum,
lots of love and many thanks.

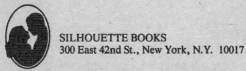

SILHOUETTE BOOKS
300 East 42nd St., New York, N.Y. 10017

ISBN: 0-373-07248-1

First Silhouette Books printing July 1988

Printed in the U.S.A.

Books by Heather Graham Pozzessere

Silhouette Intimate Moments

Night Moves #118
The di Medici Bride #132
Double Entendre #145
The Game of Love #165
A Matter of Circumstance #174
Bride of the Tiger #192
All in the Family #205
King of the Castle #220
Strangers in Paradise #225
Angel of Mercy #248

HEATHER GRAHAM POZZESSERE

considers herself lucky to live in Florida, where she can indulge her love of water sports, like swimming and boating, year round. Her background includes stints as a model, actress and a bartender. She was once actually tied to the railroad tracks to garner publicity for the dinner theater where she was acting. Now she's a full-time wife, mother of four and, of course, a writer of historical and contemporary romances.

Chapter 1

The car fishtailed and spun crazily. Brad compressed his lips in silence to bring the Chevy under control again. If he went off either side of the two-lane road, he would crash straight into swampland, into the endless "river of grass," a hot and humid, godforsaken hell on earth. He was heading west on Alligator Alley—a road that offered a weary traveler just about nothing at all except for the miles and miles of mud and muck and saw grass, the occasional cry of a bird and the silent, unblinking stares of an abundance of reptiles.

No phones here. No fast-food stands, no gas stations. Just miles and miles of nothing but the Florida Everglades.

Brad hated swamps.

Not that it mattered much now.

He straightened the car and quickly looked into the rearview mirror. Michaelson was still after him.

Glancing ahead, Brad noted that steam was pouring from the old Chevy's front. Hell, he hadn't even managed to steal a decent automobile. And now here he was in the middle of nowhere, the object of a hot pursuit, cruising in an old rattletrap of a car that was about to die on him.

Sweat beaded along his brow. Without the car, what would he do? He hadn't seen a call box for miles and miles. There was only the narrow, two-lane road, stretching through this eternity of swamp. He wouldn't stand a chance on foot. He'd be a sitting duck. They'd shoot him down in a matter of seconds.

Something popped and whizzed in the engine and a cloud of steam billowed out, obscuring Brad's view of the road. He squinted; there seemed to be some kind of a dirt road up ahead, to the left heading southward. Another glance in the rearview mirror told him that Michaelson was almost on him. He had to take the chance.

With a sudden, vicious swing, Brad veered to the left. The wheels bucked as the car bolted and groaned. It was a road—of sorts. Saw grass slapped against the body and windows as the car plunged along. Brad could hear the eternal drone of the insects, even above the groan of the Chevy's overheated motor.

The car pitched into mud. Brad wrenched hard against the steering wheel. In growing desperation he tried to floor the gas pedal, hoping to bounce out of the mire. The wheels spun; the Chevy remained stuck in the mire.

Brad slammed out of the car. Black mud oozed over his leather shoes and knit socks, soaking his trousers up to his calves.

He paused, listening.

He could hear the motor of the approaching car—
Michaelson's car. Following.

There was a sharp retort in the air. Gunfire. A bullet whizzed by Brad's ear. The sharp retort sounded again. Another bullet. Closer. *Whish*. Nearly nicking his ear, making a sick, plopping sound as it embedded itself in the swamp.

Brad turned and ran. His gun was back at the site of the drop-off, along with Taggart's body. Damn, he couldn't even go down fighting. There were three of them with Magnums and sawed-off shotguns, and there was him, without even a nail file.

What a bloody stupid way to go down. Running, unarmed, in an infested, insect-laden, swarming, sullen, putrid swamp.

The mud sucked at his feet with every step he took. He hadn't gone twenty paces before he had lost both shoes. Running was agony. There was nowhere to run to, anyway. Nothing but saw grass and rattlers, coral snakes and gators, water moccasins and mosquitoes...and swamp. Every time he put his foot down, he wondered what he would land on next.

Another bullet zinged by, close to his face. He felt the air rush against his chin. He was dimly aware that night was coming. The song of the insects was growing louder; the horizon had turned red, bloodred. Turning around to look behind him, he could see nothing but grass, tall grass, like needles, raking against his hands, raking against his cheeks. Saw grass. River of grass...that was what the Indians called this place, this Everglades. And it was. An endless river of grass, for as far as the eye could see.

Another bullet whined and whizzed by in a deadly, speeding whisper. Brad inhaled sharply and felt a stab of pain. His lungs were bursting, his hands were cut and bleeding, but he kept on running, always running. Suddenly he sank, plunging into a canal. Kicking and thrashing, he came up, sputtered and staggered onto higher land. He turned, resting his hands on his knee-caps, struggling for breath. All he could see was the grass. Were they still following him?

"Think we hit him?"

He heard the faint voice. Probably Suarez—he was the bloodthirsty one.

Someone snickered. "Does it matter? If we did not get him, Old Tom Gator will."

There was a spate of raucous laughter, then Michaelson, who never laughed, never even twisted his lip in the facsimile of a smile, spoke quietly.

"Keep still. Listen. See if we cannot lodge a bullet in his brain. I do not like leaving fate to Old Tom Gator."

Brad groaned inwardly and straightened, inhaling again for all he was worth to run once more.

The landscape had turned red, the setting sun casting a crimson pall over the flat swamp waters and the few trees straggled out upon the distant hammocks. Red...it was the color that seemed to fill his lungs as he gasped against the humid air, struggling to breathe. It was the color of the saw grass, the color of the single egret that perched in a distant tree, balanced upon one leg.

Rat-a-tat. Bullets flew by him again.

Then he felt a pain, sharp and piercing, stinging his temple. Instinctively, he reached up to touch his head, then stared at his fingers.

Red. It was the color of the night. It was the color of blood—his blood, seeping over his fingers.

He had to keep going. The hum of the insects seemed louder as he staggered along. He could hear no whispers from behind him, no laughter, no words. He gazed up at the sky and saw that the sun was falling. A coolness was descending. The breeze picked up.

Chills shot through him.

Red would not be the color of night. It would be black here—pitch-black. Florida Power and Light did not call upon the snakes and the reptiles and the birds and the wild orchids. Night would descend, and with it would come a blackness like ebony, sleek and impenetrable.

In truth, the horizon was still streaked with pinks and golds and burning reds. Yet Brad could no longer see them. His mind was sinking into the ebony darkness, just as his body was slipping into the oozing muck. All sounds around him were fading to a soft, lilting drone.

He was losing consciousness. He couldn't allow himself that luxury; he knew that. If he fell here, he would not survive the night. He would drown in the mire, become easy prey for the predators of the swamp, provide endless fuel for the bloodsuckers.

He could not fall.

But he couldn't go any farther. Besides, there was nowhere to go. Staggering, he paused. Everything blurred before his eyes.

He heard a humming sound. More bugs. Hell, he'd never seen or heard so many damned insects in his life. They were coming after him now; a herd of them, flying, floating together, in mass.

They were almost upon him. The noise suddenly cut off. Brad pitched forward, certain that he was crashing straight into the horde of insects.

But he fell against something hard. And he was dimly aware that something soft touched him.

Then the red landscape was completely enswamped by the ebony darkness.

Wendy screamed at first sight of the man. For several frozen seconds, after she had squinted against the mirage and cut the motor on her airboat, she simply stared at him.

He resembled the creature from the Black Lagoon. He was an apparition, a giant pile of black mud, rising before her.

She was accustomed to alligators and snakes and any number of slimy beings, but gigantic mud creatures were not indigenous to the Florida Everglades.

It didn't take her long to realize the figure was that of a man. A tall one, nicely built. Heavily built, she decided, grunting as she tried to drag him onto the airboat. Once she had him there, she paused again, panting for breath, trying to discern the place and extent of his injury. She checked his pulse first. Fortunately, he was still alive.

She slipped a hand into the water of the canal and tried to clean away some of the mud from his face. Against his temple she found the wound—a small gouge, still bleeding. What had he done? Tripped and fallen against something? She shook her head, and a rueful, somewhat contemptuous smile curved her lips. City slicker. It was written all over the man. Beneath the mud she could see a fashionably cut three-piece suit, silk tie and cotton shirt. No shoes at all—probably lost in the muck somewhere. She sighed, shaking her head again. When would these people learn? A swamp was a place to be respected. It was not welcoming to the unwary. And now, what to do with him?

She sat back on her heels, lost in the dilemma. He wasn't seriously injured, so he probably didn't need to be in a hospital. She had no idea where he had come from, so she couldn't really return him anywhere.

She couldn't leave the fool lying in the swamp. It would be tantamount to murder.

Wendy sighed. Maybe he should be in a hospital, but even so, she'd have to take him home first and call Fort Lauderdale for an ambulance or conveyance of some sort. Since her car was up in the garage, she couldn't take him too far herself.

"Well, sir, would you like to come home for dinner?" she murmured to her prone form, then she laughed with dry amusement. It was the first time she had ever asked a man to dinner. Well, except for Leif, and that had been different. They had never exactly asked each other to do anything; tacit consent had always seemed to rule between them.

Putting aside memories of Leif, Wendy settled the mud creature onto the boat, then started the motor and headed into the swampland. She turned on the lights; it was growing dark, and night fell quickly in the swamp.

Two miles inland, she came upon a high hammock and switched off the motor. She docked the boat, then stared at the huddled form again, trying to determine once more what to do. She was beginning to worry because he didn't show signs of coming to. Concussion? Maybe. She needed to clean him up, then she could give his condition a more professional assessment.

After a moment of hesitation, she decided to leave him while she went inside for a stretcher. He was simply too big for her to move without one.

Her house was little more than a cabin, but it was self-sufficient, and she had made it home. A generator provided electricity, and though she bought most of her drinking water, she had a purification system, too. The house itself was a square frame structure with two bedrooms, a living room and a big, eat-in kitchen. Her furniture was Early American, and her windows were dressed in earth-toned gingham drapes. It was possible to sit in the house and imagine that next-door neighbors could be found twenty yards away instead of twenty miles.

Wendy hurried through to the second bedroom and dug beneath the bed for the canvas stretcher. She had no problem carrying the stretcher out to the airboat; it was not so easy getting the man onto it. He was not only tall and very well muscled, he was unconscious, and therefore deadweight. Grunting and panting and working up a sweat, she at last managed to pull him onto the canvas.

His clothing was going to have to go before she brought him in. Not all of it, but she could strip him down to his briefs. Although Wendy lived in the swamp, she tried to keep mud out of her house. She wondered briefly what would happen if he regained consciousness while she was stripping him of his clothing, then shrugged. If he came to, he could damn well help her, and he'd better do so pleasantly. He could have been dead by then without her.

His socks peeled off easily. His suit coat proved to be a problem. She could not lift his shoulders high enough to pull the jacket away.

Wearing thin, Wendy sat back panting. Realizing that his wardrobe was ruined, she decided to cut his clothes away.

Wendy scampered back into the house in search of scissors. In the kitchen, she decided to bring out a bucket of soapy water and a washcloth. Once she had determined a plan, she set about it with a certain energy and will. Although she was handling a complete stranger, it was a little bit late to be reticent about the situation.

She hurried back outside and began cutting away his clothing with a vengeance. She rid him of his jacket, vest, tie and shirt and gently washed away all the muck and mud on his face and his shoulders. She sat back then, studying him and experiencing a shaft of acute discomfort as she did so.

She had thought his complexion was darker; it had only been an illusion created by the swamp muck clinging to his sandy-colored skin. His hair was a tawny color, the type that lightened in sunlight and grew darker in winter. He had a nice-looking face, a ruggedly handsome, masculine face. His nose was long and straight, his brow was high, and his well-defined cheekbones rose above a hard, square jaw. Even in repose, he had a determined look. She wondered how old he was, then guessed that he was between thirty and forty.

He'd been heavy and difficult to lift because he was composed of muscle, sinewed and taut. He was bronzed, as if he spent time in the sun, and he was hard, as if he spent time working with his body. Yes, it was a nice body.

Wendy recoiled quickly from touching him. She gave herself a furious shake, refusing to believe that she could be thinking this way about a stranger's body.

She searched his jacket for a wallet but found nothing except a piece of spearmint gum. When she tried to reach into his trousers' pockets, she found them glued together by dried muck. Determined, she stood, loosened his belt and tried to slip his trousers off. At first she couldn't budge them. Then they suddenly came free and she fell back, landing on her own hind end with the breath knocked out of her and more than his trousers in her hands.

His briefs had come free, too. The man was now stark naked on the canvas stretcher.

Wendy blushed profusely, then froze in a panic as the man stirred and let out a soft groan.

She hadn't been wrong to try to help him, to clean him or cut away his clothing. But she hadn't intended to go this far. What if he awoke now? What was he going to think? How could she ever explain this?

"Damn!" she swore to herself. She rose quickly, rubbing her derriere and thinking that she needed to procure a sheet before the stranger woke up. She tried to run past the man without looking at him, but something wayward within her soul tugged at her, tempting her to take a peek.

He really was a nice example of the human male.

Muscled, trim and lean, with a broad chest tapering to a slim waist and hips and long, muscular legs. His chest was furred in a mat of tawny, red-flecked hair, which became a thin line at his waist and broadened into another thick mat that nested his sexuality. Despite her usual restraint, she felt her heart plummet and hammer, and for the briefest moment she couldn't help thinking that he was, indeed, built very well. She'd been alone for such a long time...

Slightly horrified at her wandering thoughts, Wendy gave herself a shake. It hadn't been that long, and staring at an absolute stranger in such a way seemed so wanton and disrespectful. Strange, but she hadn't even thought about sex in the longest time, and now, just the sight of a man's body had made her mind start playing tricks.

Hot, fiery tears burned her eyelids and she realized she hadn't even had a good cry for a long, long time. But there was no time for that now. She needed to get a grip on herself, get inside the house and get the man a sheet.

"What the hell...?"

Too late. He was awake. The man blinked and struggled to raise himself. His gaze raked over his naked body, then he looked up, and his eyes caught hers. His eyes were tawny, just like his hair. They were neither brown nor green, nor even hazel, but a shade that combined all the colors and became tawny gold.

Tawny eyes, misted in confusion, anger, wariness— a wariness so acute that it frightened her. She took a step back, swallowing, not sure whether to be embarrassed or scared, suddenly wishing that she had left him stuck in the mud.

"Who the hell are you?"

His voice was raspy and deep and not in the least reassuring. The sound of it added another layer to the myriad emotions playing havoc in Wendy's heart. It inspired a certain fear inside of her; it also incited a definite anger.

"Wendy Hawk. Who the hell are you?"

"What?" The wary look shone in his eyes again.

"Who the hell are you?" she repeated irritably. He continued to stare at her, so she nervously went on. "I live here. You fell face forward into my airboat. I've been trying to help you."

Amusement flickered across his face, leaving a smile in its wake. And when he smiled, he was very attractive. "You were helping me—by taking my clothes off?"

She sighed, blushing furiously despite herself. "I didn't mean to—"

"They all just fell off?" he inquired politely.

"No, of course not. You were wearing half of the Everglades. I can't help it if your clothes were so tight that everything came off with one—oh, never mind. I was about to get you a sheet and drag you inside, but apparently you can—" She broke off, gasping as he hopped to his feet. It was one thing to stare at him while he was lying on the ground and unconscious; it was quite another now that he was towering over her, striding toward her with little self-consciousness. "You can walk," she murmured. "Would you stop, please? Haven't you a shred of decency? I'll get you a sheet—"

"I'm sorry," he said pleasantly. That easy grin was still in place and Wendy suddenly realized that his smile was duel-edged. He wasn't sorry one bit. "Frankly, I assumed you'd already had a good eyeful of everything."

"Wait!" she commanded, racing back into the house, spilling half of the things out of the linen closet in her haste to bring him a sheet. He accepted it and wrapped it around his waist.

"It is rather strange, waking up stark naked in the middle of a swamp," he said. His voice was still very deep, the kind of male voice that swept into the system, penetrating. Wendy trembled slightly. Perhaps it was just the night breeze, coming to dispel the dead heat of the day.

"I'm sorry. I was trying to help you."

"I noticed." He laughed, pulling the sheet tighter around his body. "Really. I was just wondering how you would have felt if it had been the other way around."

"Pardon?"

"Well, if I had been trying to help you, and you were the one who had woken up without a stitch of clothing."

"This is ridiculous," Wendy said, wondering if she should have left him in the mud. "There is no comparison. I'd never be in your foolish position. This is swampland. You were wandering around near quicksand pools! If I were you, I would just be grateful for my life."

"Oh, I am grateful. Very grateful," he said softly. He indicated the door behind her. "Were you really going to invite me in?"

Wendy hesitated, uncertain then. She hadn't felt threatened when she'd first dragged him home. Now he seemed dangerous. He might have been out of his element in the swamp, but this man was no fool. He was sleekly muscled and toned as if he were accustomed to taking on physical challenges. And there was an air of tension about him, as if, even when he smiled, he were wary and alert, ever watchful of his surroundings.

"Hey," he reminded her, as if he had read her mind. "I didn't touch *your* clothing. You were the one undressing me down to the buff."

Wendy groped behind her for the doorknob. She opened the door and went in, waiting for him to follow. When he didn't, she paused and looked back.

He'd been examining his clothing. He stared at her with reproach, holding up the bedraggled pieces of his shirt. "I would have stripped on command, if I'd known it meant that much to you," he said.

"I was worried about your life!" she snapped.

He nodded, hitching up his sheet to follow her. "Thanks."

As he came through the doorway he looked around, taking in the cool comfort of the air conditioning and the squeaky-clean butcher-block pass-through to the kitchen. He didn't seem to miss much. His gaze swept the hooked rug and the rocker, the deep, comfortable sofa and the cherry-wood coffee table. When at last he looked back at her, Wendy was glad to see the wary confusion in his eyes once again. His question was very polite.

"Where are we?"

"The Everglades," she replied sweetly.

"But—where?"

"East of Naples, northwest of Miami, almost deadset west of Fort Lauderdale."

A tawny brow arced high. "We're in the middle of the swamp. And you *live* out here?"

"Yes, I do." Wendy smiled pleasantly again, glad to feel that she had the advantage once more. She walked around him to the kitchen. Although she wasn't sure if she wanted a glass of wine, she needed one. And producing vintage wine suddenly seemed like the right thing to do. It would only baffle him more.

She took a bottle of '72 Riesling from the refrigerator and fumbled in a drawer for the corkscrew. Suddenly, she heard his voice behind her.

"Please, let me."

She was startled enough to oblige, letting the corkscrew slip into his hands while she backed against the counter. A tingling warmth swept through her as he brushed by. His chest was still bare and smelled of the soap she had used upon him.

"You still haven't told me your name."

"Bill. Bill Smith."

He was lying. She wondered why. Only criminals lied about their names. He couldn't be a criminal.

Why not? asked a little voice in her head.

The man could very well be a criminal. She had found him facedown in the swamp.

"What were you doing in the swamp?"

The cork popped out into his hand. He lifted the bottle to her and she nervously turned around, searching for glasses. They clinked together when she handed them to him. When he took them, they didn't make a sound. He poured the wine and raised his glass to hers.

"Cheers. I was lost. A fool, just like you said. I'm afraid that I don't know much about this area at all."

Wendy was determined to pry some truth from him. She lifted her glass politely but did not let her eyes waver from his. "A swamp is a strange place to suddenly lose oneself."

"My car broke down." He lifted the bottle and studied the label. When he looked at her again, his voice was soft. "I am grateful to you for helping me. Thank you."

Wendy nodded, unsure of herself. "You should take care of the gash on your forehead."

"Gash?" He frowned and touched his temple. "Oh, right."

"You probably need some stitches."

"No, I'm sure it will be all right. I'm pretty tough."

"I can at least clean it out for you," she offered.

"I'd appreciate that." He touched the wound again, then ran his fingers through his hair. "I'm still pretty muddy."

"Well, you can take a shower for yourself now."

"Is there one? May I?"

"Down the hallway, second door on your left. Please, Mr. Smith, go right ahead."

"Thanks." He handed her his half-consumed glass of wine and strode down the hallway. Wendy heard the door close.

She gnawed on her lower lip for a moment then walked down the hallway, heading for her bedroom. After a moment's hesitation she knelt down and pulled out the bottom drawer of her dresser. She dug around for several seconds and came up with a T-shirt, jeans and a pair of briefs. This man was only a little bit taller than Leif, and they had similar builds.

Back in the hallway, she could hear that the shower was still running. She tapped on the door. "I've left some clothes for you out here. I think they'll fit."

Wendy returned to the kitchen and thoughtfully sipped her wine again. Was she crazy to be helping him? No, of course not. She had known that she couldn't just let him die in the wilderness.

And yet she was wary, concerned by the effect he'd already had on her. Reluctant to think about it, she opened the refrigerator, idly picked out some vegetables and began to slice them. By the time he came out of the shower, clean and dressed with his hair still wet and slicked back, she had added diced chicken to the vegetables and was stir-frying the lot of it in a huge skillet.

He leaned across the counter. "Smells delicious."

"Thank you."

"Does it mean that I'm invited to dinner?"

"You have no choice. I don't think I can get you out of here today."

"Why not?"

"My car is in for repairs, and the garage closed at five. All I have is the airboat. Well, actually, I could take you back to the road and you could hitchhike—"

"I'd much prefer the dinner invitation," he said hastily.

By way of response, Wendy dished the vegetables and meat onto a platter and handed it to him. "Mr. Smith, if you'd set that on the table...?"

"Certainly."

Wendy took brown rice from the stove, emptied it into a bowl and joined him at the kitchen table, which she'd already set for two. He pulled out her chair, then retrieved both their wineglasses and the bottle before sitting down across from her. He smiled at her, and her heart gave a little thud again—she did like that smile.

"Thanks. For everything."

Wendy nodded, almost afraid to speak.

"Whose clothing?"

She swallowed tautly. "My husband's."

"Oh." His eyes narrowed warily. He was silent for a moment then gestured toward the table. "We're eating without him?"

"He's dead."

"Oh. I'm sorry."

Wendy nodded again. Strangers couldn't really be sorry. They couldn't really care. Especially this one. He was more relieved than anything else, she was certain of it.

"You live here alone?"

It was the question she'd dreaded. She was a prime target. And the more she saw of him, the more she became certain that he wasn't as innocent as he wanted to appear.

But her instinct told her she could trust him, that he would never hurt her. It was a foolish thought, a false sense of security, she told herself. Still, it was there, and she couldn't shake it.

"Yes, I live here alone."

"Wendy," he murmured. "Wendy Hawk." He leaned forward and reached out. Before she could think to protest, he'd curled a strand of her hair around his finger. "A five-foot-two, blue-eyed blonde named Wendy Hawk who looks like an angel and lives in this sultry pit of hell. Am I dreaming, or did I die and make it to heaven?"

"I'm almost five-four, my eyes are gray, and not even the most avid nature lover would ever compare this place to heaven."

Wendy gently tugged her hair from his grasp. Unable to stay at the table any longer, she picked up her wineglass and backed away, feeling as if a tempest were brewing within her.

"We need to do something about that gash," she murmured.

"You haven't eaten."

"I was just keeping you company. I had dinner with a friend before I found you." It was almost the truth.

She had been coming from Eric's and she had eaten lunch with him earlier. "Please, go ahead, though."

She smiled a little weakly and turned away, sipping her wine as she moved into the living room. She turned on the television and ambled back to the sofa, vaguely noticing that the news was on while reproaching herself for abandoning a guest at the table.

He wasn't really a guest. She didn't know anything about him. When he had finished eating, she would do what she could for the gash in his forehead, then return him to the road.

The word *Everglades* suddenly caught her attention, and Wendy stared at the television with interest. She frowned, trying to catch up on the story; she had come in on the middle of it.

A violent confrontation had erupted over the illegal transport of drugs. The FBI had been involved; also the Drug Enforcement Agency and the local authorities. An agent had been killed, and the drug runners were still at large. A man's photograph flashed on the screen, then Wendy's vision was suddenly blocked.

Bill Smith stood directly in front of the picture. Without turning around, he flicked off the television.

Wendy straightened, glaring at him. "I was watching that."

He stared at her intently for a moment. His chilling look made her shudder, and she wondered again if she hadn't been a fool, bringing him into her home.

Then she realized that she wasn't trembling with fear, but with a strange warmth. He was wearing Leif's clothes. He was Leif's size, she knew that, and in the darkness, in the heat of passion, he might be very much like Leif.

No. He wasn't like her husband at all.

He was arresting and appealing all in his own right, and he was stirring up long-buried desires and emotions within her, feelings she was afraid to face.

And yet he was in her house. It was going to be a long night.

"The television," she reminded him. "I was watching the news program."

"I'm sorry. I needed your help."

"For what?"

"This gash. Would you mind? Have you got some peroxide or something?"

"Sure." Wendy went into the hall, pausing to flick on the television again. The news was already over, and a game show had begun.

Wendy hurried to the bathroom for the peroxide and Mercurochrome. When she opened the medicine chest, she flinched, surprised to see his reflection in the mirror. He was standing right behind her, his eyes intense as he watched her. "Where do you want me?" he asked.

She shrugged. "You might as well sit right here."

He did. Wendy poured peroxide on a cotton ball and gingerly sponged it over his temple. Although he didn't move, she winced at the sight of the wound. Whatever he had struck had caused a deep gash. She knew it had to be painful for him.

After she had finished with the peroxide, she hesitated.

"What's wrong?" he asked.

"This stuff is going to hurt."

He nodded. "That's okay. Do your damage, please."

Blushing, she took the medicine bottle from him. Although she dabbed at his head repeatedly, he remained stoically silent. She bit her lip, dabbing carefully. "I can't imagine what you hit," she murmured. "It's almost as if the flesh were spooned out...."

"Strange, isn't it?" he murmured. He took the second cotton swab from her, tossed it into the trash can and smiled again. "I feel better already."

"I'm glad."

"Can I make you some coffee?"

She shook her head. "No. But I will have tea."

Wendy followed him into the kitchen, where he filled the coffeepot and she filled the kettle. The man had a nice manner about him. He was able to be helpful and yet not seem intrusive. She was acutely aware of him, of every move he made. She was aware of too much. His smooth jaw...he had shaved that morning, she was certain. His scent...a musky odor that mingled with the clean smell of the soap. His eyes...tawny and alert.

She was so accustomed to being alone that the mere presence of another human being heightened her awareness. Wasn't he just a normal man? A lost city slicker?

No, this man was special. This man was arresting and alluring.

"What do you do?" she asked him as they waited for the water to boil and the coffee to perk.

"Do?" he said blankly.

"Yes. For a living."

"I'm in—pharmaceuticals."

"Salesman?"

"Er—yes."

"You were heading toward Naples?"

"Yes. Yes, I was."

"Do you live in Fort Lauderdale?"

"Well, actually, I live in New York. I was just—transferred down here."

The water boiled. Wendy turned off the burner and poured the water into the teapot. When she felt him watching her, a warm sensation surged through her blood. So this was it, she thought. This was the way it felt, that spark of attraction. She wasn't sure if it was right or wrong, or if it was painful or pleasant. He was a pharmaceuticals salesman from New York whose name was Bill Smith. He'd literally stumbled into her life, and she was feeling alive for the first time in years.

She spun around. He was studying her, his eyes warm, sparkling with a strange tenderness. He shook his head, smiling. "How did you get here? Do you really live here all the time? What do you do for a living?"

"Once upon a time, I was a nurse. Then I met Leif. He was an environmental scientist. This was his home. I came out here to be with him."

"And you've stayed?"

"It's home. I love it."

"How the hell can you love the swamp?"

"There's much more here than swamp, Mr. Smith."

He cleared his throat. "Someone who has seen me in less than briefs is still calling me Mr. Smith?"

She flushed but kept her chin high. "This is a beautiful place, Bill. You haven't looked. If you spent time here, you'd see the magic, and you'd understand."

He didn't believe her, not for a minute. He hated this place: the quicksand, the reptiles, the stinking insects. And yet, there had already been magic in the night. The fact that he was alive was a miracle in itself. He had awakened to see her standing above him, blond and petite and beautiful, an angel of mercy, protecting him from the darkness.

Now it was time for another miracle: getting his man, and getting out of here alive. He sobered quickly, hoping that Michaelson and his men had really given up. He needed to see a newscast, without Wendy around.

Wendy. He even liked the name. It suggested the clean coolness of a breeze, the exciting rush of a storm. A fitting name for this tempestuous angel.

Whoa. He couldn't let his mind wander. He had to find out what else had happened that day. He didn't think that Michaelson could have followed him here, into the thick of the marshy wilderness. Michaelson wasn't any good at navigating the swamps. But still, he'd have to be careful—very careful.

If he could just keep her away from the newscasts, he would be in a good position.

He reached out and touched her cheek. It was as soft as silk, golden tan against the nearly white halo of her hair. "Are you going to let me stay here?" he asked her softly.

"Once I picked you up, there really wasn't much choice," she told him. She cleared her throat. "There's—there's a spare bedroom next to the bath."

"Maybe in the morning you'll show me why you live here," he said. "Good night."

Wendy watched as he retreated into the dark bedroom, his words an echoing whisper that stirred and rustled in her heart.

Chapter 2

When he slept, he dreamed of her.

It was probably natural. His last conscious thought was of her, of those beautiful, silver-blue eyes, sparkling with determination when she'd sent him off to the guest room. She'd stared at him with a blunt honesty and self-assurance that he had found admirable. She wasn't a coy woman; she wouldn't play games. She lived here alone, she was damned vulnerable—and he knew it. But hers was a calculated risk. If she hadn't assessed him quickly and decided that he wasn't a trustworthy character, he wouldn't be here. She would have invited him back into the airboat and right now he would be standing on the roadside with a bandaged forehead and an upturned thumb.

And of course, she was perfectly safe with him.

But that didn't stop him from dreaming.

Sweet dreams.

She was an acre of heaven in a godforsaken waste-land, a diamond among pebbles, a bolt of silk among bales of burlap. He didn't know what it was about this woman that had seeped inside him so deeply, so quickly, but she had penetrated his world.

Even her voice was music—a smooth, lyrical melody, accented with tenderness, infused with laughter. In his dreams she walked to him, and he watched her, fascinated anew by the easy sway of her soft blond hair, hypnotized by the sparkling beauty of her eyes. He smiled and he reached for her, imagining how her supple body would feel in his arms. She moved in a night mist, a dusky fog that reminded him he was dreaming.

For now, a dream would suffice. She would be perfect, with a slim waist and smooth breasts that just filled his hands, firm breasts with dark rose nipples. Her hips were rounded, too, slightly flared beneath his hands. They didn't know each other very well, but they knew the really important things about each other, things that couldn't really be said but could only be sensed in another person. He wanted her, and he wanted her just this way—in tacit understanding, in sweet, ardent, mutual yearning.

She moved closer, and he exhaled. His entire body tensed and he reached out to touch her. He felt the bed sink as she curled her long, supple legs beneath her and sat there, staring at him. He could almost feel the warmth of her breath against his face.

Suddenly the subconscious realms of dream gave way to reality.

He wasn't imagining the weight at the foot of his bed.

Slowly, still struggling against the enticing darkness of sleep, Brad opened his eyes.

For the longest time he lay still, awake but perfectly still—and absolutely amazed.

There was a creature at the foot of his bed. It wasn't Wendy; it wasn't a woman at all. And it was certainly not the stuff of dreams.

It was some kind of cat. An enormous, fierce-looking cat.

At first, Brad thought of a tiger, but he knew that tigers weren't indigenous to this swamp. The creature had tawny gold fur and menacing yellow eyes. It stared at him for a moment, then curled back its lip and let out a bloodcurdling noise.

His blood seemed to congeal, but he remained perfectly still, staring at the hundred-pound monster. Great! He'd eluded Michaelson and escaped the perilous reptiles of the Everglades, only to become catnip for some giant feline.

"Bill?"

He heard Wendy's voice just as light flooded the room.

"Wendy, no! Get out—and shut the door!" he warned her. Standing in the doorway, with her hair a soft, golden cloud about her fragile features, she even resembled an angel. Her eyes shimmered with concern.

He wasn't about to let her become cat food.

Brad sprang up on his knees, ready to meet the teeth of the animal, ready to grab for its throat. He'd never come across anything quite like this in his training, but what the hell, a man couldn't live forever. If he could get to the cat before the cat got to her...

"Baby!" Wendy chastised, striding into the room.

"Wendy! I said—"

"I'm sorry, Mr. Smith." She marched in, heading straight for the animal at the foot of his bed. "Baby has her own little door in the back of the house. She comes and goes as she pleases. Guess I forgot to warn you about her."

Crouched by the pillow and clad only in the borrowed briefs, Brad arched a brow. Wendy sat down by the cat, scratching the animal's ears, flushing ruefully as she glanced Brad's way. "I am sorry. Did she frighten you?"

"Uh, no, not at all," Brad lied blandly. "Baby, huh?"

"She's a Florida panther. An endangered breed."

And she should be! Brad thought, but he didn't think that Wendy would appreciate the sentiment. Slowly he slid back under the sheets and pulled them up to his waist.

"Baby, huh?"

"Well, she was just a cub when I found her. Someone had made an illegal game hunt of her mother, leaving her an orphan. We kind of called her 'the baby,' and the name just seemed to stick. She's really very affectionate and very, very sweet."

"I'm sure," Brad agreed.

Baby let out another sound that was something between a roar and a purr, and Wendy flashed Brad another of the smiles that seemed to cascade into his libido—and his heart.

"Honest. She's gentle, I swear it."

Tentatively, Brad stretched out a hand to pat the cat on the head. "Nice kitty."

Baby licked her chops. Brad decided that Baby's teeth could have belonged to a saber-toothed tiger.

But she didn't nip at him. She merely stretched out on her back, thrusting all four paws up in the air.

Wendy laughed. "She likes to have her stomach scratched." Brad watched her slim fingers move over the silky pelt and he longed to tell her that he liked to have his stomach scratched, too. The very thought of it made a certain heat suffuse his veins. He wondered if his thoughts were revealed in his eyes. With one glimpse, Wendy blushed and pulled at the cat, hauling her down from the bed.

"Sorry," she murmured. "Come on, Baby. We should let our company sleep awhile longer."

When the door closed softly behind her, Brad exhaled, realizing just how damned tense he had been, and just how knotted and hot he still felt. His fingers were curled into fists, and the sheet didn't provide much cover for his body. Maybe she had noticed more than the message in his eyes.

Groaning softly, Brad tossed away the covers and rose. A soft stream of pink was filtering into the guest room through the soft cream-colored curtains. Brad walked over to the window and pulled them open.

The early-morning air seemed to be colored by the sunrise in shades of glittering gold and fairy-tale pink. From the window he could see that they were on a rise of higher ground, that trees and flowers and a little fenced-in garden surrounded this side of the house. The sun reflected off a pool of water beyond the trees, though, and Brad imagined that they were probably on a hammock that stretched out perhaps an acre before giving way to the canals and muck and saw grass of the swamp.

The view from the window was pleasant, though. Wild orchids grew in profusion over the cluster of trees, in shades of lilac, yellow and pink. Closer to the house, there was a garden of roses and a bougainvillea. The flowers provided an aura of silence...and a curious sense of peace.

Brad gave himself a mental shake. The last thing that surrounded him, he reminded himself bitterly, was any semblance of peace. He had to get dressed and get moving and decide what the hell he should be doing.

With that thought in mind, he quickly donned his borrowed clothing and stepped out of the bedroom.

A glance down the hallway told him that Wendy was already in the kitchen. She was wearing denim shorts and a tank top, socks and a pair of sneakers. Her blond hair was pulled back into a simple ponytail that fanned over her shoulder as she poured water into the coffee machine.

Brad smiled at her as he ducked into the bathroom. "You could have gone back to sleep!" she called.

He stuck his head out and grinned. "Naw, I'm awake now."

He washed his face studiously and used the toothbrush she had given him. Then he stared at his features. The gash in his head was ugly, but he could arrange his hair to fall over it. He probably should have had a few stitches, but he wasn't going to die from the lack of them. With a shrug, he splashed water over his face again. He had to know what was going on. He probably needed to act, but he didn't know what he should be doing. He really needed to talk to the boss. Hopefully, Wendy would take him to civilization, where he could make a phone call and find out what the hell was happening.

A little hammer seemed to slam against his heart.

Well, then, that would be it. His blond angel of mercy would drop him off, and that would be all. So much for dreams. So much for sweet images of her coming to him in the night, smiling, reaching out to touch him...

So much for dreams of reaching out and cradling the fullness of her breast in the palm of his hand, of tasting her lips.

"Damn!" he muttered out loud, shaking his head, dousing his face again in the water. He had to break this spell, get away from this woman.

But he still needed her help.

He turned off the water and combed his hair back with his fingers, carefully pulling a lock over the ugly reminder of the gash.

Outside the kitchen, the aroma of cooking bacon filled the air, and the scent was making him ravenous.

Baby was nowhere to be seen and Wendy was poised by the counter, looking out to the living room. Brad saw that the television was on, tuned into one of the popular, national news shows. National news...

Was he safe? he wondered. He hoped so.

She turned away from the television to greet him. "Hi. Sorry you were woken up."

He shook his head. "I'm not a late sleeper anyway."

She smiled at him, and again, he liked her lack of guile. "Want some coffee?" she asked.

"I'd love it. I'll help myself."

As he stepped into the kitchen, she brushed past him, going to the stove while he headed for the coffeepot. There was a beautiful scent about—something clean and fresh and light. He was tempted to grab her, sweep her into his arms, bury his face in the perfume of her hair.

But if he did so, he thought, grinning, he would probably end up wearing his coffee rather than drinking it. He poured himself a cup, then contented himself with leaning against the counter to watch her. He studied the golden hair that played over her sun-browned shoulders, the natural sway of her hips, the easy grace that seemed to rule her every motion.

Sensing his thorough observation, she turned to face him. "How do you like your eggs?"

He grinned. "I always feel lucky if I get them cooked," he told her.

She grimaced. "Scrambled, over easy, sunny-side up?"

"However you have yours," he said firmly.

With a shrug, she cracked an egg into a frying pan. He was having his eggs sunny-side up.

"As soon as we've eaten, I'll take you to the garage. There's a phone there. No use rushing, though. The phone is inside, and the garage doesn't open until nine."

"I'm not in any hurry," he said softly.

Wendy not only heard his voice, she felt the timbre of it. He hadn't really said anything, yet his words seemed to wash over her in a gentle, beguiling caress.

Nudging an egg with the spatula, she wondered why he had such an effect on her. She couldn't forget that he was lying about his name. And men just didn't lie about their names without a reason.

But here initial instincts had been right. She had trusted him in her house, and he had proven that he deserved that trust.

Face it, Wendy! she taunted herself. You don't know a damn thing about him, good or bad. The real truth is that you're attracted to him, and though you're incapable of going about a simple sexual relationship, you just want to hold on to him and think about the possibilities....

She swallowed, trying to ignore her unhappy thoughts. The eggs were done. She strained them with the spatula and slipped them onto plates. Her guest was right beside her, ready to take them from her.

Glancing his way, she couldn't help but admire the planes and angles of his face. He was handsome, but a far cry from pretty. The texture of his skin was masculine, as were the muscled structure of his sinewed form and the calluses that lined his strong palms. Idly she wished that she could have him unconscious again. Now she would be fascinated just to explore him from head to toe.

To touch him.

He set their plates down on the table a little too sharply. Wendy frowned, aware that the television had drawn his attention.

And then she heard it.

The newscasters were still reading the national news, but it seemed that her small part of the world had gained national attention. Wendy forgot her guest for a moment, trying to concentrate on the words of the announcer.

She and Brad both rushed toward the television set at the same time.

"Stop!" Wendy ordered.

For a moment, he paused and glared at her. Wendy could feel his eyes boring into hers.

Danger emanated from him, hot, desperate danger, sweeping around her, encompassing her.

Yesterday, there had been a shoot-out. "A violent exchange of gunfire," according to the Fort Lauderdale police. A federal agent had been killed, and law-enforcement officials were still looking for the gang of men involved, a gang of drug traffickers, arms dealers and murderers.

"You don't want to hear this."

He tore his gaze from Wendy's and strode toward the television. She began to protest, but when her mouth opened, a horrified gasp escaped instead as Brad's picture suddenly flashed upon the screen.

There were five men in the picture. One tall, blond man, three medium, darker men and Wendy's guest—Mr. "Alias" Bill Smith.

"Son of a bitch!" he swore. Too late, he turned off the television.

Wendy stared at him, her gaze wide and brilliant—and condemning.

"Wendy..." He lifted a hand to her imploringly. He wished he hadn't lied to her. The whole ordeal was going to be difficult to explain. Even worse, the look of betrayal in her eyes was going to be impossible to soothe. Those shimmering, beautiful, silver-blue eyes of hers, gem hard with hatred and reproach.

And fear.

He raked a hand through his hair, wondering how to explain. "Wendy—"

She spun around, ready to escape. He couldn't let her do that. He couldn't let her leave him stranded here, and he didn't dare let her risk a panicked run back to civilization.

God only knew who she might run into.

"Wendy, please wait!"

But Wendy had already begun to flee. She was at the door, tearing it open.

Freedom, she thought. Another second and she would be free. All she had to do was fly out the door and reach the airboat. She didn't need much of a head start. The swamp would slow down the unwary man, the one who was unprepared.

She threw open the door.

It was abruptly slammed shut before she could begin to get out. Acting on reflex, she swung around to face Bill Smith—or whoever he was! Now his handsome features bore a chilling countenance. She was frightened. This man was an impostor, a liar. The way he had slammed the door had proven his speed, strength and agility. He would be a powerful adversary.

"Wendy—"

She ducked beneath his arm and raced down the hall to her bedroom. Perhaps she could escape through a window....

All the while she could feel him behind her, following close. Gasping, she flew through the door to her bedroom, slammed it shut, locked it and leaned against it, panting.

Her heart caught in her throat as she felt him try the knob. "Wendy! You have to listen to me—"

"Stinking bastard—liar!" she retorted...her eyes surveyed the room. If she was lucky, the screwdriver would still be by her dresser, where she had left it after trying to fix a brass handle that had come loose.

"Wendy, I admit that I lied to you, but you have to give me a chance to explain."

The screwdriver was there, right on the carpet. If she could pull out a screen, she could escape through one of the large windows above her bed. She just had to keep him talking for the time it would take her to do so.

"So go on! Explain!" she snapped. Carefully, silently, she moved away from the door. She picked up the screwdriver and approached the window. "Explain!" she shouted back at him as she jumped up on the bed and set to work.

"Wendy, I'm not a bad guy. Honest." She heard his voice, coaxing, sincere, from the other side of the door.

Yeah, sure.

He'd fooled her once already. He must be thinking that she was the most naive creature this side of the Mason-Dixon line.

The first screw fell away in her hand. Holding her breath, she started on another. Her fingers shook. Oh, God. The FBI and the DEA were after him. An agent had been killed. This was serious business; her houseguest was a member of a drug mob.

"I should have told you the truth from the beginning. I was trying to protect you, and at first I didn't know whether I could trust you or not. I lied about my name to protect you. I was afraid of what the media would be saying. You've got to understand. The boss can't give out the real information because he assumes that I'm still with Michaelson and his group. But they found me out when they caught Jim. Jim is the one who was killed."

What the hell was he rambling on about? Wendy wondered. The third screw gave way in her hand and the screen came careening down. She caught it as it crashed against the wall. It was harder going now. She

had to hold the screen and unscrew at the same time.
Concentrate! she berated herself.

She probably deserved this. If she wasn't so frightened, so close to tears, she would laugh at herself.
Maybe she shouldn't have stayed here, holed up alone
in the Everglades. Maybe she had spent too much time
mourning the past and licking her wounds. Because
right out of the blue she had picked up a stranger, admired his face and form—lusted after him, Wendy girl,
admit the truth! she chastised herself in silent reproach—trusted him and made a complete fool of
herself. If she'd stayed a little nearer civilization, she
might have been smart enough to smell a rat beneath
her very nose.

The fourth screw finally gave way. He was still talking, but she had been too breathless to hear him. She
set the screen down carefully, then silently hiked her
rear up on the sill. With a groan the glass pane eased
open, allowing her to slip through the window and fall
onto the soft grass below.

"Wendy, do you understand?" Brad pleaded softly.
There was no answer. Too late, with sudden, definite
clarity, intuition warned him that no one was listening.

He slammed a muscled shoulder against her door.
The flimsy lock gave way instantly and he stepped into
her room. There was only a screen leaning against the
wall and curtains that billowed in the gentle breeze
from the open window.

Bolting across the room, he leaped onto the bed and
propelled his body out the window. He fell to the grass
and rolled.

On the path below, Wendy was running as fleetingly
as a young doe, trying to reach the airboat.

"Wendy!" He tore after her, catching her just as she neared the water.

Caught by the arm, she flailed and kicked like a trapped animal. Her small, clenched fist caught him in the shoulder. Then she delivered a blow to his right eye, a punch that hurt like hell.

Now he was probably going to have a shiner to go with the cut in his temple.

Then she landed a hefty kick. He could only be grateful that she had aimed for his shin.

"Wendy—"

She wasn't listening. He was pleading; she was swearing. Brad ducked low, sweeping her over his shoulder. He ignored the hands that pounded against his back and the nails that scratched him through his borrowed shirt. Striding quickly, he entered the house by way of the front door. He had to calm this woman down.

He didn't stop in the living room, but proceeded to her bedroom at the end of the hallway, where the door with its broken lock hung open. He barged into the room and unceremoniously dropped her on top of the bed. Her fists were still flying and her hair tumbled over her shoulders in a golden cloud.

"Damn you, I'm not trying to hurt you!" Brad cried.

"And how am I supposed to believe that's not just another lie?"

"Wendy!"

There seemed to be only one way to calm her. He crawled over her, straddling, pulling her arms high over her head and securing her wrists. Her hair fell in front of her face; she tried to blow it away, growing silent at last but continuing to stare at him with a look that could definitely kill.

"You liar!" she shouted.

"I lied about my name. I'm sorry. It's Brad. Brad McKenna."

She lay still for a minute. Her body relaxed slightly, but the suspicion never left her eyes. They seethed up at him with simmering skepticism.

His heart ached for her, for the feelings of betrayal she was suffering. He still liked her, so damned much. And he was still so entranced by this silver-eyed angel. Her breasts rose and fell with agitation, and he could feel her warm body caught between his own thighs.

"Honest. Give me a chance to start over. Mrs. Wendy Hawk, meet Brad McKenna. Oh, Mr. McKenna, so nice to meet you. The pleasure, Mrs. Hawk, is completely mi—ine! Hey!"

She wasn't amused, not in the least. She bolted against him in a powerful surge that almost sent him flying, despite all his well-trained reflexes.

"Wendy!" He laughed. "Please, give me a break!"

"I gave you a break! I plucked you out of the mud and I brought you here and I fed you—"

"And bathed me," he supplied.

Her eyes narrowed and she barely skipped a beat. "Fed you and clothed you and gave you a roof over your head! I should have left you for a reptile feast!"

Brad inhaled and exhaled slowly. Deep inside, he was in anguish. What the hell difference did it make? he asked himself bleakly. So, she hated him. So what? She was going to take him to a phone, and she would never see him again anyway.

There had never been anything for him here at all. An undeniable attraction wasn't always worth pursu-

ing. He didn't indulge where he couldn't turn his back
and walk away with a clear and easy conscience.

It would be difficult to walk away from this silver-
eyed sylph. But it would be devastating to know he'd
caused her pain. And right now, she was hurting because of him. She had to understand. He didn't want
her hating him.

"Wendy, please." He eased his hold on her arm. "I
know I don't deserve your trust, but I really need it. I
need it badly."

She didn't say anything; she didn't fight him. She
stared at him defiantly. And for a moment, her mind
wandered. She saw the familiar comforter on her bed
and the walnut, antique dresser sets she and Leif had
stripped and repolished themselves. She saw the daylight streaming through the cream curtains, and she felt
the man above her.

Once she had lain like this, and laughed. And the
man above her had been no threat. He had been her
husband, and she had loved him. And now a stranger
straddled her as Leif once had, asking her to trust him.
It seemed a sacrilege.

Yet even with that thought, she realized that the
panicked beat of her heart had slowed. Despite herself, despite everything she had seen on the news, she
wanted to believe him. He couldn't be lying to her, not
here.

And he couldn't be such an awful criminal. He could
have already killed her if he'd wanted to. He could have
strangled her easily, and there were plenty of sharp
knives in the kitchen. There was even a double-barreled
shotgun hanging on the wall.

She twisted her face aside, not wanting to look into
the tawny gold eyes that pleaded so eloquently with

hers. More than his words, more than the tenor of his voice, his eyes swayed her. His gaze poured into her, like a liquid warmth, promising honor and truth and even security, when there should have been none.

She swallowed and spoke softly. She couldn't have him touching her. She didn't want to feel the power in his thighs as they locked around her, and she didn't want to feel the warm whisper of his breath. She didn't want his hands so gently but thoroughly locking her own.

"If you don't want to hurt me, then let me go."

He hesitated, then unwound his fingers from her wrists and moved away.

Quickly, Wendy edged away from him, absently rubbing her wrists while she stared at him. He idly sat at the end of the bed and met her gaze.

"Brad McKenna?" she said doubtfully.

He nodded gravely. "I'm with the DEA, I swear it. My partner—the man who was killed—and I were working undercover. We had infiltrated one of the roughest gangs running cocaine, marijuana and hashish out of South America. This area's a target zone for us—especially since the drug traffic has increased. It's hard to stop—there are just miles and miles of coastline and an endless supply of pilots willing to risk their lives for the monetary rewards of bringing in one big supply. Anyway, Michaelson—the head honcho in this little group—caught on to us. He meant to perform a quick execution, but we'd gotten some word in about our location. We'd assumed that he was planning an exchange with the buyers. It all came down too fast." He hesitated, locking his jaw and swallowing painfully. "Jim was killed. I was next in line, but I stole a Chevy and took off down the Alley. The engine died on me, and Michaelson and his boys almost finished me off. But you found me instead."

She stared at him. "Pharmaceuticals?"

"What?"

"You told me that you were a salesman. Pharmaceuticals."

He shrugged. "I'm telling you the truth now, I swear it." He wanted so badly to reach out and touch her. He wanted to assure her.

He wondered if that look of contempt would ever leave her eyes. "Wendy, for God's sake, I'm telling you the truth now. Please, can't you believe me?" He reached out to stroke her cheek, but she twisted away.

"If you're telling the truth," she demanded, "why were you in that picture with the smugglers?"

He sighed. "I told you, I was working undercover. They can't reveal my identity at the office until they know for sure that my cover has already been blown." He paused. "Michaelson is wanted for first-degree murder as well as drug smuggling. If he gets a chance, he'll kill me."

Her arms were locked around her legs defensively, and she observed him warily from narrowed, long-lashed eyes.

"Wendy! You've got to believe me!"

"Why?"

"Because," he told her quietly, "I still need your help. I have to have your help."

She kept watching him in silence. He held his breath, then expelled it slowly. "Well?"

"I don't have much choice, do I?"

He lowered his head, smiling. "Thank you," he murmured. He reached out to stroke her cheek with his knuckles.

"But don't—don't even think of touching me again!" she said vehemently. Slipping away from him, she rose from the bed and strode, slowly and regally, from the room.

Chapter 3

"Are you coming?" Wendy demanded coldly. She was waiting for Brad in front of the house.

Brad closed the front door, eyeing her suspiciously. Where was that drat cat, Baby? He had forgotten about the animal when he had chased her outside. Baby was probably more useful against unwanted prowlers than a pair of well-trained attack dogs.

"I'm not sure that I trust you, Mrs. Hawk."

"You're not sure that you trust me?" she demanded indignantly. He didn't answer her. "Well of all the nerve!"

"Where's the panther?"

"Baby?"

"Your deadly kitty cat."

"How on earth should I know," she replied sweetly. "Any cat is difficult to find, and as you might notice, Baby has a big backyard!"

Brad issued an oath at her sarcasm. Forgetting that he had promised not to touch her, he grabbed her wrist and pulled her close. Her body was warm and soft against his. He felt the taunting fullness of her breasts against his chest, the smooth silkiness of her golden tanned skin. When he inhaled, her fragrance was clean and sweet, more haunting than any tormented dream.

Afraid that she could sense his heated reaction, he wanted to drop her wrist and push her away. And he wondered what she was thinking, for she didn't fight, she simply cast her head back and scowled at him with that unique silver magic in her eyes.

Brad gritted his teeth. "What I want to know, Mrs. Hawk, is if that cat of yours is slinking around somewhere, poised to attack."

She hesitated just a minute. "No."

"Are you sure?"

"What do you want—a sworn statement?"

"Yes!"

"Dammit, I'm the one who deserves one of those!" she protested.

"I asked you to trust me."

"But you don't trust me!"

He wanted to kiss her. He wanted to know if the heat that raged in her eyes would warm her mouth and fuse their lips together. The temptation was ungodly. His fingers trembled with the desire to snake into her hair, his body shook with the very force of his longing. Maybe it was the wild, primitive appeal of the ground he stood on. Maybe it was the defiant challenge in her beautiful eyes. He had never wanted a woman more. And he had never wanted one so passionately, so suddenly. He closed his eyes, praying that God would get him out of the swamp and grant him some sanity.

Then he released her. "I'm sorry, Mrs. Hawk. You're right. I am asking a lot of you. Forgive me. Shall we go?"

For a moment she stared at him in silence, then she turned with squared shoulders and started for the airboat.

Brad followed her onto the vehicle, releasing the secure rope she kept tied around a tree. As she started up the motor, Brad let the sights and sounds of the swamp fill his senses. The day was bright now, and growing hotter. He could hear the drone of insects again. A light breeze caused the distant saw grasses to bend beneath it, and the vista did, indeed, appear to be a green sea, with ripple after ripple of wave listing through it. He heard a ruffling sound and turned to see a long-legged, awkward-looking crane soar to beauty and elegance as it took flight from the ground and entered the arena of the powder-blue sky.

Wendy seemed to be deep in thought, staring straight ahead. He smiled; she seemed so small and fragile on the airboat, like an angel driving a two-ton semi.

What kind of a love had kept her here, in the deserted marshes, all alone? Could anyone, man or woman, be so self-sufficient that he or she needed nothing but the earth and sky to survive? The land, the air—and memories?

He quickly realized that she knew this land well. Having been unconscious, he hadn't seen where he had come from last night. He could determine their direction from the sun, but he'd be damned if he understood how anyone could navigate a swamp with no distinguishing landmarks. Or were there subtle, natural landmarks, evident only to those who sought them? A clump of trees that bowed at an angle there, old trees

that had surely survived countless storms. A wide vista
of the grass, to the right, and to the left, a sudden profusion of color where a hammock rose from the swamp
to provide a home for scores of wild orchids and tall,
blue-toned herons.

Birds burst out of the foliage before them—the airboat's motor was loud. He didn't know how fast they
were going—maybe thirty-five miles an hour, tops—
but still the breeze became a wind that whipped by
them, fierce, challenging, invigorating. Brad closed his
eyes, savoring the feel of the wind on his face while the
sun beat down on his back. The scent of the swamp
that had repulsed him yesterday now seemed rich, red-
olent.

When Wendy slowed the airboat, he thought they
were idling near another hammock of high land. On
closer inspection, he could see that strands of high
grass hid the planks of a series of small, weather-beaten
docks. Wendy tossed him the rope, and he secured the
airboat.

Wisps of blond hair had escaped Wendy's neat
ponytail. They played about the soft contours of her
face as she squinted toward the small building.

"Thank you," he said quietly.

Her hands were on her hips as she continued to survey him. "The phone is inside the office," she said
simply.

They crossed a groomed lawn—regular grass that
had actually known the touch of a lawn mower—and
just ahead of them Brad could see a bright, whitewashed rectangle of a building that sported a few gas
pumps outside.

As they approached, an old man in overalls stepped
out to meet them, staring curiously at Brad. He wiped

grease from his bronzed and wizened hands, and his flesh wrinkled around a pair of light green eyes as he narrowed them upon the newcomer.

"Hi, Mac." Brad didn't realize that he was holding his breath, worrying, until she spoke. "Mac, this is a friend of mine. Brad McKenna. Brad, Mac Gleason." Mac arched a brow but reached forward to shake Brad's hand.

Brad reciprocated the gesture. "Hi, Mac."

The old man nodded, but kept staring at Brad. "You own that old Chevy that's all torn up near the Alley?"

"Uh—no, I don't own it," Brad said. That much was true. Some irate owner was probably making a claim with his or her insurance agent over the car right now.

"Brad needs to use the phone," Wendy said. "How's my car doing?"

"Car's all ready to go when you are, Wendy. Local call, son?"

"I—uh—I don't know. Fort Lauderdale." He started to fumble in his pockets, then he realized that they weren't his pockets and that he didn't have any money anyway.

"I didn't ask you for money, boy," Mac said indignantly. "I just asked you where you was calling. You want Lauderdale, you dial a one first, ya hear?"

Brad nodded. "Thanks. I appreciate it."

"Up in the office. Take your time."

Brad turned and headed for the office. He wanted to look back, but he didn't. He wondered if Wendy was whispering to the old man, sharing her suspicions that he was a murderer and a drug smuggler. Maybe the old man had a shotgun handy. Or maybe Brad would be greeted by a pair of pit bulls when he opened the of-

fice door. Here in the swamp, people were isolated, a
breed apart, and they often had their own way of dealing with things.

Don't, Wendy, please don't. Don't betray me, he silently pleaded.

The office was cool and air-conditioned inside. There
was a desk with a blotter and an old swivel chair to the
right of the door. Against the wall stood a Pepsi machine, another machine that dispensed chips and
candy, and a large glass globe full of ice water. Brad
poured himself a paper cup of the cold water, drank it
down and peered out the window.

Wendy was laughing at something the old man had
said. Her hands were on her hips, her head was tossed
back. When she glanced up at the shop and saw him,
her laughter faded.

Brad walked over to the desk and dialed the emer-
gency number. Gary Henshaw answered first. Brad
smiled, filling with warmth as he heard Gary scream
out in relief that he was alive. "Where the hell are you,
buddy? No, never mind, let me get the boss."

Two seconds later Brad was talking to L. Davis
Purdy, the man in charge of their operations in south
Florida—the Boss, as he was known with respect and
affection by his men. Purdy was no pencil pusher. He'd
worked the streets for years and had gradually risen
through the ranks of the agency. There were few tricks
he didn't know. Michaelson was one of the toughest
nuts Purdy had ever tried to crack.

"You're alive," Purdy said. The words sounded
matter-of-fact, even a little cold.

"Yeah." Brad leaned back in the chair.

"Thank God." Purdy meant it. "Jim is dead."

Brad closed his eyes. "I know. Michaelson got wind that we were both DEA."

"We figured that much out." Purdy hesitated a moment. "Your town house was firebombed last night."

"What?" Brad sat up. His home here was gone? His collection of rare forty-fives, his stereo equipment, his lumpy old recliner, his college football jersey . . . little things that meant a lifetime. They were all gone.

But he was still alive, he thought soberly. Jim wasn't so fortunate.

"We're going to have to get you in under protective custody. Brad, you're the only one who can put Michaelson away now. He wants you dead, and usually Michaelson gets what he wants."

"Doesn't sound good at all," Brad said gruffly.

"You know the ropes. You're lucky to be alive now. Where the hell are you that he hasn't gotten wind of you? I'm trying to bring him in, but you know the man, and you know the system. He's as slippery as an eel, and his kind of money can buy all kinds of favors."

"I'm in the swamp."

"The swamp? You're out in the Glades?"

"Yes. I don't really know exactly where. That's probably why he hasn't found me." Brad hesitated, sitting forward. "Come to think of it, at the moment, this is a fine place to be." He started at a sudden sound.

He was slipping, he realized, slipping badly, letting down his guard.

Wendy Hawk entered the office. She sat at the edge of the desk and stared at him expectantly.

"Purdy, will you talk to someone for me?" Brad said. "That picture that came out over the news last night almost did me in."

"We sent that out before your home was hit," Purdy explained. "Who do you want me to talk to?"

"A concerned civilian who kept me alive last night," Brad said dryly, watching Wendy as he spoke. "Now she's afraid she was aiding a hardened criminal. Say something, will you?"

"She?" Purdy murmured.

Brad gritted his teeth. In the background he could hear Gary repeating the word, then embroidering upon it. *"She?* Leave it to Brad. Even in the damn swamps he can find himself a woman."

"Tell Gary to put a lid on it," Brad said with annoyance. "I'm putting on Mrs. Hawk."

He thrust the receiver to Wendy. Curiously, she took it. "Hello?"

"Hello, Mrs. Hawk? My name is Purdy, ma'am, and I'm with the DEA. I understand that you helped one of my men last night, and I'm exceedingly grateful. Brad tells me that you saw the news. I'm sorry about that. We had to take all precautions."

Wendy was silent. Brad, listening in as best he could, realized then that there was still no definite proof of his innocence. He could have called anyone, and the voice on the other end of the phone could be spinning lies as easily as he had.

He groaned softly, slumping back in the chair. Well, she'd believe him when they sent out a car for him.

No. Abruptly, he sat back up. No, the agency couldn't send anyone near here. That would put Wendy in danger. She was safe here in her swamp, because no one would think to come here.

Unless they followed someone in, someone coming for him.

He jerked the phone out of her hands.

"Boss—"

"We'll get a couple of cars out there with our best—"

"No! No, listen to me. I'm going to get out of here by myself."

"Brad—" He could almost imagine Purdy frowning. His brow would be furrowed, and his sharp blue eyes would be squinting.

"Really, Purdy, this plan is safer. I'm calling from a gas station with an old man, and I've been staying at Mrs. Hawk's home. And, Boss, I mean, I am deep in the marshes. There's no way that Michaelson can stumble on me here. It's just impossible. This place is a watery jungle. You need a map to go from tree to tree. If I get myself out, then Michaelson won't think to go after anyone who might have helped me. I'll start wending my way out this morning."

Wendy watched him, her eyes widening. She didn't know how or why she believed in this man, she just did. For all she knew, he could have phoned the Florida State Penitentiary; the man giving her the assurances could have been working on a chain gang.

But she trusted him. She was relying on instinct again.

Her heart was beating just a little too fast; her breath was coming just a bit too quickly.

Perhaps she should simply wash her hands of the man, then and there. She owed him nothing.

But before she even knew what she meant to do, she leaned forward and gently caught Brad's hand. "Maybe you should stay here."

"What?" Startled, he stared at her.

She hesitated, wet her lips, then elaborated. "Some guy is looking for you, right? This Michaelson char-

acter. Maybe you're as safe as you can possibly be right
here.''

"Wendy," Brad said softly, staring into the soft
mystery of her silver eyes. "This guy is tracking me
down to kill me. I am the only one who can testify
against him."

She nodded. "I know. But you just said that he can't
possibly find you here."

What was the matter with her? she wondered desperately. She didn't want him here! This man made her
feel dazed and irrational. But she wasn't afraid of him.
Even when he had held her, when he had pinned her
beneath him, she hadn't been afraid. She had been
aware—painfully aware—of his build, of his warmth,
of his strength. She was captivated by the man, and it
had been okay because he was leaving, but now...

Now she was sitting here, suggesting that he stay.

Why?

Her heart seemed to skip a beat, slamming mercilessly against her chest. It was foolish, it was all so
foolish. But suddenly all that she could remember was
the sight of blood, all the blood that had once spilled
over Leif's chest. She could hear her own scream,
echoing against the corridors of her heart.

Her memories ruled her now. She couldn't let the
same thing happen to Brad. The swamp was her refuge; she knew it well, backward and forward, and it
was a good hiding place. The Indians had discovered
it years ago, but few men had charted it since. The Everglades could shield a man. The swamp was a tough
and rugged mistress, but when her secrets were learned
and respected, she could embrace and protect a man,
an ideal—an entire people.

Conflicting emotions flickered across his face. He set his jaw in a hardened twist. "Wendy, I can't just hide here with you. Running is my forte—my job."

"No one has a job that says he has to get killed foolishly!" Wendy snapped. "Do you think you'll make it out of this wilderness in one piece? Don't be a fool. The law doesn't want heroics. The law needs you alive—"

"But I can look after myself—"

"I imagine that might be true in the big city," Wendy interrupted coolly. "Were you trained to elude a gang of murderers in the Everglades?" She crossed her arms over her chest.

"Brad! Brad!" Purdy was calling him, in an aggravated voice.

Still watching Wendy's eyes, Brad spoke into the receiver again. "I'm here—"

No matter what happened, Brad was due for some painful inactivity. Suppose he did make it out of the swamp? He would have to hide out in a safe house. He'd be locked up with a group of agents guarding him day and night. Brad would be in seclusion until they managed to catch Michaelson.

He groaned, holding the phone away.

Wendy snatched it from him. "Mr. Purdy, can you prove to me that Brad is innocent?"

"I can release the details to the news media," Purdy told her. He cleared his throat impatiently. "Will you please ask Mr. McKenna to remember that he works for me—and put him back on the line. He's going to be on a forced hiatus for even longer than he thinks if he doesn't stick with me this time."

Wendy smiled. Brad noticed that she had the smallest little dimple in the center of her chin. He took the phone back from her. "I've got an idea, Boss. It will keep me safe, and her safe, too. I'm going to lie low right here."

"What?" Purdy was screeching.

Brad moved the receiver away from his ear while Purdy went on and on about the lack of control in the situation. Brad was miles from civilization; there was no help nearby.

"That's right," Brad said quietly. "I am miles from anywhere. No one knows where the hideout is, and no one can squeal. Boss, think about it."

Purdy changed his tactics. "You're going to stay out in the swamp for a good week or more?"

Brad laughed. "Can't you boys do any better than that? Come on—I'll supply the proof. All you home militia have to do is rope in the target!"

Purdy swore. But then he paused. Brad knew Purdy. The Boss was always willing to throw "standard procedure" out the window if another solution seemed to be better.

"All right, McKenna. Now you listen to me for a minute, and listen good. You might be right. Michaelson is a smuggler and a killer, but he sure isn't any Daniel Boone. Sitting tight could be your best move. But remember, he'll have men on both ends of the Alley, and I'm willing to bet he gets some air coverage of the swamp, too. I want you to check in if you see anything, and I don't want you making a single move without my approval. Got it?"

Brad's muscles tightened. He hated the swamp. What the hell was he doing?

He inhaled. He was trying to live the dream. He wanted to go back to the house and lie in the bed, and so help him, he wanted to make love to the woman. He

wanted to touch and taste her flesh, to explore the
breasts that were so firm and full in his dream. He
wanted to see her mercury eyes above him as passion
filled them. He wanted to kiss her, to drown in her...

Purdy was still talking, but Brad couldn't hear him
anymore. He stared up at Wendy, and he wondered if
his own features had gone as ashen as hers. What was
she thinking now? Was she regretting her impetuous
offer? It was a mistake. He didn't know how to sit still;
he hated to sit still. What the hell was he going to do in
the swamp for all those hours?

Except to lust after his silver-eyed angel of mercy.

He swore softly and rubbed his temple. "Hey,
Boss—"

"Not a move, Brad, unless you talk to me. They've
run a trace on the phone number, so we've got your
coordinates. I'm going to get my men out there to nail
Michaelson. You do your bit—stay alive, huh?"

There was a dull buzz. Purdy had hung up on him.

He didn't put the receiver down right away. He
swallowed, staring at Wendy. She was still so damned
white. At last, Brad exhaled, slamming the receiver
down. "You look as if you had just invited the Indians in for a scalping. I can see that you still don't believe in me. Maybe you should have kept your mouth
shut."

She hopped off the desk and her hands rode her hips.
"Ingrate!"

"Finished with the phone, son?" Mac, the old-timer
grease monkey interrupted them.

Brad shook his head, and a slow smile came to his
lips. Mac was perfect for the place. His hair and beard
were clean but shaggy, his manner abrupt but well-
meaning. It was evident that Mac was Brad's friend as

long as Wendy vouched for him. And it was equally
evident that the old man would defend her come hell or
high water. "Yes, I'm finished all right," Brad said.

Mac nodded serenely. "Wendy, you want to take
your car now? Or did you just come to use the phone?
Is he going to drive the car while you take the airboat?"

"Uh—we just needed to use the phone."

Mac nodded. "Maybe someone will get a chance to
drop it off later." He walked over to the old percola-
tor on the counter and poured himself some coffee, not
taking his eyes from Brad. "Coffee?"

"Yeah, thanks."

Mac poured him a cup. The brew was hot and
strong. Brad had just taken a sip out of a stoneware
mug when Mac said casually, "You got anything to do
with those men running around in the big black se-
dan?"

He nearly spit coffee all over the floor. Instead, he
swallowed and glanced from Wendy to Mac.

Mac smiled, enjoying Brad's reaction. "Yep, those
boys were here wanting some gas last night. Can't
rightly say I liked the looks of them, myself. They
asked about the Chevy, and for some dark reason, I
told 'em I'd never seen the thing. They were really
looking for a man—a buddy of theirs they said they'd
lost in the swamp. I told them that most things that get
lost in the swamp stay lost. Why, I reckon, too, that if
they come back, I ought to tell them that it's true—if
they're still looking for a man, they oughta count on
the fact that he's lost, deep in the darkness of the
Glades, huh?"

Brad reached out and shook Mac's hand. "Thanks,"
he said gruffly. "Thanks. It's—it's really important. I

don't know how I can prove it to you, but I'm really a decent man. And those guys are looking to stir up trouble."

"A man don't need things proved to him," Mac said. "And there's all kinds of good guys and bad guys in this world. Instinct, boy, that's what counts."

He nodded to the two of them and walked outside. When the door closed, Wendy glanced briefly at Brad, then hurried out after Mac. Through the dusty window, Brad watched Wendy give the old man a fierce hug and a kiss on his weathered cheek.

They were old friends, good friends. Brad felt a sudden stab of envy. The old man knew Wendy Hawk well. He knew the details of her life. He probably had shared her past, had listened to her dreams of the future. And Brad didn't really know her at all. He knew only that he wanted her, that she intrigued him, haunted him.

Perhaps he ought to be hiding out from her instead of from Michaelson. Michaelson wanted his life. Wendy Hawk would steal his heart and his soul.

He followed her out. She waved goodbye to Mac, then climbed onto the airboat. For a moment the breeze rustled by, and they sized one another up silently. Then she walked past him and released the tie line.

The engine came to life; its powerful roar filled the air. Birds squawked and flew before them.

Wendy stared straight ahead.

Brad sighed and settled down on the boat. They were going home, to her home, together. The die had been cast. He watched as the sun danced along the golden highlights of her hair. Light, light, ethereal gold. As he studied the bronze of her shoulders and the feminine line of her body, he remembered holding her.

How long were they destined to be together? he wondered bleakly.

Maybe time didn't matter. They both knew it already. There was something between them now, simmering and steaming, wild and explosive.

They were heading home; fate had thrown them together. He suddenly knew that he would have her, would touch her, would love her, just as surely as he knew that the sun would set in the west. Despite their individual dreams and fears, their shared destiny was inevitable.

She turned to tell him something, to point out some landmark, but when her eyes met his, her words seemed to freeze in her throat.

Their eyes remained locked together, silver melding with gold, and surely creating some ancient alchemist's magical treasure. Or perhaps it wasn't magic at all. Perhaps it was a simple pattern of nature and life, as basic and raw as the need of a man for a woman.

When she found the strength to turn away from him, neither of them cared that some vague thought was forgotten. Among soul mates the pretense of words was unnecessary.

Chapter 4

The house seemed smaller. Brad didn't know how, but the house had shrunk, closing in around them.

Wendy threw out the breakfast that they hadn't eaten and started cleaning up the kitchen. He would have offered to help her, but he was certain that she didn't want his assistance now. The kitchen had gotten smaller, too.

Brad turned on the television. It was nearly noon. He tried different stations until he found one of the major networks. A soap opera seemed to be in the midst of its final, anguished, tear-jerking scene of the day. Brad hunched down and waited. He swallowed, realizing that he was watching the soap Jim used to watch. His partner had never known quite how and when he had gotten hooked, but he had. And whenever things were slow, whenever Jim and Brad were stuck on surveillance, sitting for hours and hours, drinking coffee and waiting for something to happen, Jim would dramatically recount all the latest episodes. Of course, he had missed the soap's broadcast most of the time, but he videotaped the show religiously.

Jim wouldn't be watching any more soaps.

They hadn't worked together long. Not even a month. Brad's old partner, Dennis Holmes, had left the DEA when he'd married the college sweetheart who had waited for him for ten long years. He was teaching in Boston now. Funny, Brad thought, he and Dennis and Jim had all agreed on one thing—their line of work and marriage just didn't mix.

But Jim would never have a chance to marry. The thought cut Brad to the quick. Jim had been shot down in the prime of his life. Damn Michaelson! He would pay for Jim's life. Like a cowboy in the Old West, Brad would give his eyeteeth for a walk down a long and dusty path, and the simple chance to best the man. But this wasn't the Old West. He couldn't meet Michaelson that way. The law needed Brad alive to testify. Then the judicial court system could determine Michaelson's fate. Brad knew the rules. But for once, he'd relish the opportunity to take justice into his own hands.

Brad started, aware that the images on the screen in front of him had changed. The soap opera was over; the news had come on. He tensed, then relaxed as the personable blonde went on in grave tones about the Michaelson smuggling case.

First Jim's picture was flashed onto the screen. Brad smiled even as a bitter sadness pierced his heart. The picture had been taken at a Labor Day picnic. Jim was wearing an old football jersey. His hair was all mussed up and he was smiling unabashedly for the camera. He looked so young—far too young to be dead.

The pretty blond newscaster announced that his body would be returned to his hometown in Delaware for burial.

Then Brad's picture flashed on the television screen. The photo had been taken the same day. He was wearing a football jersey, too, and cradling a football in his arm.

In his other arm, he cradled a buxom redhead.

Where the hell had Purdy come up with these pictures? What would have been wrong with a simple ID photo showing him in a blue suit and tie, a stoic, mugshot expression and combed hair?

Leave it to Purdy.

In this snapshot, he looked like one of the good old boys. You could almost see the beer cans in the background. His hair was tousled and his eyes reflected the sultry laughter in the pretty girl's gaze.

Funny, but he couldn't even remember the redhead's name.

The reporter explained that Brad and Jim had been working undercover and that the previous incorrect information about Brad McKenna had been released to protect the agent's cover. However, it was no longer necessary. Brad had been found out. According to the newscast, Brad was missing, and authorities feared that he was dead. But Purdy had been true to his word to exonerate him—at least he was presumed dead as an agent rather than presumed dead as a drug smuggler.

The picture left the screen. The blonde came back on to state that the police and other government agencies were searching for Michaelson.

Brad realized that Wendy was behind him. He heard her exhale in relief. He was aware that she had been believing in him on instinct alone. Still hunkered down on the balls of his feet before the television, he looked up at her. Now, at least, her instinct had been somewhat vindicated.

"See, I am legit," Brad told her with a mild note of reproach.

Her gaze flicked down at him.

"Now I don't know what to think," she murmured. "They can say anything they want on the news, and we're obliged to accept the information." She smiled sweetly, and went back into the kitchen.

He rose slowly and turned the television off, suddenly feeling very awkward. What the hell was he going to do here—except try like hell to keep his hands off her?

"Hungry?"

The question came from the kitchen. He almost answered it with a sexual innuendo, yes, hungry like you'll never know, hungry for you. Instead, he forced himself to smile casually. "Yeah. Sure. We never did get to breakfast."

An accomplished cook, Wendy didn't seem to mind being in a kitchen. She flashed him a quick smile and reached into the refrigerator. Brad assumed that she was reaching for the makings of sandwiches or the like. She brought out an opaque white container and handed it to him. He frowned, then opened it up. A bunch of broken shrimp stared up at him sightlessly.

"What—"

Wendy smiled, turning away. "Let's go catch lunch." She opened the closet near the refrigerator and pulled out two fishing reels. "It's our bait."

Brad looked blankly from the fishing gear to his hostess. He grinned slowly. Thank God, they were going to get out of the incredible shrinking house. Fishing. It sounded great. "All right. In the airboat?"

She shook her head. "There's a little canoe around back. We'll try for some catfish. I've got a great Cajun recipe. You like spicy food?"

They were staring at each other again. Wendy flushed, walked past him and started digging beneath the counter. "I've a cooler in here somewhere," she muttered.

"I'll get the ice," Brad offered quickly.

In another ten minutes, they were ready. The cooler was filled with beer, ice, a block of cheese and a stick of pepperoni. Wendy had decided that they might get hungry while waiting for the meal to come along. Besides, when the meal did come along, it would more likely be closer to dinnertime than lunch.

The canoe was out back. When they walked around, Brad saw that the road was just barely discernible behind a patch of tall saw grass growing on the opposite side of the canal.

"How do you get to your car?" he asked her, puzzled.

"I take the canoe."

"You have to take your canoe to get to your car?"

Wendy laughed. "Yes. It isn't that difficult. And I don't drive that often. Most places I want to go around here are easier to reach by airboat."

"What a way to live," Brad murmured.

Wendy paused, cocking her head as she watched him with a musing smile. "It's really not so bad, city slicker. Everything that I could want or need is very close."

She stepped past him, carrying the fishing rods over to the canoe. Brad stared across the water to the saw grass and the road, trying to memorize the area and achieve a sense of direction.

Suddenly, Wendy screamed. By reflex, Brad spun, reaching to his waist for his Magnum. Then he remembered that it wasn't there, that it was lost. Without it, he felt naked. And Wendy was screaming...

He ran to her, ready to protect her with his bare hands. But even as he neared her, she was sitting back, laughing.

"Wendy, what happened? What the—"

"Baby!" she sputtered.

The great panther rose from the floor of the canoe, growled, then stretched against Wendy like any of her smaller feline cousins, seeking affection. Wendy scratched her ears, then shoved her away. "Baby, get out of here! You scared me to death."

The cat crawled out of the canoe. When she shimmied past Brad, he petted the panther's sleek coat. His heart was still pounding crazily.

Still laughing, Wendy looked up at Brad. He was not amused. On the contrary, he appeared a little gray and cold, and the contours of his face were hard-set.

"Is that shotgun the only weapon you've got?" he asked her brusquely.

She hesitated.

"Is it?"

Wendy shook her head. "I've got a police model Smith & Wesson .38 in one of the dresser drawers."

"When we get back, I want it," he told her. He lowered himself into the canoe beside her, shoving off in a fluid motion. For several moments, they drifted in silence. Wendy stared at Brad from beneath the shelter of her lashes, and she wished studiously that she had never told him the truth. She hated guns, hated them with a passion. She wished that Baby had not startled her so, and she wished that she hadn't screamed.

And she nervously wished that she had never, never suggested that she bring Brad McKenna back home. It was awkward already, and she had a feeling that it was only going to get worse. He didn't seem to understand that she had brought him back here just because her house was so damned isolated. No one could find him here; there was no danger here. He didn't need a gun.

The sun beat down on them. For miles the only sound seemed to be the dip of Brad's paddle against the water. Wendy realized he knew something about canoeing. His strokes were slow, steady and even. He'd rolled up the sleeves of the shirt, and with each of his movements she could see the muscle play of his arms beneath the bronze flesh. Deep in concentration, his face was handsome, but harsh.

It had been different in laughter, she decided. In the photo they had shown on the news, he had seemed young, and easygoing. He had appeared happy and relaxed. And...

Ready, able and willing, she finished dryly. Who had the redhead been? The sudden thought chilled her.

"Brad?"

"Yeah?" He had been paddling strenuously, becoming accustomed to the land around him, the river of grass, the calls of cranes and loons and herons. He was growing acquainted with the stillness of the swamp, punctuated by the occasional, startling cries of the birds.

"We've gone plenty far," she said. He set the paddle inside the boat. They were drifting idly. Balancing herself from years of experience, Wendy reached forward and grabbed her pole. She checked her weight and hook and secured some bait from the white bucket. All the while she could feel him watching her, silently, broodingly, watching her every movement.

"Live shrimp are much better bait," she murmured. "But these will do, I'm sure." With a skillful arm, she cast her line.

Brad took his time setting up his fishing rod. After his line hit the water, he reached into the cooler for a beer. "Ready for one?" he asked.

Wendy shrugged. "Yes, I guess so."

He popped open the can before handing it to her. She hadn't realized it was quite so hot out until she sipped the icy cold beer. It tasted good, but it hit her stomach with a churning swirl. She remembered then that they hadn't eaten anything.

She glanced across the canoe at Brad, who was staring at the water, pole in one hand, beer in the other. He wore Leif's jeans and denim shirt well, she thought. She would never forget how she had found him, not a full day ago, struggling through the swamp. A lot had passed between them since then.

Nor could she forget the way he had caught and held her this morning. She realized that her emotions were alternating between gloom because he had interrupted her peaceful life, and elation, because he excited her so. He was making her feel again. He was making her blood whistle and sing. Maybe it was wrong since he was such a stranger, but she didn't know whether she wanted to fight it or not. In one way, she felt the gravest sense of security around him. Brad McKenna would never take anything from a woman that she didn't intend to give—wholeheartedly.

But then she met his gaze and her mind grew wary, her heart raced in fear. He'd been thinking about her—

physically, sexually—and that scared her. She could almost read his precise thoughts, and awareness of those desires caused her to tremble and burn deep, deep inside.

"Brad." She was startled by the huskiness of her own voice, dismayed by the sensual undertone of it. But she had a question that had to be answered.

"You're—" This was ridiculous. She had to moisten her lips to keep talking, and the breathless quality would not leave her voice. She shook her head, then she smiled in a rueful confession, because he was staring at her again, seeing into her, penetrating her thoughts. "You're not married, are you?"

He looked at her for a long moment, then shook his head. "No."

"Who was the redhead?"

Again he paused. A dry, pained smile crossed his features, and he winced. "Honest? I don't remember. I think her name was Chrissy."

"Oh."

He set his beer on the seat beside him and wedged his pole beneath a thigh. Reaching forward, he caught her face between his palms.

She couldn't move, and she couldn't breathe. She could feel his callused touch against her flesh, and it warmed her from head to toe, just as the sound of his voice seemed to feather inside of her, touching her everywhere.

"I'm not married, Wendy. And I'm never going to be. Do you understand?"

She wanted to jerk back. Hurt and confusion raged in her heart, and still she couldn't move. The sensations that warred against her flesh would not leave her, and she sat dead still. A mocking, chilling smile curled

her lips. "Well, now, McKenna, I do remember asking you if you were married. But I do not remember
going so far as to ask you if you wanted to change your
status."

She was glad to see that he flushed slightly. "Wendy,
it's just that you have been married."

"That's right," she drawled softly. "Have been, past
tense. And I don't intend to marry again, Mr. Mc-
Kenna."

Suddenly the atmosphere between them was tense
and explosive, and hotter than the midday sun that
beat down mercilessly upon them. He still touched her,
held her with his hands. Their knees brushed, their
breath mingled.

"Why is that, Wendy? Was the experience too
good—or too bad?"

"Too good, McKenna. It could never, never be
matched."

Silence swept and swirled around them, as stifling as
the shimmering heat.

"Well, remember that, huh?" Brad murmured. "I
wouldn't want you forgetting it in the future."

"I doubt if there's a chance of that."

"Really?" His lips moved closer to hers. "You'd
better be careful. Very careful. I wouldn't want you to
care too much." He moved his thumb, drawing it in a
slow, sinuous line over her lower lip.

"And maybe you had better be careful, too, Mc-
Kenna. I wouldn't want you to care too much. I
wouldn't want you to get hurt."

"Watch out for your heart, Wendy." And then his
lips touched hers.

Bold and brash and commanding, the sensual, intimate contact was still as gentle, as tender as a brush

with morning dew. His touch was sure and steady. Wendy wondered if making love came naturally to him. The ultimate effect was devastating. Wendy didn't think about the words that they had exchanged, nor did she think about what he did for a living, nor did it even occur to her that she had known this man for less than twenty-four hours.

All she could think about was his kiss. All that she could feel was the sweet, subtle, sensual pressure of his lips against hers, his mouth, artfully claiming her own. The tip of his tongue explored her mouth, plundering the richness of it, filling it. She savored his lips and the smooth surface of his teeth, and every little nuance of passionate movement.

His kiss evoked feelings deep inside of her, where he did not touch her. She felt warmth invade her like showering rays of the sun. Passion curled and undulated in the center of her being, steaming through her limbs, sweeping into her breasts and hips and thighs. This was desire, liquid and sweet. She longed to drop everything and throw her arms around his neck. She yearned to press her body against him and feel the length of them touch and duel, as did their mouths.

Just in time, she remembered his words of warning. And she remembered that when she loved, she loved very deeply. Even if she sometimes felt desperate to reach out again for a pale facsimile, a pretense, of what she had known, this was not the time or the place.

And this cocky, overconfident city slicker probably wasn't even the right man.

His lips parted from hers. She opened her eyes and stared into the sharp, questing depths of his. Their breath still mingled. And, she noted with some satisfaction, his breath seemed to come faster than her own.

Did the thunder of his heart outweigh the tremor of her own?

He arched a brow. She smiled as sweetly as she could. "Well, McKenna," she said softly, seductively, "I think my heart is safe. Quite safe."

He was quick, she noted, but not quite quick enough to hide his surprise at her words. His hands fell from her cheeks and he sat back, watching her. "Oh, yeah?"

"Yeah."

Then he laughed, and she found herself laughing, too.

"I must be slipping," he teased.

"Happens to the best of us," she agreed consolingly.

He picked up his beer and took a swallow, still watching her. Wendy kept her eyes evenly set with his, though she couldn't control the small, wicked grin that continued to ghost her lips.

He leaned forward once again. "I'll have to try harder next time."

"You're really going to have to be careful," Wendy warned him, her eyes growing innocently large. "If you have to try so very hard, you might find yourself tripping and falling on your own effort. Could be dangerous."

"I'm a big boy, Mrs. Hawk. I do know how to take care of myself."

Wendy smiled flatly. "And I'm a big girl. Far better able to take care of myself in the present circumstances, I think."

"Next time, Wendy," he warned with a devil's grin.

He had passed the first forbidden door; he had touched her. Now he flexed his fingers to stop the tense tremors that had claimed them.

"Is there going to be a next time?" There was nothing coy to the words, nothing demure. It was a blunt, direct question, voiced with an open, amused interest. She was still smiling, and the smile lighted up her eyes to a silver-blue so bright and alluring that Brad felt himself begin to tremble all over again. His muscles were hot and tight—everything was hot and tight—and he found himself grateful that denim jeans could hide a multitude of sins.

"You bet," he promised her pleasantly through gritted teeth.

Just then, his pole dipped in the water and dug into his buttocks where he sat upon it.

"You've got something!" Wendy cried delightedly.

He had something, all right, Brad decided.

He wasn't a bad fisherman. Although these rods were a bit different, he'd grown up near Lake Erie and had done his share of fishing.

He gave the fighting fish a little space, then reeled it back. Once more, he gave the fish a little line to play itself out, then he reeled in. Meanwhile, Wendy reached for a net.

"Do we need that?" he asked her.

"You get stuck by a catfish, and it hurts like hell," she warned him. "We don't have to have it, but it would be kind of foolish to need medical care now for something stupid." She offered him a rueful grin. "I got stuck once and needed ten stitches."

He smiled. "By all means, haul out that net. I'll play macho some other time."

"Oh. Like 'next time'?" Wendy taunted, but then she bowed her head quickly, wondering what on earth was goading her.

Finally, Brad caught the line, and Wendy thrust the net out over the water. He deposited his squirming catch in the net, letting out a pleased holler. It was a hefty catfish, which would definitely rate as a dinner fish. They could even invite company over and have plenty to spare.

"A pretty damned good fish, huh?" he demanded triumphantly.

Wendy nodded serenely. "Yeah. Pretty damned good," she acknowledged. But she couldn't resist adding, "For a city slicker."

Brad conceded the point. He sat back, watching supremely as Wendy put on a glove, then carefully freed the hook and line from the fish's mouth. He enjoyed watching her. She still seemed like an angel with those silver-mist eyes and all that near-platinum hair and her slim, fragile form. But she was capable, lithe and quietly self-assured.

But like hell his touch hadn't affected her!

She tossed the fish into a bucket in the rear of the canoe.

He reached into the cooler and offered her a new beer. "You deserve it," he assured her solemnly.

"What a sport."

"Yeah, I'm a sport. I'm going to do all the paddling back, just like I did all the paddling here. And, my dear lady, you will recall, I am the one who caught the fish."

"The first fish," Wendy said.

But she never did catch anything. When the second beer made her dizzy, she decided it was time to cut up some of the cheese.

To her chagrin, Brad caught another fish, a second catfish, bigger than the first. To console her, he assured her that he had gone fishing many times before.

Sunset was coming when they headed back. The canoe streaked through the water in silence, and Brad found himself mesmerized by the beautiful surroundings once again. Gold and pink highlights fell upon the soft white of a crane, giving the bird the hues of a rainbow. The water reflected the glow of the dying light, and the waves of grass dipped to the soft, cooler breeze of the coming night.

As Wendy sat facing him, she did not see the alligator when Brad first sighted the creature. It was so still, he thought that it was a log at first.

And then he realized that it was a giant reptile.

An enormous, grotesque creature. About twelve or thirteen feet long, with a snout full of evil teeth that seemed to be a third of the length of the body.

It was ugly, incredibly ugly, Brad thought. His body tensed as he stared at the prehistoric creature.

But he wasn't going to give her another chance to call him a city slicker. He had to start getting accustomed to the creatures that roamed here. He'd been ready to battle the big cat with his bare hands, only to discover that the panther was a beloved pet named Baby.

What did she call the alligator? he wondered dryly. Junior, maybe? Spot? Rover?

He swallowed and tried to relax. When they drifted by the alligator, Brad was going to be casual—even if it killed him.

He slid the canoe up on the embankment, shoving his paddle into the muck to bring the canoe up high and secure. He started to rise, but Wendy caught his hand.

"Wait!" she said tensely.

"Wait for what?" he drawled laconically. "Oh—the gator? I saw it already."

"You saw it!" Her eyes flew to his, rounded. She grabbed his hand and pulled him back down to the seat. "Then sit still and let him go first, you idiot!"

"What?"

Wendy stood, carefully. There was a small fallen branch nearby. She picked it up and threw it hard at the alligator. The monster with the evil yellow eyes just stared at her. She tossed another one. It plunked the alligator right on the head, and the animal slunk back into the water and glided away. A moment later, it disappeared into the darkness.

Brad stared at Wendy. "You mean it isn't a pet?"

She shook her head, frowning at him as if he had lost his mind. "Who in God's name would want one of those monsters for a pet? That thing was about twelve feet long. He could have consumed both of us in one gulp. They're dangerous. I mean, you're all right if you avoid them. But I'd sure as hell never want to befriend one. They're vicious in the water if they're hungry, and bear in mind, they can move about forty miles an hour on land, too."

She smiled and rose, grabbing the pail with their fresh catch of the day. Brad remained in the canoe, watching the fluid, languid sway of her buttocks as she strode toward the house.

He smiled. Okay, so only that TV cop kept an alligator for a pet. Panthers were surely more popular. He'd learn. Surely, he'd learn.

Brad rose, collecting their gear. He'd seen a hose outside. He found it again and rinsed off the fishing gear. Then he brought the gear back into the house.

Wendy had been a quick worker, too. The catfish were already headless and well on their way to becoming fillets. She smiled up at him, then finished her task, dropping the fillets into a bowl of marinade when she was done.

"I'm going to hop in the shower. Turn on the television, have some wine, make yourself at home. I'll be right out."

He leaned against the refrigerator, popping open another beer. "Want company?"

"No, thanks."

Brad shook his head sadly. "Couldn't handle it, huh?"

She paused, rising to the taunt. "I think that time will tell, city slicker, just who can handle what around here."

He lifted his beer can to her in a toast. Wendy saw that his lashes fell lazily over his eyes, and that beneath, he surveyed her in a long and leisurely fashion.

She'd seen Baby look at birds in much the same way.

But the look warmed her, causing a hot flush to rise and tint her cheeks. Maybe he was right. Maybe she was out of her league. Maybe she couldn't handle anything that was happening to her at all. He'd given her every chance to retreat. He'd warned her that she couldn't be anything more than a friend. She didn't want to end up like the redhead in the photo; he'd remember the color of her hair, but he wouldn't remember her name.

Wendy spun around. "I'll be out shortly," she murmured.

Brad stared after her, wondering what had caused the change in her.

In the bathroom, Wendy stood beneath a warm spray and trembled with the chill that had seized her.

Perhaps she didn't want him remembering her name. She just wanted him to touch her, because she had been so lonely, and because it would feel so good to be touched again. But darkness and anonymity held a certain appeal.

The water cascaded around her. The sound cocooned her.

She wondered how he would feel if he really knew the truth. Yes, she wanted him. The chemistry was right; the attraction was strong. They had both felt it. And there had been more. They'd had the chance to know that they both believed in certain values in life, maybe in a certain sense of honor. They didn't know much about each other, but they knew the important things.

And so maybe it would be all right.

Except that he just wasn't the kind of man to stand in for another. Wendy was quite certain that if Brad McKenna even guessed that she wanted him only in darkness, as a substitute for another man, his smile would fade and his sensual suggestions would fall silent.

There was just something about him... Even if he intended to have a woman only once, he'd want her to know damned clearly just who she was with.

Wendy bit her lip. Yes, there was just something about him. And that unusual quality was drawing her closer and closer to the edge.

She jumped suddenly, hearing the bathroom door open quietly, then close.

"Brad?" she whispered. "Brad!"

There was no answer. The sound of the water cascading over her naked form and onto the tile was all that filled the room.

Chapter 5

Brad!" Panic rose high in her voice.

"Shush!"

There was a heated whisper at last. Wendy didn't have much time to worry about the fact that the man had interrupted her shower. She pulled the curtain against her body and looked out. Brad wasn't even glancing her way; he was standing at the small window over the commode, looking out into the right side of the yard.

"What is it?" Wendy whispered. He stood at the window, tense and silent as a wraith. "Brad, what is it!" she insisted softly.

At last she had his attention. He stared at her pensively, then strode toward her. He didn't touch her but came close, so that their eyes met amid the steam that poured around them.

"There's someone out there."

"If you heard something," Wendy said with a relieved smile, "I'm sure it's just Baby."

"No, no it's not."

"Really, Brad, I understand your circumstances, but we are tucked so far into the swampland. I'm sure you're just imagining—"

"I don't imagine," he said, cutting her off bluntly.

Wendy tightened her hold on the shower curtain and swallowed uneasily. He was, after all, still a stranger. He'd entered her shower without the decent grace of a quiet tap against the door. And right now he was so solidly implacable and assured that it was like talking to a rock. He had changed. He was a bundle of tension. She could see it in his eyes, in his stance, in the constriction of his muscles.

And it was frightening.

"Can you shoot?" he asked her tensely.

"Come on now, Brad—"

"I asked you if you can shoot!"

"Yes."

"Stay inside, but load that shotgun of yours and be prepared to defend yourself. Do you hear me? Stay here, and if something should go wrong, have the shotgun in your hand."

He spun around and left her. The bathroom door closed quietly in his wake.

Wendy turned off the water and hopped out of the tub, longing to call him back. There wasn't any danger out there—there just couldn't be! She had to catch him.

But she couldn't go running after him stark naked. She dried off with a lick and a promise and stumbled into her clothes. She came charging out, then paused.

There was nothing out there, but maybe, just maybe, she should load the shotgun.

She raced to get it down from the wall, then she panicked when she couldn't find the shells for the gun in the box in the closet. Pushing things around, she finally found a second box. She loaded both barrels and started down the hall. Brad, she knew, was already outside somewhere. But where? There seemed to be an eerie silence about the place.

But then that silence was shattered. "There you are, you son of a bitch!" a male voice grunted out.

"I've got you now!" a second man swore.

"Oh, no!" Wendy breathed, recognizing both male voices and realizing what must have happened. She ran down the hall to the front door and threw it open. "Stop!" she screamed. "Stop!"

She was ignored, so she raised the shotgun, and barely aiming, she squeezed the trigger. The kickback of the shotgun nearly sent her sprawling as the explosive sound filled the night—to be followed by complete, stark silence.

Brad didn't know how he knew that someone was outside, he just knew. He hadn't really heard anything, just the whisper of the breeze, the rustle of foliage, all natural things.

And yet he had felt it, sensed it.

They were being watched. Someone was watching them, watching them carefully, in stealth and silence.

That surprised Brad. Michaelson was the type to come striding right in. If he had made it to a place like this, he could quickly ascertain that he was far more powerful in terms of manpower and ammunition. And he didn't make it a habit to tease, taunt or torture—he assessed things quickly, and just as quickly he relieved himself of excess baggage.

No, this didn't feel like Michaelson.

But then, who the hell else could it be?

Dusk had fallen when he finally slipped out the front door. He locked it behind him, intending to buy Wendy a little more time to get prepared just in case the trouble turned out to be serious.

Shadows fell all around him, and the lights from inside the house made them all the worse. Brad flattened himself against the wall, straining to see against the darkness. He could hear the sounds of the night, the chirps of crickets, the occasional grunt of a frog, the wind, slight and rustling in the trees, in the long grasses that bowed low before it. Nothing seemed out of the ordinary.

But someone, he knew, was near.

Brad began to move around the house. He probably should have taken the shotgun himself, but then he didn't know where she kept the ammunition, and he had wanted the element of surprise to be on his side.

Puzzled, Brad realized that although he was still certain that someone was on the hammock with them, he didn't know how he had gotten there. The airboat was still secured where they had left it that morning, and when he came around the house, he saw that the canoe, too, was exactly where they had left it. There were no other boats of any kind on the land, nor out in the nearby water.

He heard something, and he froze. He didn't know what it was, or where it had come from, but he had heard something. He came around the corner, squinting, flexed and ready, poised on the balls of his feet. He kept moving, certain that his quarry was just ahead of him. At last he reached the front of the house again.

Suddenly, he felt a whoosh of motion. He looked up just as a heavy weight fell on him from atop the roof. Falling and tumbling beneath his attacker, Brad swore at him, and the man instantly responded.

"I've got you now!" the man returned.

And he did, Brad thought. The man was straddled over him, and he was agile and powerful. His hold was nearly merciless. Brad strained with all his might, shifting his weight, throwing his attacker.

But the man was fast—damned fast. He spun around in the darkness, a fist flying. It caught Brad cleanly in the jaw.

He responded, slamming into the man's stomach. It was like shoving against steel.

A blow struck his shoulder; Brad responded by ducking his head and butting into the stranger, a move that brought them both careening and rolling and bitterly wrestling on the ground again. Poised over his attacker for a brief moment, Brad stared down and gasped in surprise.

The guy had green eyes, but his hair was pitch-black and long against his neck. A headband kept it from falling into his eyes. He was wearing jeans and a denim shirt, but his features were strikingly bold.

Just as another blow reached his chin, Brad swore and slugged back. No, it wasn't Michaelson. It sure as hell wasn't Michaelson. He was being attacked by an Indian.

"Son of a bitch—" Brad began, but then he was thrown, and he had to gasp for air to strain against the new hold on him.

"Stop!"

Vaguely, Brad heard Wendy's voice. "Stop!" It didn't really mean anything—not to him, not to the tight-lipped man above him. Somehow they had gotten too involved in their exchange of blows. The fight had become too serious.

They were evenly matched, yet each man was determined to win.

But then it sounded as if the whole earth had exploded around them, and simultaneously, they fell back, startled.

Brad twisted around, staring in stunned surprise at Wendy. She was sitting on the ground, with the shotgun resting in her lap.

"Stop it!" she insisted, gasping for breath. "Both of you, do you hear me, stop!"

Panting, Brad stared over at the man who had attacked him.

The Indian was stretched out on the ground, pushing up on an elbow—and panting from exertion.

Brad stared back at Wendy. "Who the hell is this?"

"Who the hell am I?" the man retorted, his voice sounding much like a growl emanating from the back of his throat. "Who the hell is this guy?" he demanded of Wendy.

Brad pushed himself to his feet, staring at Wendy, and then at the Indian, who wasn't about to accept Brad's vantage point. He stood, too, placing his hands on his hips. The hostility between them still seemed to crackle in the air.

"Wendy! Who is this?" the Indian demanded.

Leaning against the shotgun, Wendy came to her feet. She hurried over to position herself between the two men. They barely seemed to notice that she was there. Their eyes were locked and she could feel the hatred that radiated from the two of them, spilling over to her. What was it with these two? Men! Let's Punch Each Other Out First seemed to be their motto.

"Brad McKenna, this is Eric Hawk. Eric, this is Brad McKenna."

"So who is Brad McKenna?" Eric said flatly, maintaining his wary glare at Brad.

"Eric! He's a friend of mine."

Brad spun on Wendy. "*Hawk?* I thought you said that your husband was dead."

Wendy saw Eric's jaw clamping even more tightly and the line of his mouth drawing into a grim scowl. "Leif is dead. Eric is my brother-in-law."

Brad kept staring at the other man, wondering why the hell it was taking him so long to assimilate it all. "He's an Indian. You were married to an Indian?"

"Well, Wendy, this is one bright boy you've got here," Eric drawled sarcastically.

"What's it to you?" Brad returned.

Fists were going to start flying again, Wendy thought in dismay. She placed a hand on each of the masculine chests, as if she could push the men apart.

"I mean it, stop it! Or both of you can get the hell off my property right now!"

They both gave her a wounded look.

She breathed a little more easily. For another long moment she waited, watching them both warily. They still stared at one another with open hostility, but at least they were silent.

"Shall we go in? Are the two of you capable of behaving decently to one another?"

Brad shrugged and inclined his head accusingly toward Eric. "He was the one stalking around the house as if he were out on a scalping party."

"Brad!" Wendy snapped.

"What was I supposed to think?" Eric asked her innocently.

"Well, Eric, you could have knocked," Wendy insisted.

Eric wasn't going to accept the blame any more than Brad intended to. "I saw Muscle Man here slinking around the windows. I was afraid for you, Wendy."

"Okay, okay!" She turned away from the two men and started toward the house. "You want to beat each other up? Fine—go to it. Tear each other apart. Just don't come here for ice packs when you're done!" She swung around and retrieved the shotgun, mumbling to herself. "Honest to God, but they deserve one another!"

Wendy stormed back into the house. Brad surveyed the man he'd been wrestling. They were almost exactly the same height, and had similar builds. A real even match. He could feel his left eye puffing up; the other man had a trickle of blood coming from his lip down his chin.

"Leif and Eric?" he heard himself query.

For a moment, the other man was silent. Then he cast his head back and laughed, and Brad felt a smile creasing his own features. "Well, I don't know who you are yet, and I'm still damned curious. Wendy seems willing enough to defend you, so I guess you're all right, but it doesn't seem that she's told you very much about herself."

Brad shrugged. "No. I guess she hasn't," he admitted. "You are an Indian, right?"

Eric grinned. "Seminole through and through."

"Leif and Eric?"

"Mom is Norwegian."

"Of course." Brad lifted his shoulders. "Norse Seminoles. Why the hell not." Suddenly it was as if the hostility had disappeared, dissipated into the evening sky. He liked the man with the sharp features, strange green eyes and rueful smile. And he felt the same respect in return. "Want to go in?"

"Yeah, I guess we should."

Eric led the way. Another little tremor seized Brad as he realized that Wendy's brother-in-law was very comfortable in her home. Eric hopped up on the counter, smiling at Wendy as she soaked pieces of fish fillet in batter before dropping them into a skillet.

Wendy kept her lips pursed in disapproval. "Are you staying for dinner?" she asked.

Eric cast a glance Brad's way. "Am I welcome?"

"We've plenty of fish," Wendy said.

Brad kept silent. He'd been worried about being alone with Wendy, but now that their privacy had been taken away, he wanted it back.

Eric watched Brad, and his grin deepened. "Well, Wendy, you know how I just love your Cajun catfish."

Wendy nodded, her eyes on her task. "Eric, would you fix yourself and Brad a drink?"

"Sure." He slid off the counter and turned to Brad. "Name your poison."

"Jack Black on the rocks, if it's available."

"You got it. Wendy? A glass of wine?"

Wendy dropped a fillet into the sizzling oil, then looked over at her brother-in-law. "Tonight? Nooo...I think I'll have bourbon, too, please."

"Your wish is my command, Wendy. You know that." He looked at her so innocently.

At this point in her life, Eric was probably her closest friend. When Leif died, Eric had mourned beside her. No one could understand her grief more than Eric, because the two of them had suffered a loss together. For the longest time, they had been each other's only salvation.

It had all happened two years ago, but she knew that seeing her with another man like this had to open old wounds for him. But then again, Eric had always encouraged her to get back out in the world again.

That had been before he had actually found a strange man in her house.

Eric handed her a Jack Black on the rocks. She sipped it quickly, savoring the sweet, burning sensation.

Brad lifted his glass to hers. "Cheers."

She nodded and started to take another sip.

Oh, what the heck! she thought. Wendy cast back her head and swallowed the entire contents of the glass. Dinner threatened to be a long and nerve-racking affair.

In the end, it really wasn't so bad. Brad remained silent at the beginning, adding a bit to Wendy's uneasiness. But Eric talked about the family and Wendy was grateful that he kept to easy topics. After a few minutes, he even included Brad in the conversation. She told Eric that Brad had caught the fish and that she hadn't been able to hook anything. Then the two men entered into an enthusiastic discussion on fishing.

However, things were bound to get sticky. They did so when dinner was over, when Wendy started to rinse the plates and load the dishwasher.

Both men went to make coffee. This time, Eric deferred to Brad, but they were both scrutinizing each other suspiciously. Sensing the tension, Wendy decided to serve some brandy and Tia Maria along with their coffee. Just as she gripped the brandy bottle, Eric asked Brad what he did for a living.

The bottle slipped from her fingers and fell to the floor. The glass bottle shattered, and the sticky liquid flew everywhere.

Both men stared at her. Wendy smiled weakly. "Slippery fingers, I suppose." She knelt to start mopping up the spill.

"Let me help you," Brad said, hunching down before her. She cut her finger on a piece of glass and absently sucked upon the wound as she stared at him in a growing panic.

"Wendy—" Brad frowned at the state of her finger.

"Did you cut yourself?" Eric demanded, concerned.

"No, I—"

"Yes, she did," Brad said. He helped her to her feet, sticking her hand under the running water at the sink. It wasn't serious, but Brad started muttering about antiseptic and Eric said he'd get some peroxide and Band-Aids.

"Brad," Wendy murmured. His arm was around her as he held her hand beneath the faucet. She smiled slightly, admiring the planes of his face, noticing the concern he showed. She was surrounded by the heat of him, and the subtle male scent that suddenly seemed to tease her mercilessly.

"Hmm?" He was still concerned about her cut.

"What do I tell Eric?"

He looked into her eyes, understanding her question. "Do you trust him?"

"Of course. I'd trust him with my life."

"That's all that matters," Brad said softly. Then he shrugged. "Tell him. Tell him the truth."

He finished speaking just as Eric returned to the kitchen. "Just peroxide—it won't hurt," Eric told Wendy, taking her hand. Brad backed away while Eric cleaned and bandaged her cut with a tender care that probably outweighed the seriousness of the situation. Brad bent down and picked up the rest of the broken bottle, soaking up the spilled brandy with paper towels.

When Brad finished rinsing his hands, Eric confronted him again. "Well? Did you decide whether to tell me what you're whispering about or not? Wendy, I hope you didn't cut your finger just for my benefit."

"No!" she gasped quickly.

"DEA," Brad told Eric.

Without flinching, Eric kept his eyes on Brad, then nodded. They all stood in silence for a moment. "I thought you had to be with some branch of law enforcement," he murmured.

"Yeah?"

"Well, you were ready for me, and I'm pretty good at stealth. It's that 'Tonto' blood in me, you know."

Brad laughed and clapped Eric on the back.

Wendy decided that they were both crazy. She turned around and started to pour coffee.

"You're involved in that Michaelson deal that went bad?"

"Yes."

"And you're hiding out here?"

Wendy had been dropping shots of Tia Maria into the coffee. Now she tightened her trembling fingers and set the bottle down. She didn't need any more alcohol on the floor.

"Yes," Brad said at last.

Noticing Wendy's hesitation, Eric grabbed the Tia Maria bottle and added another shot to each of the coffee cups. He took a sip of his coffee, then muttered, "That's dangerous for Wendy. She shouldn't be so involved in this sordid business."

"Eric—" Wendy tried to interrupt him.

"Where did you meet? How did you meet?" Eric probed.

"Eric!" Wendy protested again. She loved her brother-in-law. And it had been nice to have him care for her, to be protective. It had been nice to know that he had been close, that there was still someone out there who loved her enough to risk life and limb for her. But he was prying into dangerous territory.

"It's all right, Wendy," Brad said. "Michaelson chased me out on Alligator Alley. My car blew a gasket or something after I'd taken a side road. One of his bullets nicked me in the forehead—Wendy found me facedown in the mud."

Eric nodded slowly.

"Couldn't we have coffee in the living room?" Wendy murmured. When they both ignored her, she decided to ignore them. She took her coffee cup into the living room and considered turning the television on. Tonight, some soothing music might be a better bet. She turned on the system that Leif had so painstakingly set up and slipped in a Beatles disc. As music filled the room, Wendy sat on the couch and closed her eyes, warming her hands with her cup.

Despite the music she could still hear them talking in the kitchen, their words growing louder.

"Excuse me!" she called. "This is my house, you know. I am the hostess, you are the guests. Want to come on out here and behave?"

They both appeared, slowly. Although they apparently hadn't been able to restrain their anger in the kitchen, now they had nothing to say.

Brad wandered over to the far side of the room, studying the titles of the books that lined the shelves. With a grimace, Eric sat down beside her on the couch.

At length, he sighed. "Wendy, it's dangerous—"

"He's right. I think I should go," Brad interrupted.

"Dammit!" Wendy exploded. She slammed her cup onto the butcher-block side table and flew to her feet, spinning around to face Eric, then Brad, then Eric again.

"Eric, if you really love me, trust me enough to know that I'm not a fool. And no one knows better than you do how deeply hidden we are here!" She turned back to Brad. "If I didn't feel that I could safely help you, I'd never have asked you here. I'm a grown woman, capable of making my own decisions. Don't try to run my life—behind my back!"

Brad picked up the TV guide and began to idly leaf through it. He cleared his throat. "Wendy—"

"It wasn't behind your back," Eric said.

She glared at them both. "Oh, hell!" she groaned, falling back onto the couch in mock defeat.

"This is great," Brad said, suddenly changing the subject. "Do you get cable out here?"

She smiled slowly. "Yes, I have cable TV."

"Ten o'clock, *No Way Out* is on! I've been trying to see that movie for over a year."

Wendy got up and turned off the Beatles disc. "Go ahead, turn on the television."

Eric rose. "Got any microwave popcorn, Wendy?"

"In the top cabinet over the stove."

Brad turned on the television; Eric went into the kitchen and found the popcorn. By ten-fifteen they were huddled together on the couch with Wendy in the middle, crunching away on popcorn.

It was strange, Wendy thought. Very strange.

But then, she thought that it was nice, too. It was as if they had all known each other for ages. Considering their precipitous introduction, Brad and Eric seemed to be getting along very well.

When the movie ended, Wendy yawned. Brad stood and stretched, picking up the popcorn bowl.

Slightly uneasy, Eric stared at Brad.

Wendy lowered her head. Although Eric knew that Brad was staying here, she sensed her brother-in-law's reluctance to depart, leaving this stranger behind. "Do you have to work tomorrow?" she asked him.

"Yeah, I do."

"Do you need me?"

He shook his head. "No. It's probably better if you just lie low. I'll drop by again in a few days."

"How did you get here?" Brad asked Eric, baffled.

Eric laughed and winked at Wendy. "You've got to show him where the stones are."

"The what?"

Wendy grinned. "There's a place in the canal where Leif set boulders into the water. The depth there is only about a foot—in the dry season, you can see them. Eric drove here—his car is right behind the saw grass."

"I see." With good grace, Brad grinned. The two men shook hands. Wendy felt that Brad sensed Eric's discomfort. "Well, I'm going to call it a day. Wendy, Eric, thank you both."

"Take care," Eric warned him softly. Brad nodded, strode into the guest room and closed the door.

"I'll walk you out?" Wendy said to her brother-in-law.

He set an arm around her shoulder and ruffled her hair. "Sure."

Outside in the darkness, Eric said, "I like him, Wendy. I mean, not that it matters. You're a mature woman, and you have the right to make your own decisions. But I have to admit, I like him."

Her lips trembled when she tried to smile. "Eric, nothing has hap—"

"Wendy, don't encourage me to act like a surrogate parent. I know you've needed to get out. Hell, *I've* been out. I've been out a lot," he said bitterly.

Yes, he had, Wendy thought, but she didn't voice her agreement. They'd had their different ways of coping with the pain after the horrible night when her husband and his wife had been killed together. For Wendy, it had been a complete withdrawal. For Eric, it had been a near fall into a world of reckless delusion.

But they had both survived, she thought.

"Good night, Wendy. I'll tell the folks hi—"

"I'll be in to see everyone soon." She paused. "Think I can bring Brad to the folks?"

"Yes, I think you can."

She smiled at Eric. The breeze picked up his sleek raven hair and moved it in the darkness, and for a moment, her heart caught in her throat as he reminded her of Leif. He kissed her on the forehead, and then he disappeared in the night.

Wendy went back into the house, locking the door behind her. When she reached the guest-room door, she knocked lightly.

"Yes?" Brad responded after a moment.

Wendy pushed the door open. Brad was still in jeans, but he had taken off his shirt. The room was dark, but light seeped in from the hallway. It gleamed bronze upon his bare shoulders while his features remained hidden in shadows.

"I wanted to thank you," she said.

She could sense his confusion. "For what?"

"Eric is a good friend."

"I noticed. You're close."

"Yes, we are, but not like that. I mean, we could never be involved. He's really like a brother in the truest sense. Since I haven't dated since Leif died, you see, and—not that we're dating or anything—but I think it was just hard for Eric to leave with you and me here alone. And, well, the way you made a point of coming in here, I . . ." As her voice trailed away, she stood there, wishing to God she didn't feel quite so foolish.

"Or anything?" he queried softly.

"What?"

"We're not dating, or anything?" he repeated, and she noticed a rueful smile on his face. "Come on, Wendy, we're doing *something* together, aren't we?"

She smiled, glad that he had a way of making her feel comfortable.

"Hey. Come over here," he said softly.

Slowly, she began to walk toward him.

She paused when she reached him. The light was still shielding his eyes, while it played over the rippled muscles of his bronze shoulders. There was a rich spattering of tawny hair covering his chest. She wanted to touch it.

She did.

She laid her palm flat against his chest.

And that was when he kissed her. Threading his fingers through her hair, he lowered his head over hers. For the longest time his breath seemed to tease her lips. Tentatively, she gazed into his eyes, soft gold and fascinated as they searched her. Then his lips touched hers, very gently. Her fingers curled into his chest as she felt the force of his mouth upon hers broaden, sweeping her away. His tongue bathed her mouth in a sweet, warm invasion.

Even with her eyes closed, she saw the man, knew the man. She felt his hands, and his kiss.

A delicious weakness overcame her. It would be so easy. So easy to give way to the liquid in her knees and fall. He would catch her, she knew. He would catch her and sweep her away to bed, where she could surrender to the darkness of night.

His lips parted slowly from hers, hovering above her. She felt the golden probe of his gaze again.

"Wendy..." he murmured.

They were spellbound, locked in a magical moment. She used her free hand to smooth the tendril of hair that had fallen over his forehead.

He inhaled, and then exhaled, shakily. With stony resolve, he lifted her hands and kissed her palms. "Go to bed, Wendy," he told her.

She lowered her eyes, nodding. Neither of them was ready. "Good night."

She started walking to the door.

"Wendy!"

In an instant he was beside her again, and she rushed into his arms. This time he kissed her with passion and fire, and then his hands slipped deftly beneath her oversized shirt, finding her bare breasts beneath it. As his palms caressed her nipples a jagged sob escaped her lips beneath the sweet and savage force of his kiss.

And then, just as she had imagined, he swept her off her feet, heading with purpose for the bed that loomed huge and enticing in the shadows of the night.

Chapter 6

With grave tenderness, he eased her down upon the bed. She could feel the urgent hunger in the heated length of his body as he lay down beside her. His kiss continued to sear her, and his touch lingered upon her. His hands were everywhere, holding her face, stroking her shoulder, caressing her bare back. He was staging an onslaught against her senses, and she wanted desperately to hold on to each feeling, to each nuance of emotion and reaction. He was awakening sensations she had forgotten, feelings she had forsaken when Leif died.

His passionate assault was like the sudden surge of the tide; swept into that tide, she found that thought was difficult. She explored his chest with her fingertips, marveling at the warmth of his flesh, the tension in his muscles. She loved the coarse feeling of the short, whorling hairs that teased her fingertips, and most of all, she loved the evocative feel of his body over hers, so much of him eclipsing so much of her.

She seemed to drown in his kiss, for it was never ending, although it evolved. Fiercely, he claimed her lips ... then pulled away to press his mouth against the pulse in her throat, or the hollow of her collarbone. The inner circle of his palm fell gently against her breast, and his fingers closed slowly around the full weight of it, exploring and caressing sensitive areas.

Minutes passed ... or aeons. She breathed in the enticing male scent of his bare flesh, and she arched to meet his kiss. It was easy to respond, far easier than she had expected, for she had not known that she was starved. The darkness quietly shielded her from any sense of reality, even as the full bulge growing against his denim jeans warned her that she was plunging, falling downward into a tempest from which she could not rise. She was falling into the forbidden realm, a realm of pleasure, where loneliness was masked, and thirst was sated.

But then, abruptly, without a word, he pulled away from her. The only sound was the belabored rush of his breath. She knew from the heat of his flesh and the hardened feel of his body that he had not lost his desire for her. But it was over. Whatever it had been, he had ended it.

In the dim light his eyes seemed to gleam like a great cat's, sizzling and gold. He rested upon an elbow and stared curiously down at her. Wendy bit her inner lip, wondering what had driven him away.

"What's wrong?" she asked, her words a whisper.

He drew the tip of his thumb over her cheek, staring pensively at her face. He shook his head. "This—I shouldn't be doing this."

"But I came to you!"

They remained still. The only movement was that of his thumb, the callused pad stroking her flesh. She could read no emotion in his eyes; she had no idea what he was thinking or feeling.

Suddenly, her emotions crumbled, stung by the rejection. She had laid herself on the line. She hadn't been dreaming of the past; no ghosts had drifted between them. She had offered herself—and he had refused her. He'd dealt the supreme blow to her confidence.

"Oh, dear God!" she muttered. Humiliated, she shoved against him. Apparently, he hadn't expected her to touch him, at least not so vehemently. She pushed him so hard that he rolled right onto the floor.

"Wendy! Dammit, wait, listen—"

Brad's kneecap hurt where he'd slammed it onto the floor. His head had bumped against the bed frame and, all in all, he felt like an idiot.

It seemed that a guy just couldn't win. He had known he was bound for trouble, wanting her as he did. But he'd expected her to be angry with him for taking advantage of her, not for trying desperately, with a restraint that went above and beyond, to respect her. "Wendy!" Muttering to himself and wincing in pain, Brad scrambled back to his feet.

Wendy was desperately fighting the urge to burst into tears—not a little rivulet of damp tears, but a thunderous storm of wet, sloppy tears. She tore into her own room, but there was no way to lock the door against him—he had broken the lock that morning.

Wendy slammed the door anyway.

It didn't do any good. "Wendy!" Brad knocked on the door. When she didn't answer, he opened it and waited in the doorway, still breathless. She sat at the foot of her bed, her back to him, fiercely cradling her pillow. Soft light spilled in from the hall, falling over her, striking her hair with a golden glow.

"Wendy! I want to talk to you."

"I don't want to talk to you."

"Wendy, please, listen to me." He stood behind her and rested his hands on her shoulders, surprised to discover how much she was trembling.

She tried to shrug him away, but he sat down behind her. "I'd really appreciate it if you didn't touch me," she said stiffly.

He let go of her shoulders but remained behind her. "We've got to talk," he said hoarsely. "Wendy, if you would just turn around and talk to me—"

She spun around then, putting distance between them. She jerked the band out of her hair and golden locks tumbled down to her shoulders. She shook them out in absent vehemence, staring at him with shimmering silver eyes that reflected light like diamonds. "What? Talk. Say whatever it is and then go away."

He sighed. "Wendy, you're not making this easy."

"Well, I hope you'll forgive me. It isn't very easy from my side, either. I'm not good at this to begin with. I've been out of practice for some time."

"Wendy, that's just the point."

She inhaled, holding back a sob. He reached out to touch her cheek again, and he felt the warm, liquid tears there. "Wendy..."

"Stop it! For the love of God, will you stop it?"

He pulled her into his arms. She fought him, tensing and straining against him. He couldn't let her go, so he held her until she stopped fighting him, until she collapsed against his chest and let him wrap his arms around her.

"Brad, please," she murmured against his chest. She could taste the sweet salt of his flesh when she spoke; she could feel the beat of his heart, strong beneath her cheek.

He smoothed back her hair, somewhat awed by its color in the night. Angel's hair. So soft, so silky, so beautifully blond. "Wendy, I want you so badly, don't you see?"

She stiffened again. "No, quite frankly, I don't."

In the darkness, he smiled. "Wendy, it's just too quick. I want you, but I want it to be right. I don't want you to wake up in the morning and be sorry. I don't want to be a substitute for your husband, and I don't want you to regret what you did in the darkness. I want you to want me."

She kept silent for a moment, warmed by his embrace, feeling ridiculously secure, since she knew he offered her no real security. On the contrary, he offered her danger, in many different guises. "I did want you," she said at last.

"Did you? Did you really?" He kissed her forehead. Then, very gently, he kissed her lips again and smiled at her. "You're a very special lady, Wendy. And we are going to make love. Here I've been racking my head all day trying to figure out how not to drag you into bed. And to top it off, you wander into my bedroom when I've been a damned saint and shut myself up for the night. I'll never be able to leave you without knowing what we have to share. But I care too much now, Wendy. I care too much about you to not take it slowly. That's what we really want, what we both deserve. A night of passion with no regrets in the morning." He finished off his words with another kiss, a slow, languid kiss.

She felt as if her heart still beat a hundred miles an hour, as if her blood still raced through her system painfully. She pushed away from him, groaning softly as she twisted her head. "Brad, if you have any feelings for me, please! Leave me alone now."

"No."

Incensed, she tried to break free from his hold. He caught her arms and held her close. With one deft, sure movement, he pulled her back onto the bed. His shoulders and head rested against a plump pillow, and her head was tucked against his chest, her hair splayed in a lustrous array upon it.

He longed to touch that hair. He longed to do much, much more. But he was afraid to release her. He kept his arm around her, aware of the tension in her, aware that she could easily bolt.

"Wendy," he murmured, "want to know my middle name?"

"What?" He could see her bewildered frown, but he also felt some of the tension ease out of her. Daring to ease his powerful hold, he stroked the golden hair that spilled over his flesh, haunting his senses.

"Michael. Brad Michael McKenna. I'm a Scorpio."

She started to laugh, twisting around to sit in his arms. "Brad, this is my bedroom, not a singles bar."

"All right, well, that makes things a little more intimate. What was your maiden name?"

She frowned again, then a slow smile curved her lips. "Harper. Wendy Anne Harper."

"And how old are you, Wendy Anne?"

"That's damned nosy, isn't it?"

He shrugged. "You can't be that old."

"Thirty-one," she told him. "And you?"

"Thirty-five, next November. When is your birthday?"

"February fourteenth."

"Valentine's Day baby, hmm? Do you like sushi?"

"I hate it."

"Well, I love it, but I suppose that's a minor detail. You live in the Everglades, but you hate sushi?"

She laughed. "What does that have to do with it?"

"You're surrounded by fish."

"That doesn't mean that I have to eat the things raw."

She settled down, nestling her head against his chest again. Her breath fanned against him, just as her hair tantalized his naked flesh like a feather tauntingly stroking skin. He inhaled deeply, breathing in her perfume, the scent of her shampoo and the sweet female scent of her body.

She was gentle against him, soft and relaxed. She brought her hand against her mouth, stifling a yawn. He kept stroking her hair. "What's my name, Wendy?"

"What?"

"My name? What's my name?"

"What is this game? Brad. Brad McKenna. At least, I think it's your real name."

Her eyes—shimmering, liquid silver—rose to his. A painful desire jolted through him again. Gritting his teeth, he tried to ignore the clamoring demands of his masculinity.

"Yeah, it's my real name. But it isn't my whole name."

She twisted her jaw slightly, half smiling, half frowning. "Brad Michael McKenna."

He nodded, pleased. "That's right, Ms. Wendy Anne Harper Hawk, who hates sushi and lives with the gators and creatures and became thirty-one last February fourteenth. Oh—and who likes the Beatles and keeps a wonderfully neat, hospitable home." He touched her chin, drawing her eyes closer to his. "Wendy, it is nice to get to know you."

She smiled. He touched her lips with his fingers, and she eased her head down against his chest again.

He didn't remember saying anything else—nor did he think that she did. They fell asleep that way and woke up beside one another, in her bed, but fully dressed.

Awakened by a stream of early-morning sunshine, Brad mused that it was a damned unusual way for him to start the day.

But then, Wendy was a damned unusual woman. Unique.

Special.

He leaned over, kissed her forehead and rose. She looked like a sleeping angel, with a serene expression on her beautiful features and wisps of blond hair clouding around her. He kissed her again, then quietly closed the door.

An hour later, when Wendy awoke, she could smell the enticing aroma of sizzling bacon. She didn't rise right away, but remained in bed, pondering the night.

She didn't know what to think. She liked Brad more than ever; she admired him. There was a streak of honor in his character, a quality that was rare and unusual, and she appreciated it. But, then again, the hell with honor. It could have been so easy—a pair of consenting adults indulging in a quick affair inspired by circumstance.

But no. The man who cared nothing about marriage just had to get to know her first.

Who would have ever imagined . . . he was a lot like Leif in that sense. Leif had always had his particular sense of ethics, and nothing could ever sway him. Bright and every bit as striking a man as Eric, Leif could have traveled anywhere and accomplished anything, but his heart was pledged to his tribe and his land. Despite rich opportunities elsewhere, this had been his home.

And Leif had moved slowly with her. He would have never forced her into anything. He had just let her fall in love with him first, and then with the curious, subtle beauty of the swamp.

Yes, there was something about them that was alike, she thought, no matter how strange. Her dark, patient husband with his love of the landscape, and this tawny-haired, cosmopolitan drug agent with his total disdain for muck and mud.

A tap on the door roused her from her thoughts. Brad stood in the doorway, freshly shaved and showered, and looking as young and cheerful as a college student.

"Breakfast is almost on. You've got time for a shower if you want."

Wendy nodded. "Thanks." He returned to the kitchen, and she stole into the bathroom for a long, hot shower.

The scent of shaving cream was still fresh in the bathroom. He had wiped down the tile in the shower and cleaned the mirror and the sink. And yet, a hint of his presence lingered there. Absurdly, Wendy felt like crying again.

It was reassuring, this lingering reminder of a man in the bathroom. A second damp towel, a second mug on the counter...

A second body in bed at night.

She stepped impatiently beneath the hot spray of the shower.

Damn Brad McKenna! Things should have been left to take their course. They would have enjoyed a swift, fleeting affair of mutual passion—and nothing more. She didn't want to wonder what it would be like to live with the man longer.

By the time she came out of the shower, her mood had brewed into a volatile tempest.

Brad awaited her in the kitchen amid the aromas of coffee, fried bacon and tomato-and-pepper omelets. Two places were set at the counter. He'd done a nice job of arranging things, with place mats, napkins and even a wild orchid nestled between the plates as a peace offering.

But Wendy just didn't feel very peaceful that morning. Brad seemed too at ease, too proud of himself.

"Mrs. Hawk?" With a flourish, he pulled back one of the rattan counter stools for her. Wendy sat, watching him as she carefully unfolded her napkin. He slid into the chair beside her.

"Made yourself right at home, I see," she said sweetly, eyeing him over her juice glass as she took a sip.

He stiffened. "I guess I did. Sorry. You've led me to believe that I was welcome to anything here—anything at all."

Wendy didn't know what was simmering inside of her. She was being completely unreasonable, and she knew it. He had done her the courtesy of creating a nice breakfast. She should have thanked him. Somehow, she couldn't do it.

"I must have given you the wrong impression. I'm so sorry. I really didn't mean to."

He watched her, his jaw hard and set. "You didn't mean to give me the impression that I could fix breakfast—or that I could sleep with you? What is the point that we're making here?"

She set her juice glass down carefully, staring at her plate instead of him. Forcing her voice to remain pleasant and calm, she explained, "You're a guest here, McKenna, nothing more."

"I'm a guest here because you invited me. And I can leave. No problem."

"You really are one rude bastard, you know that? I should have left you in the muck."

"Oh, yeah! Let's bring that up again." He bolted out of the chair and stood before her. Wendy swallowed. There was a pulse ticking away at his throat, and she sensed the pulse of his heart beneath Leif's old Miami Dolphins T-shirt. She closed her eyes, trying to remember Leif in that shirt. She couldn't.

When she opened her eyes and looked up, Brad still had his jaw set in that way of his that clearly spoke of anger and hostility. His eyes were gleaming, gold as a cat's. Bracing one hand behind her on the stool and one against the counter, he leaned close to her, warm and near and threatening.

She felt his breath against her flesh, sensed the rapid pulse of his anger. "Want to leave me in the swamp, Wendy? We can go right back out there if you want. This wasn't my idea, remember? You offered. Were you that desperate to have a man in the house?"

"Oh!" She spun on the chair, ready to slap him, but he was too quick. He caught her wrist and glared down at her. Using all her strength, she wrenched free from him and slid off the stool. Ignoring him, she sped through the house to her bedroom. She found her purse and headed back down the hallway, frantic to reach the door.

"Where the hell are you going?" he called after her. When she didn't stop, he chased her, finally catching her arm and swinging her back to face him.

"I'm going out."

"Out where, damn you?"

She freed her arm again and backed away from him. "I'm going into work."

"Work?"

"Yes, work! People do work."

"Who do you work for?"

She didn't want to answer him for various reasons: sheer perversity, perhaps, or the bubbling black cauldron of her temper, or the raw wound of hurt and rejection. "I work for Eric!"

"You work for Eric—where? Doing what?" he demanded suspiciously.

Wendy hesitated, feeling her anger sizzle and whirl inside of her again. It was the most awful feeling. She was being so unreasonable, but now she was trying to salvage something of her pride by leaving.

"I'm not one of your suspects, Mr. G-Man," she retorted, but he took another step toward her, grabbing her arms, wrenching her against him.

"I'm not a G-Man. Now tell me, *where* do you work for Eric, and *what* do you do for him?"

"My God, what does it matter to you?" She pulled back her wrist, but he wouldn't release her. At that moment she realized just how strong he was. He could be powerful and ruthless when he chose.

"I asked you a question," he hissed. "Why didn't you tell me that you worked? Why didn't you go to work yesterday?"

Wendy sighed, making a great show of exaggerated impatience. "I work for Eric, but I only go in a day or two a week. He spends some time working with the tribal council, but he also sold a book last year on Andrew Jackson's campaign against the Seminoles. This year he's doing one on the relationship between the Seminole Indians and the Miccosukees. I'm his research assistant."

"What?"

"There are two tribes down here, McKenna. Not just Seminoles. The Miccosukees have some tribal land south of here, fronting the Trail. But I'm sure you didn't know or care. This whole place is just an infested pile of wet mud to you, isn't it? Muck and savages, huh?"

Her cutting remark caused his lip to tighten. He pulled her even closer. "That's another thing. Why didn't you tell me that you had been married to an Indian?"

"What?" Wendy said blankly. Something inside of her ticked and then exploded. "Because I don't owe you any explanation! I didn't tell you that he was Norse, either. Did that matter? Does any of it matter?"

"Yes, it matters! Had I known the details, I wouldn't have gotten into a fight with your brother-in-law. I wouldn't have been frightened half out of my wits, thinking I'd enticed a criminal to your home!"

"Bigot!" Wendy snapped, trying to wrench away with all of her strength. It did her no good.

He gritted his teeth and held her even closer. "No, Wendy, I'm not a bigot, and you damn well know it. I may be ignorant about a few things that you surely know backward and forward, but that doesn't imply any lack of respect for a people. Honest to God, Wendy, I think that you do know that. Now would you mind telling me what this morning's fiasco is about?"

"I've got to go. Get your hands off me."

"Not until we straighten this out. Okay, you're mad. You're furious at me over something. You did invite me here. And I have a hard time believing that this whole temper tantrum thing is over the fact that I made breakfast! So what can it be? Oh, I know. I disappointed you last night. You thought you'd invited some stud in, and you didn't get quite what you really wanted."

"Damn you, McKenna, let go of me!" Wendy warned him. Her temper began to cool as she realized that his had risen. His eyes sparkled with a menacing sizzle, and every muscle of his body seemed to have tightened.

Wendy tossed back her head, narrowing her eyes. "I want to leave the house, all right? You're a guest. I asked you to stay. Foolish me, I thought that you might consider your life to be a valuable quantity. Now—let me go!"

He didn't let her go.

Instead his mouth bore down on hers with a startling and savage determination. His lips encompassed hers, his teeth grated against hers until she surrendered with a little whimper. His tongue plunged into the depths and crevices of her mouth so intimately that she shuddered, feeling as if her very soul had been invaded. Blind rage turned the world black to her, but then that blackness dissipated. His fingers threaded through her hair, forcing her against him.

But, despite herself, she melded to him. Despite herself, she felt her heart race, beating raggedly. Despite herself, she inhaled the scent of him, marveled at the sweet tension of his body, surrendered to the fierce and yearning power of the man.

His ankle twisted around hers; suddenly she was off her feet, swept to the floor. He lowered his weight over her. He stared at her for a moment, then his fingers plunged into the wings of her hair, and he held her still while his mouth ravaged hers again. His body was hard against her. Rigid and hard.

Hot tears played behind her eyes. She wanted him, but she didn't want the commitment. She was afraid to get to know him, afraid that she'd enjoy the smell of shaving cream in the bathroom, or tremble at the sight of a wild orchid beside her plate. She was deathly afraid of loving him . . .

Wendy twisted away, breaking the kiss. "Brad! Brad, damn you, this isn't right, this isn't . . ." Her voice trailed off painfully.

He went dead still. For endless moments, she felt only the soft, heated whisper of his breath against her throat. Then he moved. He hunched to the balls of his feet and then stood. He offered her a hand, and when she didn't take it, he reached for her, pulling her up to stand in front of him.

Wendy couldn't face him. She lowered her head, wishing that he would free her fingers. Suddenly, he dropped them.

He crossed his arms over his chest and stared at her until she felt compelled to face him, eye to eye. "This isn't what?" he demanded bluntly.

She shook her head. "I—"

"It isn't what you wanted, right?"

"Brad, please! Can't you just leave me alone to be humiliated in peace!"

He stared at her and shook his head slowly. The tension began to ease away from him, and a rueful smile worked its way into the line of his mouth. "No. You shouldn't be humiliated. Come here, Wendy." He reached for her, gently easing her into his arms. Tenderly, he kissed her nose and lips.

"Did I ever thank you?"

"What?"

"Did I ever really thank you? You did save my life."

"It was nothing," Wendy murmured raggedly. Her hand fell against his chest and she stared up at the gentle smile on his lips. "Still, I think I should go to work today. You are very welcome to make yourself at home. I just have to get out for a while."

He stared into her eyes and nodded. "I understand," he said softly, and she thought that he did. He grinned ruefully. "Think that the food is still edible?"

"This is the second breakfast we'll have to trash, I'm afraid," she murmured. "Well, maybe it's still edible, but I don't think that I can eat."

He nodded. "Well, worse things can happen than breakfast trashing."

"Yes."

"Wendy, seriously, where are you going?"

"Not far from here. Eric has a house on a plot of land that he owns."

"On the main road?"

She frowned, wondering at the question. "Well, the land itself fronts the main road. But the house is far back."

He stared at her, then sighed. "I should come with you."

"Not today!" she whispered.

"Wendy, Wendy!" He pulled her close, moving his fingers through her hair in a fervent massage. Then he held her away, searching out her eyes again. "Wendy, I really shouldn't be here. I'm afraid for you, Wendy. And I'll be afraid for you until this is over."

She smiled, touched by the timbre of his voice. "Brad, no one knows who I am. If your Michaelson character happened to be looking for you, he wouldn't know me. I've never seen him, he's never seen me. And I won't be passing any public places on the way. I go near the small family village where Eric and Leif's grandparents still live, but that's all. I'll be very safe."

He stared at her a moment longer, then exhaled slowly and nodded.

"All right."

"I need you to move away from the door," she told him.

He nodded again, but it took him a minute to move. Then, when he did, he pulled her into his arms.

"Wendy," he murmured seriously.

"What?"

He gently smoothed back a wild strand of hair. "We are going to make love."

"Are we?" she queried, raising her eyebrows.

"Yes." He opened the door for her and grinned. "And don't worry. I'll be sure to let you know exactly when."

"Pompous ass!" she muttered to herself, hurrying to the airboat.

She didn't realize he was behind her until he caught up with her. He was laughing as his hands descended upon her shoulder. She swung around to face him.

"I heard that."

Wendy shrugged. "Well, it's true. You are decidedly too sure of yourself."

"Shouldn't I be?" he demanded innocently.

"You'll tell me when," Wendy mimicked. "I just might change my mind about this whole thing, you know."

He shook his head. There was a grave expression on his face. "You won't."

She set her hands on her hips, cocking her head at an angle as she returned his scrutiny. "Ah, yes! You think I'll fall apart and fly into your arms by darkness again."

He shook his head, that slow smile lifting his lips. "No. It will be broad daylight, lots of light—or not at all."

"Oh, really?"

"Really." He started to return to the house. At the door, he paused and called back to her in a sensual drawl. "Don't worry about it. As I said, I'll make sure to tell you when." He grinned and closed the door.

Not sure whether to laugh or refute him, Wendy merely turned away and continued down to the airboat.

Chapter 7

Wendy stared down at the page she was reading and shook her head in annoyance. A history book lay open before her, and the information in it was inaccurate. She flipped back to the front of the book, looking for the copyright date. When she realized that the book had been written before World War II, she was able to take some of the misinformation more philosophically. The U.S. government hadn't recognized the two different and distinct tribes living in the Everglades back then—why would a white schoolteacher-turned-author know any better?

She set the book on the table and scratched out a note to Eric. A glance at the cypress clock on her brother-in-law's handsomely paneled study wall indicated that it was well past six. She should be heading back.

Just the thought of going home made her palms begin to sweat and her stomach churn. It was her house! she reminded herself. She had every right to go home.

She straightened all of her materials on the desk, turned off the computer, covered it—and sank back into the chair. She gnawed idly on her thumbnail. It was her house. Yes, the rights were hers. But she didn't have a right to act the way she had been acting. She had invited Brad to stay.

She'd actually invited him to a whole lot more. He was right about one thing: she needed to decide exactly what she was willing to offer.

The front door opened and closed. For a moment, Wendy sat up in panic, thinking that she'd been an absolute fool not to lock the door. But then, peeking down the long hallway that led to the front of the house, she saw that Eric was coming in.

"Wendy!" he called, spotting her from the end of the hall. She waved to him, smiling. He wore jeans and a colorful Seminole shirt, woven in various shades of red. The color contrasted with the warm bronze of his face and the startling shade of his eyes.

You need someone, too, brother-in-law, Wendy thought suddenly. He was a special man, so striking in appearance, so proud and ethical, so warm and generous to those he trusted.

Like Jennifer, his wife.

"Let me get something cool to drink," he called to her, "and I'll be right with you."

She heard the refrigerator door open, then seconds later, he appeared carrying a Sol for himself and a wine cooler for her. She smiled, thanking him. Eric knew her. Beer for fishing, wine with company dinner, ice tea or water if she was thirsty. Diet soda if she was determined on a diet, but her diets would seldom last long because she loved the taste of real sugar. She had known her brother-in-law for a decade. All those years bred real friendship, real closeness.

And Brad, who would go away very soon, wanted to know her birthday and her middle name. He should have been a dream, she thought. An imaginary lover, tan and sandy and agile and beautifully formed. A midnight visitor who would dissipate with the morning light of dawn.

"What are you doing here? I thought that you weren't going to come over while you were hosting the DEA." Eric studied her with frank curiosity.

Wendy shrugged, but she couldn't keep her eyes level with Eric's. "I—uh—I don't know. I guess I needed a little breathing space."

He took a long sip of his beer, set his booted feet comfortably upon the edge of his desk and leaned back. He surveyed her from beneath half-closed, jet lashes, then closed his eyes completely and smiled. "Sparks are flying too hot and wild for you to handle, huh?"

Wendy stared at him until he opened his eyes again. She wanted to tell him to mind his own business, but she shrugged instead. "No. I just needed some space."

"Get out of the kitchen if you can't take the heat," Eric quoted gravely.

"Eric," Wendy moaned.

He sat up, letting his feet fall to the floor. Reaching over, he tilted her chin upward. "There's something there, Wendy-bird," he teased her lightly. "I could feel it all night long. Palpable, thick." He released her, rose and stretched with the grace of a cat. His back was to

her when he said, "So did you run over here because
you did go to bed, or because you didn't?"

"Eric—"

"Well?"

He turned to look at her, and she felt the depth of his
concern for her. She smiled. "Because I didn't. Eric, I
don't know what to think. I don't know what I feel. I
mean, he's going to go away again, right? He's just
here for a few days. Until they catch this Michaelson
character, or until something else breaks. I like him a
lot, Eric—"

"So do I, for whatever that's worth."

"I hate what he does for a living. And he doesn't intend to get married—"

"Well, if you haven't made it into bed yet, why are
you worrying about marriage?"

"I'm not! I don't want to get married again."

"So?"

She shook her head, then blurted out, "So then why
doesn't it just happen? Why do we have to go through
twenty questions?"

Eric stared at her for a long time. At last he spoke
very softly. "Because he does care, Wendy. Because he
didn't meet you on a bar stool, because he thinks highly
of you."

"But he said—"

"Trust me, Wendy." As he sighed, a skeptical glaze
clouded the lime color of his eyes. Wendy could almost see time rolling away in the shadows of his eyes.
"Trust me," he repeated hoarsely. "When a man just
wants solace, none of it means anything to him. Not
the day or time or date, the color of the woman's eyes
or her hair. Hell, her name doesn't even matter." He
sensed he   ng at him. He was remembering his own

wild pursuits, just after Jennifer had died. Ultimately, he'd found little peace in physical satisfaction. "He cares about you, Wendy, and I'm damned glad. I know this sounds sexist, but hell, I'm an Indian, and we always had our trouble keeping up with the times. If he weren't a decent man, I'd probably be over there trying to throw him off your property. Maybe you won't ever marry him. Maybe you'll never even fall in love, but—"

"You don't understand, Eric. I don't want to get married again. And I don't want to fall in love—especially not with a DEA agent!"

He ignored her. As if she hadn't even spoken, he continued, "But what you will have, Wendy, will be good, and it will be caring."

"You might want to try that yourself," she retorted.

He slid back into his chair and took another long swallow of his beer. "Wendy, I don't want—"

He broke off, aware that he was about to repeat her words. He laughed and shrugged. "So how did work go? Did you get anything done?"

"Yeah. I found a couple of books that you can refer to for total misinformation."

"There's a lot of that, but thanks. It's just as important to know where the bad stuff is as the good." He grinned at her. "I was over at the Miccosukee center today. Things are going full speed ahead. They're planning even more on their reservation lands. Billy was telling me that it's hard to hone in on the Seminole bingo, so they're going to try and battle the Hyatt instead."

Wendy grinned. She'd also heard the Miccosukee leader speak about his ideas, and she liked the plans as

much as she liked the young man making them. It was
true, the Seminoles had managed their money well. The
tribe did well with bingo, and with cigarette sales. The
Miccosukees were looking into those enterprises, but
they were also interested in catching business from the
new linkup with Interstate 75.

"So you were fooling around all day, huh?" she
said.

"Yes, and no." He leaned his head back and stared
at the ceiling. "We were talking the same old route.
Money, education, housing. I never know quite where
I stand myself. I like my house. I like owning this land.
Then again, I enjoyed going to school. The years I
spent in the service were traumatic—bloody and—yet,
they were somehow important. Now I stand here on a
crossroad. I don't want to lose the value of our cus-
toms or traditions. But I don't want to see the children
of the tribe growing up without every benefit of white
America. Where is the right place to be, Wendy? What
is the right stand?"

She stood up and gave him a hug. "I really love you
alot, Eric, you know that?"

He laughed. "I didn't mean to give a soapbox lecture."

"And you didn't. You're super, and I'm going
home."

"I love you, too, Wendy." He looked into her eyes
for a moment, then told her, "I think you should
know, everyone seems to be commenting on all the activity going on. Along Alligator Alley, along the Trail."

"What activity?"

"Well, knowing what I know, I assume that some of
the men driving around and hovering around the airboat rides and villages work for the government. There

have also been a lot—I mean a lot—of cops around, and you know that the police stations are really good about letting our own forces handle our own problems." The Seminoles had a police force of their own, just as the Miccosukees did. Eric had always said that Florida was a fair state when it came to respecting the tribal laws of the Indians. The city and county police from Miami and Fort Lauderdale and the other communities seldom interfered with the Indian forces.

"Well," Wendy murmured, "I guess that it is reasonable for the government to have men trying to keep an eye out for Brad—and for Michaelson."

Eric nodded, watching her. "There's something else, Wendy."

"Yes?"

"Some of our men seem to think that something big is going to happen. They say there have been seaplane drops in the swamp, down toward the Trail."

Wendy shrugged impatiently. "Twenty miles south! Eric, think about it! Think about the size of the swamp! You have to know what you're doing to find things out there!"

"That's true. But we don't know if these are just petty crooks, smuggling in a kilo of pot—or hired assassins, hunting for Brad."

"I'm not worried."

"You should be. At least tell Brad what I've told you. I don't believe that they can just walk in and find Brad, either. Only you and I know that he's there."

"And old Mac up at the gas station."

Eric shrugged. "Mac never says a word to strangers. Never. So your secret is safe. But I'm afraid that they might stumble upon you by accident."

"They'd be idiots to molest me."

"Wendy, they're criminals." He sighed, exasperated. "You of all people should know the danger of innocence!"

Duly chastised, she lowered her head. "I'll tell Brad," she promised.

"Just warn him, that's all. He has the right to know what's going on, the right to protect you both." He laughed suddenly. "Don't worry. I'm sure you won't have to give him up—yet."

"Very amusing, Eric," she retorted, but when she saw his grin, she smiled, too. "Want to walk me out?"

"Sure." Arm in arm, they followed the lawn to where it began to level and fall toward the canal.

"Want me to come home with you?" he teased her.

Yes! Wendy thought, but she had to fight her own battles. "I'm all right."

"You're better than all right, Wendy-bird. You're perfect."

She kissed his cheek. "Flattery is great stuff. I'll see you soon."

Distractedly, Wendy waved and started for home. The wind rushed around her and lifted her hair, gently calming her spirit.

Maybe Brad was right. He knew what she wanted, but he wouldn't give it to her, because he wanted her to have something better. And maybe someday, if she ever lay upon a psychiatrist's couch and poured out her life's story, she would be glad of it. Yes, I had a very bad time learning to step out again after my husband died. For two years I could do nothing. But then I met a man, and though he passed briefly through my life, it was something precious, and something very special.

As Wendy neared home, she made a few resolutions. She was not going to act childish as she had today. She liked Brad, and she was going to enjoy him. The teasing was fun, and it was fun to get to know him.

Of course, she'd be damned if she'd ever take another step toward him. If he really wanted her—whenever he decided to let her know when!—he'd better plan on coming to get her.

Humming softly as she cut off the motor, she wondered if he might have discovered something to cook for dinner. She walked across the lawn to the house with a jaunty step.

It wasn't until she reached the door that she began to sense something was amiss. Emptiness and silence abounded through the house. Carefully, she opened the door.

Nothing was disturbed—nothing at all. The house was neat and tidy. Rushing down the hallway, she discovered that Brad had straightened the beds. She flushed slightly, realizing that he had found the laundry hamper and the washer and dryer behind the slotted doors in the hall. He had washed the clothes that he had been borrowing—and her things. There was ample evidence of the chores he had done.

Only the man himself was missing.

Wendy let out a soft cry of fear, spun around and went tearing back out of the house. In dread she searched the yard, praying that she would not find a bloodied body. Pain glazed her heart. It was impossible. They couldn't have found him. Not here. She lived too deep in the swamp.

She kept telling herself that as she ran back into the house and found the shotgun.

Wendy loathed weapons, but she wasn't foolish. Brad was out there—perhaps in the custody of murderers. She cocked the gun and slung it over her shoul-

der. Fighting back the tears that stung her eyes, she set
out to find him.

Nothing, absolutely nothing, should have surprised
Brad about Wendy Hawk's house anymore. He had
been accosted in bed by a wild panther and attacked
from the roof by a green-eyed Seminole. He'd learned
that the Florida panther did belong, but that only
madmen kept alligators.

And yet, when he came into the living room to discover the very tall, withered old man, standing dead
center in the room, Brad still didn't know what to
think. There was no mistaking the fact that this man
was an Indian. Half of his hair was white, the other
half was blacker than midnight, long and straight. His
face was near brown and weathered from constant ex-
posure to the sun, and his features were solid and
strong. His eyes were as black as onyx.

Brad thought of all the things he had learned in
school. This man had the simple pride and dignity of
a Chief Joseph. He had the unfaltering stare of a
Cochise or a Sitting Bull.

Or an Osceola, Brad thought. This man was surely
a Seminole.

I'm definitely slipping, Brad thought. He hadn't
heard a single sound.

But the old man didn't seem to expect violence from
him. In fact, he seemed to know that he would find him
there.

"Hello," Brad said.

The Indian nodded. Brad fumed uncomfortably as
he realized that he was being scrutinized, from head to
toe. What if the old fellow didn't speak English? Brad

raised a friendly hand, palm outward in friendship. "Hello," he repeated.

"I am old, not deaf," the Indian told him.

Brad felt like a fool. "Sorry. You didn't answer me."

"I hadn't decided what to answer."

"I didn't think it was that difficult a question."

"Where is your respect for your elders?"

"I meant no disrespect, truly," Brad returned evenly. He paused, "Uh, sir, who are you, please?"

A smile revealed a million wrinkles in the old man's face. "Hawk. Willie Hawk." He was dressed in faded dungarees, boots and a beribboned Seminole shirt. He stepped forward, offering Brad a hand.

"Mr. Hawk, my pleasure. My name is—"

"Yes, I know. You are McKenna. I have heard."

Brad frowned. He had heard? Hadn't he stressed the importance of his anonymity to Wendy? Had she told this man about him today? Or hadn't Eric realized that he was betraying Brad to give him away. Maybe Eric hadn't understood—

No. Eric was too bright not to understand the situation.

Willie Hawk seemed to have read the quick wanderings of his mind. His smile deepened and his face seemed to crinkle even more. "They have not betrayed you. Not Wendy, not Eric."

"Surely—"

Willie Hawk dismissed Brad with a wave of his gnarled hand. "You have judged them well. They have not betrayed you. I know the swamp, son. I know what happens here. I can listen to the earth. Even the alligator speaks to me."

Just what he needed, Brad decided—an Indian, and senile to boot.

Willie Hawk lowered his eyes, and Brad realized that the old man had read his mind again. "So Wendy has gone to work, and you are here alone?"

Brad nodded. "Yes, sir. Can I get you anything? This is your grandson's house. You are probably at home here."

"My grandson is dead. It is Wendy's house," Willie said, and Brad could not fathom with what emotion he spoke. If there was pain, it was well hidden. If there was love, that, too, was well hidden.

"Well, then—"

"You are alone here. There must be very little to do. The inactivity must weigh heavily upon a man who is accustomed to movement."

Brad laughed. "Yes, I guess it does get bad. The laundry is all done, and Wendy is too neat a lady to leave much else to do."

There was something intriguing about the old man's face. It suggested an ancient, enigmatic wisdom. The onyx eyes never seemed to leave his own or to cease their slow and careful assessment. He turned around suddenly. "Come with me."

"What?"

Willie paused. "Are you deaf, young man?"

"No, it's just that—"

"The Indian wars ended many, many moons ago, you know."

The old man was a bit of a dramatist, Brad decided. He saw the twinkle in Willie's eyes, and this time, the Indian laughed with him.

"What the hell," Brad said. "I'll live dangerously. But give me a minute, please. I want to leave Wendy a note. Under the circumstances, I don't want her to worry."

Willie nodded. "Yes, write a message. Tell her that you are with me, and she will not worry."

Brad scribbled out a note. He started to attach it to the refrigerator, then worried that she might get scared outside if she called him and he didn't answer. He followed Willie out the door, thinking that he'd stick his note in the mailbox. Then he realized that there was no mailbox. "How does she get her bills?" he wondered out loud.

"P.O. box," Willie advised him sagely.

"Of course," Brad murmured. He tried to shove the note beneath the door. It seemed to stick, more or less.

Willie had come by canoe. He pointed the hand-made vessel out to Brad, and they started toward it. Brad offered to paddle, but Willie would have none of it.

"Sit still," he advised Brad. "There are not many times in life when you may enjoy the journey with no effort, with your eyes and ears and heart open."

"Right," Brad said. "Thank you, sir." He still worried that he should be doing the work, but knew that Willie would not appreciate his worry.

Just as they rounded out to slice westward along the canal, Brad noticed a black figure lurking around the house. On closer inspection, he relaxed. It was only Baby, prowling around the house.

"I wonder if I was supposed to have fed her something," he murmured aloud.

"She came by the village this morning. My wife gave her a chicken. Baby is fine."

Brad nodded. But Baby, he saw, wanted something. The cat was crawling up on her hindquarters to let out her savage meow. Baby wanted to go in.

Brad couldn't imagine a bag of Tender Vittles big enough for such a cat anyway. He was glad that she'd eaten elsewhere.

The canoe moved through the swamp.

Brad dismissed all thoughts of Baby, not realizing that the panther had clipped his note with one long toenail, and that, when she finally walked away, she shredded his note as she went.

Three hours later, Brad discovered himself sitting at the base of a tall pine. His hands were loosely tied behind his back, and he was smiling as a group of wild Indians danced and war-whooped around him.

As a kid he'd played cowboys and Indians. Sometimes he'd been an Indian, and sometimes he'd been a cowboy.

To the best of his knowledge, there hadn't been any cowboys in the swamps, but that was okay. He had met Marna Hawk Panther and Anthony Panther—and all the little Panthers. He had met Mary Hawk, whom Willie referred to as his raven woman because of the ink-dark tresses that still adorned her head, despite the fact that she had turned eighty on her last birthday.

Mike, Dorinda, David and Jennifer—the four little Panthers—suddenly ceased their war whoops. They raced over to hug their father, who gave them each a hug and a pat on the back. He whispered something to the children, and they all ran back to thank Brad for playing with them. Dorinda blushed and came close, giving a kiss on the cheek. "You're very, very nice, Mr. McKenna. I'm going to tell Aunt Wendy that, too."

He smiled. She was a very pretty little girl with her great-grandfather's onyx eyes, Mary Hawk's raven hair and her mother's lovely, golden skin. Brad nodded to her gravely. "Thank you," he told her. She blushed again, then ran off to join her siblings.

Tony Panther sat down beside Brad, leaning against the tree. He was a young man, dressed in a business suit that seemed somewhat ludicrous in the clearing of thatched-roof chickees. The clearing itself seemed to Brad to be a moment out of time.

Of course, there were cars nearby. Tony's Dodge was just beyond the tree. He was an accountant, who worked for the tribe. He drove in and out of Fort Lauderdale daily.

"That was nice, letting the kids play that way," Tony told Brad. "We didn't get to win very often in real life, you know."

Brad laughed, idly running the rope that had held him so loosely captive through his fingers. "I enjoyed them." He ran his fingers through his hair. "I remember playing cowboys and Indians when I was young. At the time, it was a total fantasy—pow-wows and peace pipes and scalpings."

"I'm just proud to still be here. It meant our Hawk ancestor was willing to fight and brave the swamps, rather than be sent west. But don't worry—we haven't scalped anyone in ages." Tony looked at him a long moment. "Did you really enjoy the afternoon?"

Brad mused over the question. He had. Mary had told him how the tribe had once raised pumpkins to survive. She had made him taste the old staple of their people, koontie bread, made from the koontie root. He had helped repair a chickee, and—since it was alligator season, he had also tasted the smoked meat of the creature. Tony, he had learned, was a Miccosukee, and from him, he had learned quite a bit about the two tribes who had coexisted in the Florida swampland.

They shared their green corn dance and other festivals.

Then, sitting there against the tree, Brad felt the peace of the area sweep through him. The sun was setting beautifully. Out on the water, a great blue heron rose and swept into the sky. The entire horizon reflected the golden sunset.

Brad turned and nodded to Tony. "Yeah. I've enjoyed it very much."

"I wonder why Wendy hasn't shown up yet," Tony murmured, then he shrugged, seeing the worry that sprang into Brad's eyes. "She might know what Grandfather is up to. He came over to kidnap you on purpose, you know. Just to rile Wendy."

Brad laughed. "Did he really?"

He nodded. "I hope you don't find this too strange, but we are Wendy's family. Wendy and Leif met in college, when they were just kids. They married before they graduated. Her mother had died when she was a child, and her dad passed away right after they were married. She has been with us for a long time. We love her as if she were our blood."

"I'm glad," Brad said. Although he shouldn't be prying into her life, Tony Panther was willing to give him answers, so he decided to ask a few more questions. "What happened to Leif Hawk?"

Tony appeared startled. "She's never told you?"

Brad shook his head.

Tony stared off in the distance. "He was killed. In cold blood. Eric's wife was killed with him."

"What?" Brad demanded huskily.

He didn't get an answer. From the water, there was a sudden commotion. He looked up to find that Wendy had come at last.

She seemed to fly out of the airboat. She didn't seem to see anything or anyone—until her eyes lighted on him. Her eyes were huge and sparkling and silver and—quite suddenly—sizzling with fury.

She was running toward him with all the lean energy of a pouncing tiger. Warily, Brad stood up. A moment later she catapulted herself against him, half screaming and half sobbing in fury. "You son of a bitch! You stinking—cop!"

"Wendy!" She took a swing at him and he ducked. She flew around in a circle with the force of her blow, and he caught her, pinning her arms to her sides.

"Hi, Wendy," Tony said lightly.

She ignored him, and her fierce glare bored into Brad. "You inconsiderate, careless weasel! You scared me half to death!"

"Wendy! Wendy Hawk!" She tensed and swallowed, apparently aware that Grandfather was approaching the scene. "Wendy, you calm down."

Far from calm, she struggled against Brad's hold and managed to turn. "Grandfather! You wily fox! How could you do this to me! I was so frightened."

"Wendy!" Brad swung her back around again. "I left you a note—"

"Liar!"

"Wendy!" Grandfather said sharply. Immediately, her anger softened, and Brad realized how much she loved and respected the old man. Still staring at Brad with a look that could kill, Wendy exhaled slowly.

"Wendy, he did leave the note. You do not call a man a liar unless you know it is truth to do so. And to deny a friend, that is even worse. He is a man of his word. You must have known that, or else you would not have him at your house."

Wendy nodded, trembling in Brad's arms. "I even remembered the shotgun."

She had been truly frightened for him. Her concern was reassuring, though he hadn't meant to scare her. "Wendy, honestly. I left a note."

"I was scared to death." She tried to retain some of her anger, while regaining her dignity. Her words were still a whisper, and he longed to touch her, to kiss away her worry right then and there.

"I'm sorry, Wendy."

"Come on, Brad. Wendy, please? We're tucking the kids into bed, and they'll be heartbroken if they don't get to see you."

Wendy forced herself to tear her eyes from Brad and smile at Tony. "Of course, Tony. I'm dying to give them all great big hugs."

Brad lagged behind for a moment, wondering about the story Tony had been telling him. He needed to hear the end of it. Leif Hawk and Eric's wife had been killed—in cold blood.

The very thought of it was tragic. Wendy and Eric had shared a great deal, an ocean of sorrow, and Brad couldn't help the tug of pure sympathy that tore at his heart.

A young man, and a young woman, cruelly taken from life. What the hell had happened, and who did he ask?

"Brad, are you coming?"

They were waiting for him. "Yes, yes, I'm coming. Thanks."

As Brad caught up with them, the gold remnants of twilight left the sky and night fell, a blanket of darkness.

Chapter 8

It was late when they returned to Wendy's house. They'd spent the evening huddled around the cooking fire. By its eerie light, Willie Hawk had woven tales of the past, of a people forced to run away from a white government that had betrayed the Seminoles at every turn. Brad thought it appropriate that the name Seminole meant "runaway." He'd spent most of his career running from dealers and mobsters.

His head was fuzzy from folklore and brew. Brad wasn't sure what he had been drinking all night. Tony called it a "black" drink and assured him it wouldn't do anything to him that Jack Black wouldn't. But it was potent stuff—very powerful.

In the darkness of the clearing, a blackness alleviated only by the camp fire, he could almost see a mist around old Willie. And in that mist he could see the past: warriors, feathered and oiled, shaking knives and rifles in the air, clad in the colorful garb they had borrowed from the Spanish and adapted to their own use. He could see a million fires. He could hear a cry on the wind. He was entranced.

The night was black, but the wind felt refreshing against his face as they drove back to Wendy's place. Brad reveled in the quiet of the swamp when the motor died. They were sounds that he was coming to recognize and understand.

When they stepped back into Wendy's house, he felt comfortable, as if he were home. Wendy wandered into the kitchen, and Brad went to the stereo and began to browse through her collection of tapes and discs and albums. "Okay if I turn on the stereo?"

"Whatever you want," she called back.

Whatever he wanted.

Brad found an old album by the Temptations. He carefully set the needle on the vinyl record, then collapsed upon the couch. She had an impressive music system, with dynamite speakers. He closed his eyes as the music filled the room and soothed his spirit.

When he opened his eyes, Wendy was leaning against the counter, smiling at him tolerantly. He grinned at her, then rose slowly.

Whatever he wanted. That was what she had said. He wanted to hold her in his arms.

She was a vision of loveliness. Her hair fell free about her face, and her silver eyes sparkled. She was wearing jeans and a tailored shirt. Her shirt collar angled around her smooth throat in a manner that Brad found enticing.

Her smile was the killer. Her smile revealed her essence, the sweet, elusive quality that drew him to her, that excited him, that elicited the tenderness and the yearning.

He lifted a hand to her. His head was spinning, either from the Indian drink or the devastating effect of her beauty. "Want to dance?"

"Dance?"

"Move around on the floor. Step to the music. Dance."

He caught hold of her hands. There was silver laughter in her eyes as he drew her to him, enfolding her into his arms. The Temptations were singing about "sunshine on a cloudy day" as he held her close.

"See? Dance?"

"In the living room?" She laughed.

"Anywhere."

He released her slightly, swinging her out, then back into his arms. She was still laughing as he sang off-key to the music.

"This is a classic album," he told her, pulling her close. "You've good taste in music."

"Thanks."

The music faded, then another song began. He moved with the soft, slow tempo, grateful for the lovely woman in his arms. His left hand caressed the small of her back. He could feel her flesh beneath the cotton shirt. The softness of her breasts brushing against him caused a definite reaction inside him.

The music...it seemed to be a part of them. It was so very easy to move with Wendy in his arms. But suddenly he realized that he wasn't moving at all. He was merely staring down into her eyes, her beautiful eyes, with their startling silver color and their dark, sweeping lashes. She had to know what he was feeling, everything that he was feeling.

She smiled very slowly. The little vixen, he thought.

Did she know that his pulse was pounding hope-
lessly out of control? Surely she could feel that he was
taut and tense and that his muscles were constricted
with desire. She was so close, he could feel her softness. He could feel the fullness of her breasts, the peb-
ble hardness of her nipples through their clothing. He
could feel the trembling that swept her, the supple
length of her thighs, the angle of her hip, the soft and
almost indiscernible swell of her femininity.

She just had to feel the evidence of his desire,
straining against his borrowed jeans. She just had to…

She did. He knew by the soft, silver clouds that filled
her eyes. By her slightly parted lips, by the ragged
whisper of her breath.

She moistened her lips with the tip of her tongue,
and they somehow became even more tempting. Glossy
and sleek and still tempting. Lowering his head while
the Temptations serenaded them, he kissed her.

The feeling was riveting. Their mouths fused in a
passionate union, hot and electric. For a moment, they
broke apart, then he held her face, searched out her
eyes and kissed her again. Gently, his palms kneaded
the soft flesh of her back until he reached her buttocks. Lifting her against him, he fitted her to his form
while her arms clung tightly to his neck and their
mouths continued to meet, exploring, melding.

She broke away, gasping for breath. He stared at her
with the rage of his passion naked in his eyes.

Had she ever felt like this? she wondered. So excited
that it hurt? So sensually alive and aware that his kiss
seemed to reach into her body and soul, warming her
through and through.

She had been married to a man she loved, and theirs
had been a passionate relationship. Maybe this desire

was heightened by the loss of her only love. Maybe it was due to her loneliness.

And maybe it was just Brad, the man himself.

But she had never, never felt like this. Desperate to have more of him, she longed to latch her arms around his neck again and savor the sizzling heat that flared between them. She'd waited too long. She wanted to feel her flesh naked against his.

"Brad," she whispered against his mouth.

He paused, staring down at her.

"Brad, is this 'when'? I mean, you said you'd let me know when, so if this isn't it..." Her voice trailed away and her body grew heated and flushed. She didn't know if she was shamed by the bluntness of her query, or merely so hot with desire that fever was spreading through her limbs.

"Yes," he told her huskily. "This is 'when.' That is, if you're willing. You said I could have whatever I wanted. I want you, Wendy. God, do I want you. Now. Here. If—you're willing."

This time there was tenderness as well as fire in his gaze. She was willing, and he knew it. He didn't wait for her answer, but drew her into his embrace again, desperately moving his hands to mold her body to his. "Dear God, yes, this is when!" he murmured.

He kissed her throat and teased her earlobe. The brush of his lips grew more heated, more sensual, as he searched out the buttons of her tailored shirt. In seconds, he had cast the shirt aside. Deftly, he removed her bra.

His callused hands cupped the firm fullness of her breasts. At his touch, the pink, tawny nipples immediately hardened. Lowering his moist lips to her, he laved his tongue around a nipple, then sucked it hard into his mouth.

Wendy let out a little cry, arching against him. The staggering sensation swept like swift white lightning from her breast to her pelvis. The yearning pain between her legs intensified, so that she could barely stand. His hands splayed across her back, holding her up.

But she could not bear it. She tugged wildly upon his hair, whispering his name. Somehow she was borne to the floor. As she lay there, her heart thundering, he cast his shirt aside in such a fervent hurry that several buttons were torn away. His breathing was torn and ragged as he knelt by her side.

She couldn't stand to wait any longer. His chest was naked with its planes of muscle and tawny hair, and she had to know the feel of that nakedness against her own breasts. Whispering her wild desires, she reached for him, brushing her naked body against his. His muscles were rock hard. His hair titillated her throat and breasts, already so sensitized to his touch.

He was whispering to her, giving her hoarse little commands. His desires were burning like a flash fire, out of control. All the little things that he'd wanted to do, all the nuances of slow seduction, all were swept away amid a sudden tempest of need.

He had tried. God knew, he had tried.

Now, he couldn't wait any longer.

He pressed her to the floor and pulled off her boots and socks and jeans. Only then did he pause for the slightest moment to relish the sight of her. The spill of golden hair about her shoulders and the rise of her breasts made him wild with desire. His eyes lowered to take in the arch of her hips and the golden nest at the juncture of her thighs, visible beneath the lacy string bikinis she wore.

He looked from her supple form to her face. Her eyes were still silver, and her lips remained parted, wet and moist. And so inviting.

He let out a groan, a guttural cry of appreciation and raw need.

Burying his face against the soft, smooth eroticism of her belly, he let his tongue trail over her flesh, and then he kissed it.

"Brad!" She arched and writhed beneath him. His fingers slipped off her panties and curled over the apex of her thighs. She was hot and sweet and damp.

"Please!" She tugged at his hair. Desperation filled him again. They wanted the same thing. "Please, please," she whispered, tossing her head. Her hands gripped his jeans, tugging at them.

A roar rose in his head. Almost blindly, he brushed his fingers against that web of gold. Desire shot through him, as hot as molten steel. The roar in his head thundered, and the pulse inside of him throbbed to a frenzied pace.

He stripped off his shoes and jeans, then stared down at her again.

He towered above her, naked and very male. His thighs were well-formed columns over his long legs. His shoulders and chest were bronze, his masculinity was shockingly brazen, yet enticing.

Wendy closed her eyes, dazed at the sight of him, stunned at the intensity of the passions that swirled inside her.

Although her eyes remained closed, she could feel his hot flesh against hers as he lowered himself over her.

He had become naked, removing her husband's clothing.

Leif. She had loved him. Didn't she owe him more?

"Wendy!"

Brad spoke her name so harshly that she opened her eyes wide, startled and guilty. His gold and amber gaze, penetrated her, inciting a new panic. Could he read her mind? she wondered. If he knew what she was thinking, he would go away.

He didn't go away.

He wedged himself between her knees, stroking the sensitive skin along her inner thighs. She gasped as a wave of searing desire raged through her. She closed her eyes.

"Wendy!"

She gazed at him again. There was no tenderness about him now, but neither was there cruelty. "Lift your legs around me, Wendy. Meet my eyes. Wendy, look at me."

She moistened her lips. She couldn't have begun to disobey him.

"Now look at us, Wendy. Watch where we come together. Watch how we make love."

She cried out as her entire being seemed to rock to a new, blinding pulse. In that languid moment of ecstasy, he plunged himself within her, driving deep, deep, until he filled her, until he was completely sheathed. He stayed there for a moment, keeping his eyes fiercely locked with hers.

Then he moved.

"Watch, Wendy..."

She watched until the excitement spiraled in her so deeply that she cried out again, reaching for him. She felt him inside of her, stroking her. She cast back her head, and he trailed kisses along her throat. He tucked his hands beneath her buttocks, bringing her ever more flush. Again his lips trailed over her breasts, leaving a lingering euphoria wherever they passed.

He brought himself to the edge of her, and she writhed madly to catch him. Then he would plunge again, deep, deeper. The ache inside of her was swelling, the anguish building until she passed through the wild storm, and sunshine seemed to burst upon her. Beautiful sunshine, in golden droplets, seeping into her, sating her, filling her.

He whispered her name, he demanded that she draw her legs higher. She could scarcely obey, and yet she did, and it all began again. His movement inside of her. His touch, guiding her. His kiss, wildfire burning her flesh, raking her nipples.

Fire flared once again. Wendy gasped, caught in the whirl of a second thrill, shuddering as she felt Brad's traumatic release, rich and hot. She lay gasping, her eyes closed, savoring what had happened. She felt the weight of his body, heavy over her now, and yet she loved it. She loved the warm, rich scent of him, she loved the slick feel of his naked flesh. She loved the way that they lay, entwined.

"Wendy, look at me again."

Wendy glanced up and smiled lazily. When she reached up to touch his cheek, he caught her hand.

They both became aware that the needle on the stereo was sweeping over empty space, making a strange sound. All the lights in the house were still blazing.

Wendy stared up at Brad and her smile faded. The hardness was still there about him. She couldn't understand it. She was still feeling after-tremors, feeling so close to him, and yet he seemed so distant from her.

She had been open and honest with him. She had wanted him; she had gladly given herself to him, trusting in him. And now, even as she lay there, naked and still filled by him, fear began to sweep into her. "Brad?" Her voice trembled slightly as she questioned him.

But then he smiled. Opening her palm, he pressed a kiss against it and lay back down beside her.

"I don't understand—" Wendy began.

"I just wanted to hear you say it. My name."

She inhaled, closing her eyes. She could have told him that she had known from the beginning that he would be no substitute for another man. Brad McKenna was in a class all his own.

"We were both afraid, a little, weren't we?" she asked.

He lifted his weight from her and stretched, resting on one elbow. His gaze remained on her, intense.

"Yeah. Afraid of Leif Hawk entering in here."

She couldn't quite meet his eyes. And when hers shifted, he abruptly straddled her, catching her cheeks between his palms. Intimacy seemed rampant between them again. She felt his thighs, his nakedness, keenly. She stared up at him, then her gaze fell away.

"You loved him very much," Brad said.

"Yes." She opened her eyes and met his at last, anger suddenly burning in her own. "But I made love with you, and you know it. So get off me, you oaf."

He caught her face in a tender hold. "That's why I made you watch me. Watch *us*. I wanted to be sure you were making love to me—not the ghost of another man." Now his kiss was slow, leisurely, yet thorough.

He rose then, a man completely at ease with his nakedness, naturally graceful in his movement. He picked up the stereo needle and set it back to the beginning of the album. Once again the room filled with music. Wendy watched him for a moment, then started to reach for her panties.

"No, don't," he told her, noticing her movement. A smile played across his features. "Please, don't."

She hesitated. He knelt down behind her, slipping his arms around her and locking his hands beneath her breasts. "It's nice just to hold you," he whispered, resting his chin upon her shoulder.

She let her head fall back against his shoulder. "It's nice to be held," she said.

Nuzzling her neck, he added, "And we have to make love again. Tonight. Maybe a few times, maybe several times."

Wendy twisted, trying to see his face. "For a slow starter, you do get quickly into gear once the motor is running."

"Slow starter?"

"I've been willing for some time now," she teased.

"Wendy, we haven't known each other for 'some time.'"

She leaned back again, slipping her slender fingers over his rougher, callused ones. "I knew that I wanted you."

It took him a minute to answer. "Last night you wanted a body in bed. Tonight, you wanted *me*. There's a difference."

She didn't reply; maybe it was true.

He hummed to the music. "We used to have sock hops back when I was a kid. Everybody used to go.

This was what we played. I never did learn to disco. Did you?''

Wendy shook her head. "No."

"Want a glass of wine?"

"That sounds good. I'll get it." She didn't know if she could be as easy as Brad about walking around her house naked with all the lights on. Of course, no one would be near, and they couldn't possibly see in if they were.

She was just out of practice.

But it wasn't bad, not really. Although she keenly felt Brad's eyes on her while she moved, it was a nice feeling. She poured two glasses of white wine and brought out a platter of cheese, salmon and crackers, too. Brad was waiting for her, leaning against the bottom of the couch. She set the tray between them.

"Salmon. Perfect. I was starving."

He picked up a piece of the pink fillet with his fingers and popped in into his mouth. Wendy started to cut cheese for the crackers, but was interrupted when she realized that Brad was dangling a piece of salmon in front of her mouth. She licked it from his fingers, her tongue sensually bathing his fingertips. He flashed her a crooked smile. Blushing, she turned back to the cheese again.

"Oh, Wendy," he murmured. His eyes studied her intently. She had never imagined she could feel such a rush of warmth, just from the way a man looked at her.

When she handed him a cracker with cheese, her fingers were trembling.

He slipped an arm around her while they ate and sipped wine. Although their conversation was casual, Brad never passed the opportunity to add a few sexual innuendos. Every time he sipped his wine or nibbled on a morsel of food, he somehow intimated how the mouth could be used effectively on flesh. He promised to demonstrate.

"Brad!" Wendy protested at last. She was laughing, amazed at what words and looks could imply. But then again, he was touching her, too. His arm was around her shoulder and his hand dangled idly over her breast, his fingertips teasing her nipple. His whisper fell against her hair, her throat, her ear.

"What?" he asked innocently.

"You're making me crazy!"

His gaze was lazy, his tone sultry. His tawny lashes lay half-closed as he looked at her. "Why? I'm not going anywhere, you're not going anywhere." He paused for a moment, suddenly becoming serious. "I didn't mean to be so selfish. I just—I just couldn't wait anymore."

"Selfish?" Wendy echoed blankly.

He kissed her forehead. "Yes."

"But you weren't—"

"I intend to make up for it."

"Brad—"

"Cracker?" He slipped one in her mouth.

Wendy chewed it, watching him gravely. "Brad, I know that you're not married. But what you said about Leif... well, you were right. It wouldn't be fair to anyone if I tried to find a substitute for him. And maybe I did want to do that at first. But you'd never stand for that." For a moment her voice trailed. "I know you don't have a wife, but I really don't want to be a stand-in, either. Your lover, just because of this 'convenient situation.'"

He lifted her chin and kissed her lips lightly. "There's no one special in my life, Wendy. Honestly.

Just you." He didn't release her but kept studying her eyes. "Wendy, what happened? To your husband—to Eric's wife?"

Wendy inhaled sharply. She wanted to wrench away from him and crawl into the darkness. His words brought the past rushing in on her and despite the healing effect of time, the wounds of the past still hurt.

"They were killed."

"I know that. How did it happen?"

She shrugged. "We—we were having a party at Eric's. It was his and Jennifer's third wedding anniversary. Jennifer was partial to a certain burgundy, so as a surprise, Eric and I had ordered some from a friend who owns a liquor store."

She paused, swallowing. She hated remembering that night. Hated it. The last time she had seen her husband and her sister-in-law, they had both been laughing. The four of them had been so close, she and Jennifer, Leif and Eric.

She told Brad about how stunning Jennifer had looked in her white dress. Her honeyed skin had posed a striking contrast, as had her waist-length, jet black hair. She'd been so happy, and so in love. Leif had also been clad in white, a white dinner jacket. The shirt he wore beneath it had almost matched the unusual shade of his eyes.

At the last minute, the friend who owned the liquor store in Fort Lauderdale had been detained at the shop. Wendy had been cooking, since she had ordered Jennifer not to do a thing for the party. Eric had been trying to help Wendy with the outside grill.

And so Leif and Jennifer had gone together to pick up her present. Jen had been so pleased with the gift, the picture of giddy innocence in white. The two of them had left, arm in arm.

"They walked right into an armed holdup," Wendy explained. "The owner of the store was already dead. When one of the robbers slapped Jennifer to the ground and aimed the gun her way, Leif sprang upon him. He strangled the assailant with his bare hands, trying to buy Jennifer some time. But there were four robbers, and Leif was unarmed. As she turned to flee, Jennifer was caught."

Later the police told Wendy that the first shot had killed Leif instantly, piercing his heart.

They'd shot Jennifer three times. She had suffered slowly, bleeding to death.

I shouldn't have asked, Brad thought. He shouldn't have done this to her. And yet the story went on as Wendy continued in a strange monotone.

She and Eric had had to visit the morgue to identify the bodies—the hollow shells of Jennifer and Leif.

"And all I could remember was the blood. So much blood, staining the beautiful innocence of their white clothing. So very, very much blood." Wendy swallowed down her wine in a gulp.

Brad saw that her eyes were wide and unseeing. He understood why she had hidden herself here in the swamp for so long. And this certainly explained the closeness between Wendy and Eric.

But she had reached out, leaving the past behind. She had wanted him.

And now, he saw, they'd lost that special warmth. Wendy was shivering now, reaching for her clothes, ashamed of the way that she sat with him. She set her glass down. "I'm going to take a shower." She stood up. Brad reached for her, trying to catch her fingers.

"Wendy, wait—"

"Damn you, Brad! Leave me alone!" She ran down the hallway.

He sat back, brooding in defeat. He couldn't let her retreat to the past she had begun to leave behind.

Brad picked up the remnants of their meal and brought them to the kitchen. Deep in thought, he stared down the long hallway. Despite her denials, he knew that Wendy was trapped in the past, haunted by the memory of her husband. He couldn't let her wallow in that misery.

The shower was still spraying loudly when Brad strode into the bathroom and ripped open the shower curtain. With a bar of soap in her hand and her hair plastered over her face, Wendy turned to him. "Brad, damn you, leave me alone! Don't you understand—"

She gasped as he stepped into the shower. The water hit his hair and his back but he seemed not to feel it as he stared down at her.

"Brad, get out of here!"

"No, I don't think so, Wendy." Her skin was wet and slick and fragrant with the clean scent of soap. The shower water slid over them as he slipped his arms around her waist.

She twisted away from him. Tears stung her silver eyes. "You made me remember! Can't you understand—"

"I'm sorry. Yes, I made you remember the past. But now I'm going to help you forget." He planted a kiss on her neck. "Come on, Wendy. Let's wipe the slate clean."

Her eyes narrowed in amazement and fury. "Well, now, McKenna," she spat out, "you can damn well guarantee that I'll be thinking of him."

"Oh, no, Wendy," Brad assured her with confidence. "I can damn well guarantee that you won't."

Holding her squirming form in his arms, he kissed her with his mouth and his teeth and his tongue. He clung to her naked, dripping body with his left hand, while using his right to explore and caress her. He followed the pattern of her spine, kneading her buttocks. Tracing the curve of her hips, he found the soft apex of her legs and gently explored the feminine flesh there, seeking and finding the soft button of greatest pleasure.

Overcome by sensation, she went limp against him.

Then her body tautened. Her lips parted willingly to his, her tongue met and mated with his. Rising up on her toes, she buried her head against his shoulder. He leaned to whisper against her ear. "Everywhere I touch you, I will love you."

The water was hot as it pelted their skin. With the drive of the water against his back, Brad tasted her lips again. Then he cast her into a sea of trembling as he slowly, determinedly, kissed her breasts, taking his sweet time, his sweet pleasure. Bracing herself against his shoulder, she whispered his name, and then moaned in ecstasy.

As he lowered himself against her, she could feel the texture of his wet body against hers. Beneath the cascade of the shower, he knelt, gripped her buttocks firmly and buried himself against her.

Fire swept through her loins as she trembled fiercely and fought to hold on to his shoulders. The sensations were so overpowering that she could barely think. All she could do was feel and arch and undulate and burn.

"Brad!" She tore at his hair. He knew no mercy. "Please, really, I'm collapsing."

Her words had no impact. Breathlessly, barely able to form a coherent sentence, she continued. "Please! I'll fall against the tile. I'll die of a concussion."

Finally her words reached him. He rose, wet and gloriously handsome.

He did turn off the water.

But that was the only concession he gave the shower, or their drenched state. He swept her off her feet, dripping and naked, and carried her into the bedroom.

When she was safely nestled upon the bed, he continued his assault. She tossed her head and cried out his name. And he reminded her that she could not fall, for she already lay before him.

In seconds she soared to a volatile climax, and then he climbed atop her, parting her thighs to slide inside her. Exhausted and spent, she whispered that she could not go any further.

But he proved that she could. He touched her, inside and outside, and she felt the heat kindle inside of her again. He was the match to set her aflame. She ached again, she wanted again.

And she burst with the sweetness of it, once again.

She fell asleep in his arms, exhausted.

Brad lay awake for a long while, stroking her hair. Listening to the velvety sounds of the night, he felt the peace of the swamp surround him.

Chapter 9

Brad woke late. The sun was high in the sky when he opened his eyes. But then, it had been very late when they'd gone to sleep. Wendy was still sleeping.

She was curled halfway upon his chest, her hair a teasing cloud fanned over his shoulders. He carefully shifted her head to the pillow, then he watched her as she lay there. Her skin was as smooth as honey and cream against the sheets, and he was tempted to touch her all over again. She looked somewhat like an angel, he thought, a tender smile curving his lips. It was the color of her hair, he knew, and the classic lines of her face that reminded him of a heavenly spirit. And also, perhaps, her inner purity, her essence, that had warned him that Wendy was someone special, someone unique. A woman not to be taken lightly.

A woman to whom a man could lose his heart.

Warmth invaded his system again. No angel last night, he mused, but a siren, a tempest, stirring him up, beguiling him. Of course, he had wanted her. He had wanted her from the start. They'd been destined to come together. But it was wrong. He didn't belong here. He would have to leave, return to his own life in a world miles away from this marshy refuge. He swallowed fiercely, remembering his partner who now lay dead. Wendy did not belong in his life. He did not belong in hers.

She opened her eyes slowly, her dark lashes blinking over soft silver-and-gray eyes. At first she studied him with a misted confusion, then she smiled with a soft, almost shy welcome.

She yawned and shifted, and the dusky crest of her nipple became visible to him. He groaned inwardly. It was his fault. She had just wanted to be held; she had wanted a figure in the darkness, a man to hold. He had insisted on knowing her. He had wanted her to know him, to make love with him, and not with some forgotten dream.

Yes, he had wanted to know her. He had wanted it to be slow and careful, a union that mattered. But now the mere sight of her smile sent him plummeting into a downward swirl that gripped his loins and his heart in a painful vise. He should be running for his sanity.

Yet he could not leave her. He didn't know how much time they had in this strange Eden, but while it lasted, they were entwined, and he could not give that up.

She reached out and stroked his cheek, running her fingers slowly down his torso. She paused at his waist, drawing circles idly with her fingers, then her hand curved seductively and plunged lower as her fingers locked around him. She edged toward him. The tip of her tongue played over his chest.

Spasms of desire stabbed him like a white-hot lead. He leaned over and kissed her.

This was no angel, he thought as he lifted her above him. Her hair fell in golden sheets over her rosy breasts. She was as beautiful as an angel, but she moved with an ancient, earthy wisdom. And she gave herself to him, completely.

"Wendy..."

He pulled her down. Hers was the kiss of a total temptress, a seductress who made love with her body, her soul and her heart. Soon, Brad forgot that there was a world beyond them. All that mattered was the steaming crest they rode, in a writhing glory of kisses and whispers and slick, entangled limbs.

When it was over, she smiled at him. So sweetly. An angel again. She curled up just like a kitten and fell asleep against his chest.

Later, Wendy reflected that it was one of the best days of her life. She'd never known what it was like to have so much fun doing so very little.

She was more of a sleeper than Brad. She woke again to the scent of sausage. He was lingering in the doorway, naked, a tray of food in his hands, a wild orchid held in his teeth. When she laughed, he nearly dropped the tray. Instead, he deposited it on the floor to leap on top of her, mercilessly tickling her and demanding that she show more respect.

She laughed all through the meal.

When breakfast was over Brad turned on the news, but there was nothing reported about the case. Then an old-time mystery came on, and they watched the show, lazily entwined. An hour or so later, Wendy decided she wanted a shower. Brad decided to shower with her, and they made love once again, with Brad promising

Wendy that he could do so in the shower without killing her or causing a serious concussion. She laughed until she cried out with the ecstasy of it, until she was breathless and spent, until his gold-and-amber eyes locked with hers and the world went still.

They sat in the living room and pored through her music collection. He told her grimly that his home had been destroyed, and Wendy was painfully reminded that Brad was a stranger here, that he belonged elsewhere. She told him that he was welcome to begin a new collection with some of her old albums. He shook his head with a rueful smile, then reached out and stroked her golden hair. He whispered that she was incredible, and then he kissed her and made love to her again.

Wendy prepared stuffed Cornish game hens for dinner, and despite the fact that Brad kept pulling her out to the living room to dance to some old treasure that he had found, she managed to put the meal together rather well. Baby made an appearance at the door soon after. After consuming a hefty slab of raw beef, the panther settled down at the foot of the couch.

Later on, Brad led Baby back outside. He didn't want that much company tonight.

When Wendy locked up for the night, Brad was waiting for her in the darkened hallway. He kissed her there, lifted her into his arms and carried her off to bed. They made love again, before drifting into a deep and peaceful sleep.

The next morning, when Wendy awoke, Brad was no longer with her. Worriedly, she jumped out of bed, wrapped the sheets around herself and hurried down the hallway. Finding the house empty, she opened the front door and breathed a sigh of relief. He was there.

Baby had come prowling home. Brad was petting the panther's head as he stared out over the swampland, watching as morning burst upon it.

The sun was radiant, glittering in diamonds upon the water. The sound of silence was awesome, until some distant gator let out a grunt—very much like that of a pig, Wendy had always thought—and a mockingbird let out a screeching call.

He was wearing a pair of Leif's faded jeans, along with a Seminole cotton shirt, richly colored in deep blues and crimsons. Mary Hawk had made it for her grandson, as a Christmas present one year. Wendy bit her lower lip, remembering how tenderly Leif had thanked his grandmother. Leif had always shown Willie and Mary deep devotion and respect. That was one of the things that had always made her love her life here, despite the fact that her in-laws were so near. The members of the Hawk family cared for one another. They knew an ancient courtesy and a tender wisdom.

But Brad shared some of those qualities. She had been in a flying fury the other night when she had found him—she had been so worried by then. And it had taken her a while to realize that Willie—that sly old fox!—had been determined to find Brad, introduce himself in his unique way and make his own assessment.

And it seemed that Willie had judged Brad well. Brad had been a natural in Willie's small village. Willie was an old man who liked the old way of life, and many of the younger people, too, were now trying to maintain tribal traditions. Brad hadn't made judgments. He had fitted right in.

A sledgehammer suddenly seemed to slam against her heart as she watched him. She truly admired Brad

McKenna. It was difficult to believe that it had not quite been a week since she had met him. And yet it was all too easy to remember that first night, to remember removing his muddy clothing and thinking with inner tremors that he was really beautifully built, powerfully male. She had admired him then; there was no denying the way she'd been drawn to him. Perhaps her loneliness had contributed to the attraction. But since then she had discovered so much more to respect, so very much to like.

And he was going to leave. He'd warned her not to care too deeply; he'd warned her that he would never marry.

And she had assured him, and herself, that it didn't matter.

But it did, now. It mattered so much.

It was easy to live with him, easy to adjust to the extra damp towel in the bathroom, his coffee cup in the sink. It was easy to share things with him—meals and laughter and conversation—and most of all, it was easy to sleep beside him, held tight in his arms.

Don't fall in love...

I'm not in love, Wendy assured herself. As an independent woman, she had opted for this. When he walked away, she'd hold her head high.

And it would be all for the best, wouldn't it? she demanded silently to herself. If she had ever thought that he could stay, she had been living in a fantasy.

Suddenly she found it difficult to breathe. Horrid images flooded her mind as she remembered the violence that had made her a widow. Leif had stumbled upon that violence. Brad made a living at it.

If she and Brad were to fall helplessly in love, it would still be a dead-end relationship. She wouldn't be able to bear it. Every morning when he left for work, her palms would sweat and then she'd begin to tremble...

Brad turned around suddenly, as if he sensed her thoughts. She wanted to raise a hand in cheery greeting; she wanted to smile. She couldn't. Something in his somber gaze warned her that he had been having similar thoughts. Those thoughts were causing harsh lines to become ingrained upon his features. In silence, she merely held the sheet closer to her as a soft breeze whispered against her flesh. Then she returned to the house.

When she had showered and dressed, Brad was in the kitchen. He had made coffee, scrambled eggs and toast. Solemnly, he sipped his coffee.

"Thank you, that looks delicious," Wendy said. She slid onto a stool and tried to take a bite of the eggs. Unfortunately they stuck in her throat. She set her fork down and swallowed some orange juice.

"I need to go back to the gas station and make a phone call," he said.

She put her fork down. "I'll take you in. I need my car anyway. I want to drive into the city and buy some groceries and things." She stood and picked up her plate to take into the kitchen. She couldn't even pretend to eat.

Brad leaned across the table and caught her wrist. She paused, looking down at him. "Wendy, I don't think I should stay any longer."

She forced herself to shrug, pulling at her wrist. "Whatever you think."

"Wendy—"

"Brad, do whatever you think is best."

He stood in annoyance, taking the plate from her hands and setting it on the counter. His eyes burned a passionate gold, and his face was strained and tense. "Don't. Don't do that to you, or to me."

"Don't do what?" she demanded, trying to retain the coolness of her first words. She wanted to remain aloof and above it all.

"Don't pretend that it doesn't matter!" He was nearly shouting. She couldn't quite meet his gaze, but she managed to speak with extreme impatience. "Pretend what, McKenna? You're the one who made the big deal out of this. 'Let's get to know one another.' You're the one—"

"Wendy, I care about you, you little idiot. You just weren't made for one-night stands—"

"Why not, if I so chose? Damn you, I made a decision." Both their tempers were rising. Although Wendy was trying to hide her emotions, they spilled from her. Anger seemed the only way to combat them. She so desperately wanted to hold on to her pretense of sophisticated distance. But sarcasm entered her voice, a sharp, sharp edge that rang out like a call of battle.

"I made a decision, Brad!" she repeated. "That first night. Yeah, it's been a while. I took one look and decided, an attractive guy. Just what I need—a little uncomplicated sex. When you warned me not to care too much, it seemed so perfect. A mature, adult relationship... a consenting man, a consenting woman—"

"Wendy, stop it! We both know—"

"We don't know anything! What is your problem? If you want to leave—leave! There's nothing keeping you here! You are the last person I want as a permanent fixture in my life. My God, you kill people for a living—"

"That's not true!"

"Your partner was just killed, for God's sake!"

"Yes! And planes crash, and trucks kill people crossing the road."

"But you ask for it!"

"Wendy, other than target practice, I think I've actually fired my gun three times in almost ten years."

She backed away from him, her hands on her hips. "Why are you trying to convince me—"

"You're making it sound like I'm some kind of contract killer!" Two steps brought him back to her. He gripped her shoulders, staring furiously down at her. "I try to keep crack off the streets, Wendy, that's what I do. I try to keep drugs from high-school kids. And I try even harder to keep them out of the grade schools. Ever see a twenty-year-old dead on a cocaine mix? Or a kid in junior high with needle tracks on his arm? It doesn't do any good to arrest that poor kid— you can only pray that he kicks the habit. You have to get guys like Michaelson. The guys who orchestrate the big deals—and make big bucks on the drugs."

The heat that emanated between them seemed to crackle like dry lightning. "Fine, Brad. You go after the Michaelsons in the world, and quit worrying about me! I've gotten what I wanted from you—"

"What?"

His tone was so sharp that she paused for the fraction of a moment. She was trembling, rocked by fury and fear. The truth had descended upon her like a falling weight. She was falling in love; she *had* fallen in love. But she could never use that to hold on to Brad.

"I said, I've gotten what I wanted—"

"Sex?"

"That's right."

He stared at her incredulously. "Just sex?" His temper was roiling and boiling, but it didn't change the way he felt about her. He still wanted her. He had desired her when she laughed, and when she stared at him with tender, sultry eyes. And now, despite the way she lifted her chin and scowled at him with cool, complete disdain, he still wanted her.

Her cool facade was a hoax. He could swear that it was all a lie. Brad wanted to rant and rave; she could evoke such extreme reactions in him! But he didn't. Even while a hot, soaring pulse took hold of him, he forced himself to smile lazily. He wanted so much from her, and he was desperately afraid that this fantasy would end. Couldn't he touch her soul? Couldn't he reach her heart? He had to find out.

"Just sex, huh? Is that it, Wendy? You took one look at me and decided that I'd do for a fling?"

Something in his tone warned her. "Brad—"

Fiercely, he pulled her into his arms. His kiss was sweet and savage; his hands moved in torment.

Although she wanted to lash out at him, she was losing the desire to fight. His lips nearly bruised hers; his tongue ravaged her mouth. His body was white-hot, fevered. The anger, the tempest, the sudden blinding need exploded from him and filled her. A surge of urgent longing seized her, spiraling into her loins. She knew she should twist away from his kiss, but she could not. Instead, she pressed more closely to him. And with the desperate, lingering assault of each kiss, the idea of protest faded from her mind. Instinctively, her fingers curled into his hair. They played over his neck and raked his back. She felt his hands beneath her shirt, freeing her breasts from her bra, stroking them.

He unsnapped her jeans, then slid his fingers beneath the waistband, searching for her most sensitive area. She wrenched his shirt from his pants, touching his bare back, moaning softly.

Somehow, together, they lowered themselves to the floor. For a moment she was a tangle of clothing, and then she was naked. She prayed that he would come to her swiftly, that he would assuage the yearning, the desperate longing.

He did not. With a feverish pitch, Brad made love to her more thoroughly than he ever had before. She whispered to him, pleading and crying out . . . begging him. But still he explored her, finding new erogenous zones, leaving no sweet inch of bare and vulnerable flesh unaware of his touch, of his kiss.

When he came to her at last, it was instantly explosive, but he did not let it lie at that. He moved while she lay limp, until he roused her again. Then her cry mingled upon the air with his, as they soared above the earth.

Their descent was slow and leisurely. Time had no meaning for Wendy when she was locked in Brad's warm embrace.

"Wendy, I know it's—"

He broke off, and they both jumped at the sound of a tapping against the door.

"Dammit!" Brad swore, casting her a quick, angry glance as he moved to the window. "I am slipping to hell since I've met you!"

"Wendy? Brad? Anyone home?"

Although Brad relaxed at the sound of Eric's voice, Wendy was overcome by a sudden panic. She knew that Eric liked Brad. But still, a terrible feeling of guilt swept over her, dark and poignant. Like a high-school girl caught necking in the car, she scrambled for her clothing.

Brad watched as she stumbled quickly into her clothes. She was such an enigma to him, this sultry, silver-eyed angel. After all, she had claimed that she wanted sex only. She had hurt him with her callous words. But what else could she have said to him? *I understand, please do go, we are getting too involved. Yes, you're right, please do get out of my life before I fall irrevocably in love with you.*

"Would you please get dressed!" Wendy whispered hoarsely.

He looked at her as if he were weighing her words for a moment, then he shook his head and pulled on his jeans. Wendy had barely tucked her blouse into her jeans before he smiled with sarcastic sweetness and strode over to open the door. His shirt hung open, and his feet were bare.

"Hi, Eric," he said, opening the door.

Eric hesitated in the doorway, looking from Brad to Wendy. Eric's emotions were always almost impossible to read. Wendy unwittingly put a hand to her hair, trying to smooth back the wild disarray. Eric glanced at Brad. "Bad timing. I'm sorry."

"Don't be ridiculous—" Wendy began.

"The timing is just fine," Brad interrupted her. "In fact, it's good to see you. We were heading off to the garage to use the phone in a few minutes. Come on in."

Sensing the tension, Eric offered Wendy a curious frown. She smiled at him as innocently as she could. "Want some coffee, Eric? Ice tea, a beer?"

"I'll have some coffee, thanks."

Eric noticed their breakfast plates, barely touched.

Wendy was relieved that he made no comment, but accepted a cup of coffee and turned to Brad. "Willie enjoyed taking off with you, you know. He did give Wendy quite a scare, but he enjoyed having you so much that it was worth it, I think."

Brad told Eric that he had enjoyed meeting his family. When the two men moved into the living room Wendy exhaled, relieved. She picked up the breakfast plates and mournfully realized that they seemed to have a serious problem with breakfast. No matter who made it for whom, the meal had a tendency of winding up in the garbage.

What are we going to do? she wondered in a fleeting panic. Then she realized that she had no choice. Their future was in Brad's hands. Whenever he left, it was over.

A glance over the counter told her that the men were still engrossed in a discussion. Retreating to the bathroom, she brushed out her hair and splashed cool water over her face. As she stared at the reflection of her own wide, silver-gray eyes, she was certain that they wore a telltale glaze, the glow of a woman in love.

"Wendy!"

Brad's voice came to her like a roar. She was sure Baby had never sounded more menacing. The sound of it irritated her, and she gritted her teeth.

When she squared her shoulders and strode out to the living room, her hands on her hips and her brows arched in an irate query, she discovered that Eric was staring at her the same way Brad was—as if she were a child.

"What?" she snapped. They exchanged glances with one another.

"Eric said that he gave you a message for me. About strangers in the swamp—possibly here to hunt me down."

She hesitated, feeling mortified that she could have forgotten such an important warning. But first, she had come home to find him missing. Then they had spent the evening in the village with Willie and Mary and the family, and then when they had come back . . .

She shook her head. "I—I forgot."

"You what?" Brad said, his eyes narrowing.

"Wendy, it was important," Eric said mildly.

"I'm sorry."

"Sorry!" Brad looked as if he were about to go through the roof. He spun around, hands on his hips, his head lowered, as he fought to control his temper.

But she didn't think that he was so angry about the omission. Even a minor problem would test the limits of his temper right now. Because nothing had been settled between them, nothing at all.

He turned around again, looking at Eric. "You think they've got seaplanes coming in to the swamp? Near here?"

Eric nodded.

Brad shook his head. "That's why we were here, trying to infiltrate his organization. We knew he was securing his stuff out of Colombia, but we could never get a fix on the checkpoints. I knew that he was up to something out here. We were trying to trap him...that's when I wound up out here." He glanced Wendy's way. His eyes were dark, unreadable. His gaze lingered upon her, then he returned his attention to Eric. "But I don't understand how our agents haven't caught him if he's still operating here."

Eric interrupted him with a soft laugh. "Brad, you're not considering the size of the swamp. The grasslands go on forever. There are endless miles of marshes, deep canals and high, dry hammocks with pine trees. There are also lakes, large lakes, with plenty of room for a small seaplane bearing millions of dollars worth of white gold to land."

"So Michaelson's got a drop spot near here," Brad said, calculating. "I've got to find it." Tension constricted his muscles as he studied Eric appraisingly.

"Oh, no!" Wendy swore suddenly. "McKenna, you royal son of a bitch! You haven't the sense to hide out from a man who has one purpose in life besides the pursuit of money—killing you! And if you think that you're going to take my brother-in-law—"

"Wendy!" Eric stopped her furiously.

"No!" Tears stung her eyes. "You idiots! Eric, it would kill your grandfather if something were to happen to you! And, Brad, damn you, I know your boss didn't hire you to act stupid! To foolishly get yourself killed—"

"Wendy, stop it!" Eric insisted. He reached for her, but she twisted away. "Wendy, I prowled the jungles of Asia. If I'd been killed, Grandfather would have understood."

"We're not going anywhere or doing anything," Brad murmured. He paused. "But I told you this morning, Wendy. I don't think that this is safe for you anymore."

She didn't believe them. She was convinced that Eric intended to take Brad deep into the swamps, deep into all the villages to meet with his friends, Seminoles, Miccosukees and the whites who made their homes out there. Michaelson was hunting him, and Wendy realized that Brad was growing tired of it. He was ready to hunt Michaelson instead.

"Well, maybe leaving here is the best thing for you," Wendy said softly. Then she went back to her bedroom and snatched her purse and the airboat keys that sat on her dresser.

Brad was in the hallway when she emerged. He still looked angry, but not as angry as she was becoming.

"Get out of my way."

"Wendy, you have to understand. We have to talk."

"Talk? No, I don't think so. I don't want to talk, Brad. I want to get out of here. I want to go talk to some store clerks and salespeople—maybe a bartender or two. Someone who doesn't make a living at violence!"

"Wendy, I told you—"

"Yeah, yeah, yeah, you never draw your gun. I found you with a bullet hole in your forehead. That's what it was, right, Brad? A bullet hole. And you're ready to leave, right?" Tears were as hot as molten lead behind her eyelids, and she was afraid that she would shortly grow hysterical and throw her arms around his legs and tell him that she couldn't bear it, she couldn't let him go anywhere, she couldn't let him go away and get himself killed. She was in love with him.

But she was the fool; she was the one losing control. Brad could handle this. He had warned her that he couldn't love her. He had warned that he had to leave.

"Wendy—"

"No!" She shoved past him. "Eric will take you to the gas station. I'm sure that he and Mac will see that you make your phone call—and that you're able to get wherever you want to go."

The tears were about to spill over. Blindly, she spun around. "Goodbye, Brad."

Not wanting to break down in front of him, Wendy ran out of the house to her airboat. Eric would understand, she thought. Eric would see that Brad got wherever he wanted to go.

She doubled over, listening to the drone of the motor, barely seeing the grasses that dipped and swayed as she passed them, barely aware of the wind that dried her tears.

He had been safe. He had been safe at her house— surely, no one would have found him there. But he couldn't stay put, he just didn't have the patience to keep hiding out.

He was gone. He was out of her life. She had claimed that she had gotten all that she wanted, and he was gone now.

No, he wasn't gone—not when she could close her eyes and feel him with her still. The subtle scent of him lingered against her skin. She could imagine his touch in each lilting breeze. She could remember his laughter, his tenderness, his raging passions.

She would never forget his golden eyes and his soft words. There had been so very much between them.

But no amount of passion could deny the disparity between their chosen lives. He wasn't a killer. She knew that. She understood his job. And she understood that he could have no room for her in his life, while she couldn't bear to live with a man in his profession.

She scarcely knew him, she tried to tell herself.

But it didn't matter. Imagining a future without him now seemed as cold and austere as an arctic plain.

Chapter 10

L. Davis Purdy had been silent on his end of the phone for so long that Brad began to think that they had been disconnected. When he answered at last, he chose his words carefully.

"What do you know?" he asked Brad.

"What do I know—for fact? Very little. Except that I have a—a friend—" He paused, looking out the window. Eric Hawk was leaning against the building, listening to old Mac go on while he waited for Brad to finish the call. Eric wore a low-brimmed hat, jeans, a denim shirt and cowboy boots. His jet hair fell over the collar of the shirt, but even with the brim of the hat covering his eyes, there was an air of quiet confidence about the man. Yeah, Brad decided. If Eric Hawk had said that something was going on, then it was going on. Hawk would make a good partner. More so than many men Brad had worked with, he felt as if he could trust the Indian with his life.

He cleared his throat and continued. "I have a friend who knows this place like the back of his hand. He says that the deal is going down in the swamp, and I believe him. Michaelson is out here. He's waiting for the next drop, and it's going to happen here. I'm sure he's still looking for me, too, but money means more to him than revenge."

Brad vaguely heard Purdy warn him to investigate, but not to make any moves without checking in. Somberly reminding Brad of his partner's death, Purdy admonished him to be careful. Brad clenched his teeth in anguish, reliving that moment. But then as Purdy's voice went on about procedure, Brad's mind wandered.

He had meant to leave today, to go back to the city, to do it by the book, live under constant guard until they could do something about Michaelson. He'd meant to leave Wendy, to get out of her life. To leave her safe and alone. To leave her, before...

Before they fell in love.

She had told him to go ahead and leave. When she'd stormed out of the house, she hadn't even looked back. She wouldn't expect him to be there. Maybe he shouldn't be there, maybe he should stay with Eric. But he wasn't leaving. Purdy had agreed that Brad was better off staying in the swamp—especially since his agents were getting closer to Michaelson.

Brad had to talk to Wendy; he had to see her again. They couldn't just leave things the way they had.

He realized that Purdy had finished his lecture, and that he was hanging up. Just in time, Brad made the proper response. Promising to stay in touch, he hung up the phone.

He left the office and came upon Mac and Eric still involved in conversation. "Can't tell me these guys are all here for gator season," Mac insisted. He spat on the ground. "No sirree, I know the hunters when they come. I know the office boys who dress up in khaki and shoot up beer cans and sit around in their skivvies, and I know when I see a horde of people comin' through here that don't belong. They just don't look right. They look like they're still wearing suits, no matter how they try to dress like hunters."

Brad winced. He was sure that half the guys who looked so ridiculous in khaki or denim were either FBI or his own associates from the DEA office. But all the telltale signs were evident. The swamp was crawling with men—bad guys and good guys. Brad hoped to God he would know the difference when he came across someone.

"Well, if anyone asks, remember—you've never seen this man," Eric instructed Mac.

The old man grinned at Brad. "I've seen the news, Eric. I know when to keep quiet."

"Thanks a lot, Mac."

"Nothing to thank me for." He looked at Eric again. "You going to be out on the swamp today?"

"Yeah, I thought maybe we should check out a few of the canals."

"You want me to fill up the cooler?"

Eric laughed. "Sure. Fill her up with some cool brews, and some mullet, if you've got any. And throw in some snacks—cheese balls, corn chips—whatever you've got handy."

Mac loaded the airboat with supplies from his limited stock of grocery items. When they stepped back into the airboat, Eric suggested that Brad pilot the vehicle. Within a few minutes, Brad had more or less mastered the craft, and he loved it. Eric grinned tolerantly as Brad let out a whoop and raced pell-mell across the open water.

When Eric warned him that they were coming into a narrower channel, Brad cut the speed and Eric took over.

They spent the morning traversing a myriad of hammocks. They came upon a few isolated Indian villages and a few deserted shacks that weekend hunters had built but didn't really own because the state had taken over the land. Although they didn't run into any hunters, they did discover one shack that had been recently inhabited by someone who smoked expensive cigars and drank high-grade brandy.

Setting an empty bottle back on the rough table, Eric arched a brow. "Michaelson?"

Brad nodded slowly. "Maybe. Though I can't see Michaelson coming this deep into the swamp. He's a city boy all the way. He likes his conveniences—brushes his teeth with mineral water. But it might be a couple of his boys, copying his habits."

"We'll wait it out a while, see if they come back," Eric said.

They waited on the airboat, hidden behind a pine hammock a few yards from the rustic cabin. Eric broke out the beer and a bag of potato chips. After casting fishing lines into the water, they both leaned back.

Brad took a long look at Eric. "Thanks. I realize I'm taking up a lot of your time."

Eric shrugged. "I don't live a nine-to-five life. I use my time when and where I think it's important."

It was hot and humid as a summer day in Hades. Brad swallowed down half a can of beer, then shook his head. "Still, I appreciate what you're doing."

"Sure thing."

As the strange silence of the swamp surrounded them, Brad realized that it wasn't silent at all. He could hear the buzz of insects, the chirp of birds and the rustling sound of the breeze. When he heard a grunting noise, he knew it was the sound of a distant gator.

"She's right, you know," he said.

"Wendy?" Eric grinned.

"Yeah. I have no right dragging you into this."

Eric swore. "Look, I'm here because I want to be, all right? This is my land those bastards are screwing up. My territory. I'll deal with Wendy."

Brad nodded, enthralled by the sight of a long-legged crane that stepped delicately over a patch of marshland. He finished his beer, and Eric tossed him another.

Brad nodded at Eric. "Wendy told me what happened. To her husband—and your wife. I'm sorry."

Eric's muscles tightened as he swallowed. "Thanks. It was a long time ago. I guess we've dealt with it differently, Wendy and I. I spent months alone, then I went wild. Eventually, I settled down, finding peace in this land, getting support from my family. Wendy has just stayed home—alone." He hesitated. "I wanted to find those guys myself. I wanted to bring them out here and kill them my way." He looked across the water. "I did find the one guy in the end. I managed to turn him over to the cops. Then I knew that I could go on. Wendy, well, Wendy never had the same satisfaction, but she goes on. I think you've been good for her. Damned good for her." He shrugged, managing to smile again. "So, I may have a bit of an argument on my hands. But, come to think of it, you're going to have more to explain to Wendy than I will."

Brad looked back at Eric. "I—I don't know if I should even go back there."

Eric appeared amused. "She doesn't bite. Or does she? Whoops, wait a minute, none of my business."

"You sure about that?" Brad grinned.

"About what?"

"It being none of your business."

"All right. It is my business. But only in the sense that I care about her happiness."

"So what do you think I should do?"

Eric shrugged. "What do you want to do?"

"You heard her this morning," Brad said huskily. "I don't think that she wants me around."

"I'm willing to bet that she'll open that door for you if you go back to her."

"She thinks I'm a killer."

"She knows you aren't a killer. She's scared, and in defense she's lashing out with accusations. She has a right to be scared. She's been hurt before. She's had her heart and soul severed. Tolerate her."

Brad laughed. It was so much more than a matter of tolerating a nervous streak! "I don't know, I have no promises for her."

"No one really has promises these days. I think you owe each other more of your time. While you've got it, you owe it to one another."

"Maybe."

Eric grinned suddenly. "Grandfather has a great saying for any dilemma. He says that life is a river, and we chart out that river with our hearts, our minds and our souls. When it matters most, he says, the heart should be the guide. The mind is made of logic, the soul is saddled with pride. Only the heart has no logic, and only the heart can bypass pride. You're welcome to come back home with me tonight. Or else I'll take you back to Wendy's. You decide. Just let me know.''

"Yeah, I will," Brad answered, though it was only a pretense that he needed to make a decision. They both knew where Brad was going for the night.

"Hey!" Eric cried suddenly.

"What?" Brad set down his beer can.

"I've got a bite on my line!"

"Oh," Brad said in relief. Then he laughed. "Oh."

Eric looked up at him, realizing that Brad had thought someone was near them, stalking them. He grimaced. "Sorry." Then his line plunged, and he rose to battle it out with the fish. But it was too late. The fish had cleverly slipped off the hook.

"You made me lose him," Eric complained.

"I made you lose him?" Brad protested.

Amid an easy chorus of laughter Brad took out two new cans of beer, and they settled down to wait again.

Dusk came, illuminating the canals in shades of gold and red and mauve. The white cranes on the water seemed to be bathed in pink. Then darkness fell, nearly complete.

"I don't think that anyone is coming back here today," Eric said.

Brad shook his head. He could barely see Eric in the darkness, but his eyes were starting to adjust to it. "They've got something going here, though, I'm sure. Maybe every third day or so. How the hell did they ever find this place?"

"Airboat. There are shacks all over the Glades. Somebody found it to be a convenient spot. Maybe they're gone for good, maybe they'll come back. We can check it out again tomorrow."

Brad nodded. "Thanks."

"Quit that, will you?" Eric charged him. "I told you—this is my territory your man Michaelson is messing with." Eric started the boat motor, and they began to sluice through the canals, the headlight on the airboat their only illumination except for the stars above. There was barely a sliver of a moon that night.

Although he still hadn't said anything to Eric, Brad realized that they were heading for Wendy's house.

But as they came upon Wendy's, Eric quickly cut the motor. The house was too empty; it was too dark.

"We'll go around to the marshy side where there's more saw grass to hide us," Eric whispered.

As Eric secured the airboat, Brad stepped off into deep muck that pulled at his borrowed shoes. He hurried through the marsh until he reached dry land. Eric joined him shortly, moving more easily in his high boots.

"She isn't here!" Brad said tensely.

"Well, maybe—"

"It doesn't take that long to go shopping!" Brad insisted. Fear clawed at his throat and ravaged his gut. What if Wendy's cabin wasn't hidden deep enough in the swamp? If someone had been biding time in an old wooden shack, couldn't they have also discovered Wendy's handsome home with all the modern conveniences?

He tried to swallow down his fear for her; he tried to think professionally and rationally.

"I'm sure," Eric said very quietly, "that she just hasn't come home yet. She might have gone out to the village. And she might have visited some friends in town. There are any number of things that she could be doing."

Sure, Brad thought. Any number of things. All he knew was that she wasn't nearby, where he could touch her and see her and know that she was safe. "Let's check it out," he said softly.

By instinct, they nodded at one another and stealthily crept around the house in opposite directions, Brad going left, and Eric moving to the right.

Although Brad's instincts told him that there was no one there, he couldn't control the pounding of his heart, the naked fear that Michaelson might have snatched Wendy.

At last he reached the back of the house. He sensed movement, then heard a birdcall. Despite his tension, he smiled. It was Eric. It was a damned good birdcall; a week ago he would have thought that it was real. One week in the swamp had sharpened his senses.

He stepped out around the back. Eric joined him.

"Nothing?" Brad asked him.

Eric shook his head. "Nothing. I don't think anyone has been here since we left earlier today. But come on, we'll check the house."

"Think we really ought to break in?"

"No." Eric grinned. "I have a key."

When they surveyed the house, Brad quickly saw that nothing had been touched since they had left that morning. He expelled a long sigh and sank onto the sofa.

"What if Michaelson grabbed her?" he said out loud. "What if he somehow figured out that she was sheltering me, and he grabbed her out in the swamp?"

"Come on, Brad, she's a big girl. She was upset. Probably wanted to talk to Grandfather, or maybe a friend, as I said." He grinned. "Ordinarily, she would have talked to me, but hell, it looks like I've joined the enemy. That meant she had to find someone else. She's all right. I'm sure of it."

Was he so sure? Brad wondered. Despite his words, Eric was pacing, too.

Then they both froze.

There had been no sound of a motor, no sudden flash of headlights.

But someone was outside now, moving around the house in secrecy and stealth.

They looked at one another and rose quickly. Silently, they headed for the front door. Brad opened it cautiously, then both men paused to look out. There was nothing there. The lawn was covered in a soft glow of light from the house, but the edge of the yard was surrounded by shadow. The high pines to the right seemed like a dark forest where a million demons could dwell—a million Michaelsons.

Eric motioned to Brad, who nodded. They started to retrace their earlier steps, silently circling the house.

When Brad came around the back, he saw the form, dark and huddled low, trying to look in one of the windows. Quickly, silently, Brad began his approach. The figure started to turn, to rise, but he was already upon it.

With impetus in his last step, Brad hurtled himself against the form. A low growl issued from his lips. Then he heard a whoosh of air and a soft scream.

He was on the ground, straddled atop her, before he realized that the figure in the darkness was Wendy. With her wrists pinned to the ground, she looked so frightened and helpless.

"Wendy!"

"Brad!" Her eyes opened wide, and then narrowed. "Brad! You slimy son of a bitch—"

"Well, what a nice reunion!" Eric interrupted brightly. He was leaning comfortably against the wall.

Wendy cast him an evil glare, then turned her furious stare upon Brad once again. "What the hell—"

"Where were you?" he demanded hotly.

"What?" she returned.

"Where were you? Where the hell were you?"

"That isn't any of your—"

"You scared me to death!" Brad shouted.

"*I* scared *you*! You muscle-bound Kong—you attacked me! You're sitting on me. You—" She paused. "Eric! Tell him to get off me."

Eric smiled as he hunkered down on his toes near her head, chewing on a blade of grass. "I'll bet if you just ask him real nice, he'll get up on his own."

The grate of her teeth was audible.

"Dammit, Wendy, where did you go?" Brad insisted.

She exhaled. "This is ridiculous!" Despite her anger, there was a glaze to her eyes, as if she had been crying. Dimly, through the maze of fear and relief and anger, Brad wondered if she had been crying because of him.

Then he wondered what the hell he was doing here, making the situation worse. But wasn't this better? If someone had stumbled onto his trail, they would find Wendy—whether they found him or not. Now she was better off with him than without him. Now they would both be better off not to take any chances at all.

"Wendy!" Nervous energy racked his body. She meant so damned much to him.

"You . . ." Her teeth grated again as she struggled against his hold. Her eyes grew brighter, as if she were on the verge of tears.

"Not that my whereabouts are any of your business!" she hissed, twisting her head to stare at Eric. "Or yours!"

"I'm just an innocent bystander."

"Could you go stand somewhere else?"

Eric laughed, but he didn't move. Wendy stared from one man to the other—Eric, who seemed to be having the time of his life, and Brad, who still seemed deathly pale in the darkness.

"I went to the damned store!" she spat out.

"All day?" Eric queried politely.

"Where's the airboat?" Brad demanded.

"I have my car!" Wendy snapped. "The boat's across the water. I went into the garage, I talked to Mac. I got my car. I drove into Fort Lauderdale. I went to the drugstore, and I went to the grocery store. You want to know what aisles I perused? I bought a can of Pepsi from a vending machine. I stopped for a copy of the newspaper."

"That still doesn't take all day! Dammit, Wendy, you scared me half to death."

"Well, dammit, Brad, you did the same to me! How the hell do you think it felt to know that someone was in the house?"

"You knew that Eric has a key."

"But neither Eric's car nor his airboat were visible. Why the hell am I explaining this to you?" Wendy exploded. She swallowed, wondering whether to laugh or cry or keep screaming. She was shaking, trembling inside and out because he had come back, because he was still with her.

Grandfather had told her that he would be there. He had smiled and told her to be patient. He had told her to go home and wait, to trust in her heart.

Although she had told Brad to go away, she had prayed that he wouldn't. She had bought groceries for two. In the drugstore she had tried not to indulge in fantasy, but she had bought extra shaving cream and toothpaste and soap...

For two.

Which had been foolish. Eventually, he had to go away.

Eventually, but please, God! Wendy silently prayed, not now. Let us have some time. I need that second damp towel in the bathroom just a little longer.

"You're explaining it to me because you worried me to death!" Brad yelled back at her.

"You're not even supposed to be here!" she reminded him.

Eric cleared his throat. "Maybe we should hassle over the finer points inside." He cleared his throat again. "Brad, er, I think you're about to cut off her circulation at the wrists."

Brad instantly released Wendy's wrists. Then he took her right hand in his own and began to rub it. "Did I hurt you?"

"No," she replied. "Just move, will you please?"

Slowly, he came to his feet, then reached a hand down to her. She took it, eyeing him warily as she stood.

"Did you leave packages in the car?" Eric asked.

She nodded, then smiled sweetly. "Except for the bag that I was carrying. I dropped it in the bushes there when the G-man jumped me."

"Oh, well, no harm done," Eric said, shaking out the tattered brown grocery bag and collecting the canned goods and cereal boxes that had fallen out.

Brad and Wendy were still staring at one another heatedly. Eric shoved the bag into Brad's arms. "Why don't you take this into the house," he suggested. "I'll go for the rest."

"Yeah, thanks," Wendy said. Brad was still staring at her. Rumpled and handsome, his tawny hair was all askew. She brushed by him and headed for the front.

He set the bag down on the kitchen floor. By then, Eric had returned with two more sacks. "On the counter, Wendy?"

"Yes, thank you."

Brad stood by the counter. "Wendy, where were you?"

"I wasn't out making a million-dollar coke deal, if that's what you're asking," she said flippantly.

"Oh, jeez," Eric groaned.

Brad grabbed her arm. "Wendy, I'm asking you a civil question! I want a civil answer!"

"Civil!"

"Wendy—"

"I told you, I went to the stinking store! Then I came back and I went out to see my family. I went to the village. I had dinner with Willie and Mary and the kids. That's it, that's all! And it's none of your business, anyway! You told me that you were leaving!"

He swung around on his heel. Wendy glared at Eric, who merely shrugged and followed Brad outside.

Brad was on the lawn, still tense and angry—but deflated. He looked at Eric. "Where the hell is her car?" he demanded.

Eric laughed. "Come on. I'll show you."

He led Brad to what looked like dark water, but there were stones beneath the water, which was barely an inch deep. It seemed that they walked across water, but of course they didn't. There was even a trail hacked through the tall grass on the other side, and there, high on a dry clearing near the end of a dirt road, was Wendy's small station wagon.

Together, the men collected the rest of the groceries, then returned to the house.

Wendy was putting things away, slamming every door she touched.

Eric set the last of the grocery bags down. "Want some help, Wendy?"

"No," she said curtly.

"Suit yourself. You want a beer, Brad?"

"Sure," Brad said.

Eric sauntered casually past Wendy and reached into the refrigerator, helping himself to two cans of beer. He tossed one over to Brad.

Wendy stood at the sink, separating a pack of steaks into individual freezer bags. She sniffed. "The two of you already smell like a brewery."

"What?" Eric protested. "I'm crushed."

Wendy swung around to face him. "All right, where the hell have the two of *you* been all day?"

"Fishing."

"Fishing." She paused in her efforts and stared at him. "Fishing. All day. *All* day?"

"Fishing. Shooting the breeze. Swilling beer. You know. Having a good old time."

Wendy turned back to her steaks. "Liar," she said softly.

"Ask Brad. I had a catfish on the line that you wouldn't believe. He made me lose it. City slicker."

She looked up at Eric. He smiled blandly. "You going to let him stay on here?" he asked her bluntly.

"What?" She flushed.

"Well, I'm going home. I was wondering if I should take him with me?"

Brad's eyes opened wide in amazement. "Eric, I can sink my own ship!"

"Stop it!" Wendy snapped. "Brad can stay."

"Stop shouting. I just asked a question," Eric said defensively.

Brad swallowed a sip of beer. Wendy was alive and well, and they were together. Heat filled him at the idea that their time together wasn't over yet.

"Good night." On his way out of the kitchen, Eric offered Brad a wink. "Just watch out! She's dangerous."

Wendy swung around. "Watch out? *He* tackled *me* out there, and I'm supposed to be the dangerous one."

"I think I can handle her," Brad said.

Wendy glared at him. A curious golden light was in his eyes as they swept over her. It made her feel warm. No, it made her feel hot, as if she would melt to the ground. Just seeing him there, tall, ruffled sandy hair, bronze and sinewed, made her remember the morning. She remembered what it felt like to run her fingers over his shoulders, over his back. She remembered watching the play of his muscles as he held her, remembered seeing the taut flicker of passion in his face as he gazed down at her...

"Yes," he said softly, "I think that I can handle her."

"Maybe," Eric said. "Maybe not. You know, friend, she could be trying to trap you."

"What?" Wendy and Brad said simultaneously. They both stared at Eric, who maintained his facade of a friendly calm.

"Trap you, Brad. She's always wanted a baby. Did you know that? Did she ever tell you? She was trying to get pregnant before Leif died. Maybe she's using you. Maybe she intends to trap you into marriage."

"And on the other hand, don't you think you're misleading her? You're not the kind of guy to settle down. You've got important work. A hell of a job. And heck, any damn day of your life could be your last. Do you use that as a ploy to take advantage of lonely women?"

"Eric!" Wendy snapped in disbelief and horror. No. Eric was her friend, he loved her. Why would he ever say such things? "Eric!" Her voice was small but strong, and it was laced with anguish. "Get out of my house! Get out! How could you—just get out!"

She was as white as chalk.

Eric nodded. "I was just leaving."

He walked out the front door. She heard it close. In absolute dismay, she let her eyes meet Brad's at last.

He was staring at her, staring at her hard. He started walking toward her.

"Wendy..."

"No!" Knowing that she was going to burst into tears, Wendy turned to run down the hallway. She just couldn't stand any more, not today.

Brad caught her by the shoulders, then swung her around into his arms.

"No!" She struggled against his hold.

"Use me, Wendy, if you would," he whispered softly. Then his lips caught hold of hers, hot and searing, and she gasped at the power of his hands moving over her. He was lifting her, lifting her high into his arms, she couldn't help but respond to the feverish heat of his body.

Chapter 11

It was so good to touch her, so good to kiss her, to hold her soft and pliant in his arms. Her lips fused to his, seemingly as hungry as his own. He could have held her all night, drinking in a kiss such as this...

At first he ignored the sound that came to him from the swamp outside.

But then it came again, that sound in the darkness of night, and it penetrated Brad's mind. It was a birdcall, soft but clear, cutting through the night, cutting through Brad's desire and causing a prickle of danger to streak along his spine.

Brad slowly lowered Wendy until her feet touched the floor. Her arms were still around his neck, but her eyes met his. She, too, had sensed the danger.

"Eric?" he asked.

She nodded. "Yes, it's Eric."

"You said you had a pistol. What about ammunition?"

She nodded and quietly slipped away from him. He stayed in the hallway, listening. Concentrating, he tried to clear away all other sounds. Then he heard the footsteps outside.

He knew that Eric was out there . . . somewhere. But Eric had called to him, warned him, because someone else was out there, too.

Wendy returned with a Smith & Wesson .38. He took the weapon from her and cocked it. "Stay here," he whispered. "I want you to find a sheltered corner and stay low. Hold on to the shotgun. All right?"

At last she nodded. He turned away from her and hurried down the hall to the front door. The lights were on in the kitchen and the living room. He turned them off and went to the window, where he stared out across the lawn. Nothing moved. He went to the front door and slipped out.

Perched on his haunches by the corner of the house, Brad hesitated, then sprang around. His weapon was aimed straight ahead, at the ready. There was no one there.

He moved silently along the side of the house. The night was dark, so damned dark.

The birdcall sounded again. Someday, Brad decided, he was going to have to ask Eric what kind of bird it was supposed to be. An owl?

It didn't matter now. What was important was that he knew that Eric was moving almost opposite him, on the other side of the house. Within a few minutes, they'd both be at the rear, and their prey would be caught between them then.

Their prey . . .

He knew that someone else was there. He could feel it, smell it, sense it. All he had to do was turn the corner.

At the edge of the wall, Brad paused, his heart thudding against his chest. He held the gun steady with both hands, and then he sprang smoothly around, prepared to shoot.

A man was there, in back of the house. He hadn't heard or sensed Brad or Eric yet—he was busy at work on Wendy's bedroom window.

"Hold it right there. Get your hands up—up high, clear in the air!" Brad demanded.

The man dropped low. Brad saw a glint of the pale moonlight gleaming upon something in the man's hands. He had a gun, too, and he was getting ready to shoot.

Brad shot first. Carefully, very carefully, he squeezed the trigger. The gun went flying and the man screamed, clutching his hand.

Eric flew around the corner, stooping silently to retrieve the thrown gun even as the fallen intruder tried to reach for it. Brad came forward, keeping the .38 aimed at the man.

"Three fifty-seven Magnum," Eric observed. "He meant to plug a few holes in you for keeps."

"Yeah," Brad said softly. "Michaelson's men do play for keeps."

"Cripes! I'm bleeding to death down here! You're supposed to be the cop, McKenna. You'd better get me to a hospital quick, or I'll be screaming my head off about police brutality."

Brad squatted down by the man, seeing a swarthy, pockmarked face. He'd thought he recognized the voice.

"I'm not a cop. I'm worse than that, Suarez, and you know it. I'm DEA. A fed. And you know what? We've been losing some good guys to scum like you lately. We don't take the same heat as the poor local cops. I don't care if you rot away of gangrene, Suarez."

"You know him?" Eric asked.

Brad nodded, careful to keep the gun aimed at the slender but dangerous man on the ground. "Tommy Suarez. He's so high up with Michaelson that he rarely has to take on the dirty jobs these days. We think that he killed a lot of people to get to his position. He used to give me my 'order'—where to pick up cash, where to drive, that kind of stuff." He hesitated. "This bastard killed my partner." He pulled back the trigger so that it clicked.

In a timeless moment he gritted his teeth, realizing he had to stop. He was emotionally involved here. But this guy had been the triggerman who killed his partner. Suarez had also been working away at the window to a bedroom where Wendy might have been sleeping.

Sleeping, all alone. If Brad had left, Wendy would have been there—alone, innocent, vulnerable. And God alone knew what Suarez might have done with her to extract information about Brad—or just for the hell of it, because she was a beautiful woman.

He aimed the gun straight at Suarez's temple.

"Hey!" Suarez whined. "You can't do that! You're—"

"Who else is hanging around here, Suarez?" Brad demanded.

"No one," he said sullenly. "Hey, my hand is bleeding. You've busted it all to hell, you ass—"

"Hey!" Eric grinned. His teeth were a bright white slash against his bronze skin in the pale moonlight.

"My turn, Brad. I'm not with the government. I don't have a scruple in the world, dealing with this swine. You hear that, Suarez? I'm not a cop, and I'm not an agent. I'm an Indian. And you know what, buddy? I've had enough of you guys slipping that rotten crack to our teens. They're not starting out with a real fair deal to begin with. You know how many overdoses we've had out here in the last year? Since your friend Michaelson decided to make a septic tank out of our swamp?"

Suarez licked his dry lips. Eric held him by the lapels of his shirt. His eyes darted nervously from Brad to Eric and back to Brad again. "Tell him to let me go. Tell Mr. Rain Dance there to get his hands off me!"

Eric's laugh was harsh and bitter. "Rain Dance, Sitting Bull, yeah, you got the message, Suarez!" Brad hadn't known that Eric carried a knife until he saw the flash of the steel blade pressed against Suarez's throat. "Mr. McKenna asked you a question."

"Please!" Suarez whined. He seemed afraid to even swallow. "Please, tell him to get the knife away. He's going to kill me."

Brad nodded to Eric. Eric sheathed the knife beneath the edge of his boot. "Hell," he moaned. "And I thought I was going to get to see if a rat could live after it had been scalped."

"Who knows you're here? How did you find this place?" Brad asked. Suarez remained silent, his eyes wide with panic. Brad swore softly. "So help me, Suarez, start talking or I'll just turn my back and let Rain Dance experiment on you."

Suarez kept stalling, until Eric brandished the shiny blade of his knife once more. Ultimately, Suarez believed the threat. He started talking. No one knew where he was; he'd come out on his own. He'd been holed up in a hunter's shack, but some hillbillies in an airboat had been hanging around all day, guzzling beers and trying to catch fish. He hadn't dared go in anywhere close, so he'd done a little exploring on his own.

"Come on, Suarez, you weren't out here alone."

"Charlie Jenkins is supposed to be with me. He had to take a ride this morning. I'm alone, I swear it."

"Okay, okay. You and Jenkins have been hanging out in a shack in the Everglades." That rang more true. Charlie Jenkins had grown up in southern Georgia, in the Okefenokee swamp. He would know how to get around down here.

"Why are you guys staked out here?"

"We're looking for you," Suarez said.

"There's more," Brad told him.

"Yeah, all right, yeah. Michaelson has been using the Everglades. You knew that—hell, half the law enforcement in the state knows that." He sneered, revealing tobacco-stained teeth. "Everyone knows that. But Michaelson is slick, real slick. He can't be caught. Just like the water moccasin, he slinks away when he doesn't want to be found."

"When is the next shipment coming in?" Brad demanded.

"I don't know—"

Quick as lightning, Eric pulled his knife out and pressed it against the man's throat. The blade glinted even in the dim moonlight. "I swear it! I swear it!" Suarez screamed, looking apprehensively at the blade so near his jugular vein. "Charlie Jenkins is supposed to know, when he comes back."

Convinced that Suarez was telling the truth, Brad nodded to Eric. Eric backed off, silent as the night.

"I've got to take him in," Brad said.

"You mean we don't get to kill him?" Eric sighed deeply in mock disappointment. When Suarez shivered, Brad was barely able to suppress a grin. "Not this time, Tonto. Sorry."

Eric grinned. Suarez started blubbering again. "I swear, I'd tell you anything. I don't know nothing else, honest."

"Let's go tell Wendy—" Eric began, but just then an explosion rent the darkness of the night.

"Hands up, everyone. All the way up."

Apparently, Wendy had waited long enough. She had silently crept around the house, but the kick of the shotgun had announced her arrival and sent her stumbling backward. Fortunately she hadn't lost her grip on the weapon; she still held it cocked and aimed.

"Wendy!" Brad snapped. "Dammit, I told you to stay in the house!"

"I told you she had definite problems," Eric warned.

"I was worried when you didn't come back."

"But I told you to stay inside—"

"Like a sitting duck. You might have needed me."

"Well, we didn't! Everything is well in hand." Or it had been, Brad thought. Now he was trembling again. Maybe it was a damned good thing that he had come here. Suarez had just been exploring in the night. He would have stumbled upon Wendy, and she would have been completely unaware. He would have attacked her in the night, and she could have screamed forever, and no one would have heard her....

Wendy. His angel. She held the shotgun with poise and regal grace. Her hair gleamed in the dim moonlight with a splendor all its own. She seemed so small and slender, and yet so feminine. It was strange how something like denim work jeans could hug a woman's figure, making her appear so sexy. And it was strange, too, how a simple cotton shirt could hang so evocatively upon a body.

Suarez inhaled sharply. Brad looked down at the man. He was watching Wendy with a sizzle in his eyes.

"Wendy, get back into the house, now!" Brad ordered.

"I am not your personal lackey!" she protested. "Damn you—"

"Break it up, break it up," Eric interrupted. "We've got to deal with this guy. Brad, his hand is shot up badly."

"You shot him?" Wendy accused Brad.

"Well, excuse the hell out of me!" Brad returned. "I shot him before he could shoot me, do you mind?"

When she rushed over to examine Suarez, Brad stopped her. "It's not a pretty sight."

She stared at him, then pushed his hand away. "I told you, I was a nurse. Trust me, I've seen worse."

She hunched down on the balls of her feet and examined the man's hand. Suarez stared at her in that same way that made Brad so uncomfortable, and yet he blessed her in Spanish and in English and told her that she was an angel of mercy.

She scowled at Brad. "This wound is serious. He needs to be in a hospital. You shouldn't have kept him here so long."

"So long!"

"I heard that shot a long time ago," Wendy said.

He wanted to grab her and shake her. She didn't realize that this sleaze might have friends, nor did she even seem to realize that he meant to break in through her window and . . .

"Don't pull a Florence Nightingale act on me. This man meant to come through that window, and rape you. And hell, he might have even killed you."

"C'mon, break it up for the moment, huh?" Eric suggested lightly. "Wendy, this guy isn't exactly Mr. Rogers, you know, dropping in on the neighborhood. Let's get him in—"

"I'll take him—alone," Brad said. He didn't want Wendy along, and he wanted Eric to stay with her.

"That's well and fine, but I'm not sure you can find your way around at night," Eric reminded him.

That was true, Brad thought dismally. Although he'd become familiar with the swamp, he couldn't safely navigate at night.

"What about the car?" he asked Eric.

Eric shrugged. "You still shouldn't be venturing out alone. Why don't you call your boss. I'll turn this thug over to the tribal police. From there he can be transferred over to your people."

Brad nodded. Eric's plan made sense.

Wendy turned around. "I'm going to get some bandages."

"I don't want her left alone," Brad said to Eric.

"Want me to take him in?"

Brad shook his head. "I'll have to call Purdy and see what he wants to do with this scum."

"That's some *chica*," Suarez said nastily.

"Shut up." Brad kicked him, then turned away. "I don't want her left alone, Eric."

"Then we'll all go. I'll drive. Wendy can ride up front with me, and you can ride in the back with our friend here."

Brad thought about it for a minute. He didn't want Wendy anywhere within reach of Suarez, but Eric's plan seemed like the best solution. Brad didn't want her left alone, either. He definitely didn't want her alone. Jenkins was coming back somewhere along the line— according to Suarez—and Brad wasn't going to take any chances.

"All right," he told Eric.

Wendy returned with a bottle of antiseptic and white gauze bandages. A true professional, she knelt down by Suarez. In a no-nonsense tone, she warned him that it was going to sting like hell, then she poured the contents of the bottle over his hand. He screamed in pain, trying to clutch his hand away, but Wendy didn't let him. Deftly, she wrapped the injured hand in clean gauze. She handed him a little white pill and told him to swallow it. "Percodan. It will help the pain."

"Let's get him a suite at the Biltmore," Brad murmured sarcastically.

"Brad, you did put the man in pain," Wendy said.

"Yeah. And he meant to put me six feet under."

"Are you two going to take him into town?" Wendy asked, smoothing back a loose strand of her hair.

"No, *we three* are going to take him," Brad said.

Her eyes widened. "I don't want to go."

"You're going."

"The hell—"

"You're going." His teeth were grating and his muscles were tightening. It had been such a damned explosive evening that he was ready to throw her over his shoulder and carry her into the car. Of all the damned times for the woman to be so stubborn!

"Okay, okay!" Eric stepped between them. "Wendy, give the guy a break, will you? He's worried

about you. Brad, I'm glad that you're in law enforcement and not the diplomatic corp. Now, for God's
sake, let's get this show on the road!''

"I'm all for that, Rain Dance," Suarez agreed. The
Percodan was working fast, Brad thought. The guy's
eyes were already glazing over. Suarez almost looked
agreeable.

"Rain Dance?" Wendy's eyes widened. Brad almost smiled. He could see her fury growing. She'd
fight anytime for someone she loved, and she loved her
brother-in-law. "Why, you slime mold!" She hissed to
Suarez.

Her love was so fierce, so loyal. *I want you to love
me with that fury, that passion,* Brad thought. *But like
a lover.*

Eric groaned. "Wendy, I've got it in control, okay?
Can we please go?"

"Let's do it. Suarez, up," Brad said.

Brad was holding the gun, so Eric gave the man a
hand. He struggled to his feet. Brad stared at Wendy
fiercely.

She returned his stare, then her rich lashes fell over
her cheeks. "I'll be just a moment," she said, hurrying back into the house. When she returned, she was
still carrying the shotgun. Brad was sure that she had
more shells for it, too, probably packed away in her
brown leather purse.

Suarez was convinced that they were trying to drown
him when they told him to walk over the stones. Then,
when Eric showed him how it was done, Suarez was
convinced that Eric was an Indian god.

"What the hell did you give him?" Brad demanded
of Wendy.

"I told you—Percodan!" She proceeded over the stones herself. "See? I swear, you'll barely get your feet wet."

Suarez followed her at last. He looked back longingly at the canoe, drawn up on the shore, that had brought him to the house in the woods. "I shouldn't have come here. I should have shot those hillbillies in the airboat and drank up their beer."

"Nothing like hindsight, is there, Suarez?" Brad said, prodding his prisoner with the barrel of the gun. "Let's move."

At last, Suarez gingerly walked over the stones. When they reached the car, Brad helped Wendy into the front seat, then pressed Suarez into the back. Eric asked Wendy for the keys, and she tossed them to him.

The car was eerily silent as they started out. Eric flicked on the car radio. A latino tune came on, and Suarez decided to sing along.

Brad was getting a horrible headache. He tried to watch the terrain as Eric drove, but the headlights of the small car didn't alight upon any recognizable landmarks.

By car, it was a long trip. Brad understood Wendy's affection for her airboat. It took less than forty-five minutes to reach Mac's garage by way of the airboat. Now time seemed to drag horribly. They drove for more than an hour before they pulled up beside the garage.

"We're going to have to wake up Mac," Wendy said. Eric turned the car off, and she hopped out.

"I have to go," Suarez said.

Eric and Brad exchanged looks of annoyance. Eric came out of the driver's seat and opened the door. Brad followed Suarez out, keeping the gun trained on him at all times. He knew these people too well to trust even a simple call of nature.

Between them, they led Suarez over to a clump of bushes. Brad looked toward the station and saw that the office door was opening. Wendy had managed to rouse Mac from his bed in the back room of the office.

He handed the gun to Eric. "Don't trust him."

"He won't pull anything," Eric said, "if he values his life."

Hurrying toward the station, Brad smiled, shaking his head slightly. Suarez was thoroughly convinced that Eric was probably worse than the entire Indian contingent at the battle of the Little Bighorn.

"Come on in, Mr. McKenna. Come in and make whatever calls you want," Mac said, opening the glass door.

"Thanks, Mac," Brad said.

"Wendy, you want some tea or something?"

"Sure, I'd love some tea," Wendy murmured. It would give her something to do while Brad started dialing numbers.

Brad phoned Purdy, who agreed that it was a good idea to bring in the tribal police. His people would meet them at the entrance to the swamp and extradite Suarez. Purdy planned to interrogate Suarez as soon as he had received medical attention.

Brad glanced over at Wendy. "I—I can't come in now."

Purdy was quick, Brad gave him that. He hadn't gotten where he was by being stupid.

"You don't want to talk? You're worried about your friend? The girl you're staying with?"

"Yes. Exactly."

"Fine. Hand Suarez over to the tribal police and go back with her. Call me tomorrow at noon. Maybe it's time to get some backup out there."

"Yeah. I think it might be."

"But play it smooth, huh? You've got a nice trap sitting out there. Maybe we can bag something else."

"Carefully."

"Carefully, beyond a doubt. We won't let the woman get hurt, Brad."

"Thanks." He dared another glance at Wendy. She was talking to Mac, but he was sure that she had heard everything he had said. He was glad that he had kept it simple, glad that Purdy was perceptive.

He hung up. Purdy was going to contact the tribal police.

"Everything taken care of?" Mac asked.

"Yes, thanks. Thanks a lot," Brad told the old man.

Mac smiled. "Tea?"

"No, thanks just the same." He shook Mac's hand. He wondered if there was any way that he could repay the old guy, if there was anything that Mac wanted. In many ways, Mac had helped keep Brad—and Wendy safe.

When Brad left the office, Wendy started to follow him.

"Stay inside with Mac," he told her.

"Don't you—"

"Please! Stay with Mac."

Wendy looked into his eyes, so fiercely gold, so powerful. Her rebellious nature balked at the order, but she swallowed her pride and went back inside to wait with Mac. It had been such a rough day! She'd been trying so hard to pretend that her life was entirely normal.

But life wasn't normal anymore. Brad had entered into her world, and she had fallen in love with him. She had cried as she'd strolled down the aisle in the grocery store, and despite herself, she'd bought enough food for two. She'd burst into tears in the drugstore, and again, she'd bought supplies for two.

And at first she hadn't been able to go home to her empty house. She'd gone to see the family, because she had needed them so badly. She'd needed Grandfather's wisdom, and Grandmother's support. Willie had held her when she cried, and she'd known with an even greater strength than ever before just how much they loved her. Leif was dead, but the Hawks still loved her. They were such good people. Blood was a strong tie to them, but love was even stronger. She was Willie's granddaughter, blood or no, for he claimed her as so. He knew that she had loved Leif.

And he knew that she loved Brad now.

"He is a good man," Grandfather had told her.

"He is gone."

"Go home. Wait for him. He will come back."

"What if he doesn't?"

"Then you will cry, but life will go on. And you will be richer for the time that you have shared."

And now, looking out the window at Brad, she didn't know whether to laugh or cry. He had returned to her house, he had returned to her arms. But danger had come between them.

She was a fool. Brad McKenna lived with danger— it was an occupational hazard.

And yet she loved him anyway.

A while later, Wendy saw the flash of headlights. When the car parked outside, she recognized the emblem of the tribal police. After a very brief conversation with Brad and Eric, the tribal police took Suarez away.

Then Brad opened the door and stretched out a hand to her. "Wendy, it's time to go back home."

Back home. Yes, it was time to return to her home— with him.

Eric drove again. Wendy sat in front with him; Brad sat silently in the back. The only sound was the music from the radio, though Eric switched the station a dozen times.

At last, they were home. Still in silence, they parked and locked the car, then traveled over the stones to reach the house.

"You need to give Brad a decent pair of boots," Eric commented. "He's soaking his shoes on those things."

"They're your brother's shoes," Brad said.

"Yeah, well, my brother had boots, too. And he can't use any of them now. Boots are a necessity in swampland. Leif's old leather pair were strong enough to break the grasp of a rattler or a cottonmouth."

Ahead of the two men, Wendy was unlocking the door. "Leif's boots are in the closet. Take them."

It had been a long, long night, and it was nearly three in the morning. Too tense to be tired, Brad glanced at Eric, wondering when they were going to tell Wendy what they had decided while waiting for the tribal police.

Wendy went in and set her purse on the counter. She looked at the two men invading her life, her brother-in-law and the lover she was so afraid of losing.

"Do you two want anything?" They were staring at her so expectantly, like two big dogs.

"Yes!" Brad said, suddenly realizing that he hadn't eaten a decent meal all day.

"Yes, please!" Eric echoed.

She opened the refrigerator. "Like what?"

Brad requested two of the steaks she had just brought home. Eric agreed with that, and he also wanted broccoli in cheese sauce. Brad thought a salad would be great. Eric said they should add some micro-wave baked potatoes to the menu, too.

So at 3:00 a.m., they started cooking.

The conversation remained casual and polite. Wendy kept her distance from Brad, who seemed careful to do the same.

When they had eaten and cleaned up the dishes, Eric still remained. Wendy looked at him curiously.

Brad cleared his throat at last. "Uh, Eric is taking the first watch."

"First watch!" Wendy looked from Brad to Eric and back to Brad again.

"First watch, Wendy." Eric reached over and squeezed her fingers. "I'm going to stay awake, while Brad sleeps. Then we'll switch. It's safer that way."

"I see." Wendy set her dish towel on the counter and turned away from them both. "Well, then, good night."

She walked down the hallway. Maybe she was just so tired that she felt like a zombie. Maybe she was so desperately in love she was losing her spirit. She showered and dressed for bed in a long cotton gown. She was so overtired that she was afraid she would throw some ridiculous, childish fit if she encountered either of the men, so she hurried into her bedroom and closed the door.

Sleep eluded her. She heard someone go into the shower—Brad, she assumed. The water roared on, then there was silence.

A few moments later she heard a soft knock at her door.

Brad leaned in, his hair still damp and glistening from the shower. "Good night," he told Wendy softly, then closed the door.

"Good night," she called after him.

She sank back against the pillows for a moment, then threw back the covers and raced to the door. She opened it and saw Brad standing in the threshold. Her heart skittering away, Wendy ran to him. She leaped off the floor, hurtling herself into his arms, locking her legs around him.

He held her to him, kissing her hungrily. Holding her so, he walked straight to her bed. Together they fell backward onto the billowing sheets.

Wendy broke from his kiss. "The door. We're not alone."

Brad got up and closed the door. When he reached for her again in the darkness, she was naked.

And she was waiting for him.

Forgetting the turmoil of the day, he buried his heart, his soul and his body into her never-ending sweetness.

Chapter 12

Brad was beside her, sound asleep, when Wendy woke, late in the morning. She assumed that he had spelled Eric, staying awake for the second part of the night, and that he'd come to bed after that, to sleep for the first time.

She showered and dressed. Eric wasn't in the living room when she came out. Looking out the window, she saw that he was sitting on the lawn, sipping a mug of coffee. Apparently, he had just fed Baby; the big cat was curled up next to him just as sweetly as a Persian kitten.

She watched Eric for a moment, remembering what he had said before all the commotion had begun last night. He'd made some lousy accusations! She went into the kitchen, poured a glass of ice water and went outside.

She couldn't sneak up on him; she knew that. When he looked up and flashed her a smile of greeting, she smiled back. She came up behind him, then squatted down to pat Baby.

"Sleep well?" he asked her innocently.

"Fine," Wendy said sweetly. Then she poured the water directly over his head.

He sputtered, swearing and jumping to his feet. "What the hell was that for?" he demanded in outrage.

"You know damned well what that was for! Your wonderful little performance last night!"

Annoyed by the whole thing, Baby stretched and walked away in search of peace and quiet. Dripping, Eric stared at Wendy, then started to laugh.

"Well, apparently it didn't do any harm."

"Eric! How could you say those terrible things about me? You're supposed to be on my side!"

"Wendy, Wendy..." He opened his arms to give her a big hug.

Wendy quickly realized that he only wanted to drench her, too. "Eric!" She eluded him, but sat down on the lawn a safe distance from him. He sat down beside her. The sun was high in the sky; he would dry quickly.

"I *am* on your side," he told her.

"Then what was that all about? Brad's going to leave. We all know that."

"Do we?" Eric arched a brow to her and she flushed. "Oh, yeah, that's right. You don't want anything to do with a fed agent, do you?"

"Eric—"

"Well, whatever I said, it didn't seem to do any harm to either of you. Seemed to me that things went well enough."

"Eric—"

"You know, Wendy, your life is your business. And Brad's life is his business. Your decisions have to be your own."

"Then—"

"I just wanted to make sure that you were both playing with a full deck, that's all."

Wendy groaned. "You're making me crazy!"

He grinned, glancing over his shoulder. "Well, morning has broken. Here comes the fed. Excuse me. I think I'll make more coffee."

Wendy twisted slightly. Brad was coming out the front door, shirtless, shoeless and clad only in a pair of jeans. His hair was still tousled, and though she could see that he had shaven, he still looked somewhat bleary-eyed and disoriented. He was carrying a coffee cup. Eric, heading back into the house, paused. The two men exchanged a few words, then Brad joined Wendy outside. He cradled his coffee cup in his hand and smiled at her. "Good morning."

"Good morning."

They didn't say anything else for several long moments. He took a sip of the steaming coffee and stared out over the terrain. Baby reappeared and curled up beside Wendy.

Brad slipped an arm around her. She watched his profile, setting a hand lightly on his knee.

"None of that was true, you know."

He looked her way again, a small smile playing against his lips.

"What Eric said."

He paused. "You didn't want a baby?"

She looked down at the ground. "Well, yes, I did. That was true, but the rest—was absurd. I would never try to trap you."

He set his coffee cup down and threaded his fingers gently through her hair, kissing her tenderly. "Would you want to trap me?" he asked softly.

She shook her head. "No one should ever be forced into anything. I wouldn't, I just wouldn't, and I hope you believe that." She spoke flatly, trying to escape his hold. He laughed and pulled her tightly against him. His hand lay beneath her breast, and they could both feel the pulse of her heart.

"I know that you would never force anyone to do anything. Sometimes it's difficult to get even an opinion from you."

"What do you mean by that?"

"You don't want to admit how you feel."

Wendy scratched Baby's ears and looked out over the water. "I let you know how I feel," she said softly. "You know that I care." She turned and stared searchingly into his eyes. "You know that I'm afraid of your work. You're afraid of what it can do to two lives—you've warned me not to care too deeply. Nothing has changed. This—" She hesitated. "This will end. But I want you here with me, for as long as possible. I'll never regret this time. I—"

She wanted to be open and honest. But she couldn't tell him that she had fallen in love with him. She knew that he cared about her, but love was another story altogether. And because she loved him, she would let him go. What she had said was true. She was afraid of losing him . . . but he had set his priorities long ago.

His fingers curled tensely around hers. "What were you going to say?"

She shook her head, looking down at Baby again. Fortunately, she was spared when the door opened loudly.

Eric had come out. "Hey, Brad, aren't you supposed to call in at noon? We've just got time to make it in to the garage."

Brad was still studying Wendy. "Yeah," he said with a soft sigh. "I guess we'd better go."

Before he could slip into the house for a shirt and shoes, Wendy caught his hand. "Brad?"

"What?"

"I take it that you and Eric were the 'hillbillies' sitting out there fishing and watching that shack that Suarez was talking about last night?"

He hesitated. "Yes."

"Is that what you're planning to do today?"

"Wendy, it's my job. Charlie Jenkins will probably come back to the shack. He's my link to Michaelson." He ruffled her hair, then reached down to take her hands. "Come on."

"Come on?" She raised her eyes to his.

He exhaled again in a soft sigh. "Wendy, I can't leave you here alone."

"It's broad daylight. I know how to use a shotgun. And Baby is with me. People don't argue with her."

"Baby is a big cat, but Michaelson moves around with big guns. He's been known to carry M-16s. I want you to come with us."

She opened her mouth to protest.

"Please!" Brad said before she could say anything more.

"All right." Wearily, she rose with him. The sun cast a golden sheen along the ripples of his shoulders. She didn't want to argue with him, and she didn't want to dread the future. She wanted to run her fingers and her tongue over that sleek bronze flesh and feel him come alive to her touch.

She couldn't do that. Not now—not ever.

She was losing him. She felt it. Some force beyond their control was tightening its grasp around them, surrounding them like a writhing python. They had discovered something, and now they were losing it, before they could ever hold it tightly and give it a name.

"Brad?"

He paused.

Placing her palms against his chest, she rose onto her toes. She kissed his lips softly, then slid to her feet against him.

"What was that for?"

"I just needed it," she told him.

He gave her a quick hug. "I needed it, too. I needed it, too."

They headed for the house together. As Brad went into the bedroom to dress, Wendy called to him that he really should be wearing boots.

"Where are they?"

"In the closet."

Five minutes later, he still hadn't found the boots. Wendy came into the bedroom and began searching through the cluttered closet. When she glanced up at Brad, he was sifting through the collection of Leif's clothing that still hung in the closet.

He shook his head, looking down at her. "Wendy, you've got to get rid of these things, really."

She nodded, finally locating the box with the boots in them. "You should be glad that I kept this stuff," she said, handing him the boots. "I don't think that my jeans would have fit you."

He smiled at her, leaned down and brushed her cheek with his knuckles. "Very cute, smarty-pants. But seriously, I hope you don't plan on stripping every stranger who crash-lands on your doorstep."

"What an interesting possibility to explore," she said sweetly.

He pulled her to her feet and kissed her. She let out a surprised cry as his palm circled around her rump. "Not amusing, Wendy," he told her. "Now, behave."

"I was behaving!"

He sat at the foot of the bed and pulled on the boots. They were a little tight, but the rugged leather would provide necessary protection in the swamp. Brad gazed at her curiously. "Want to suggest a shirt?"

She turned around without a flicker of emotion and pulled out a red plaid. It still hurt, she thought. Even discovering that she was in love again could not completely release the past. She'd never been able to get rid of Leif's things; it had seemed so cold, so final. She couldn't throw away Leif's clothes any more than she could throw away his memory.

But Brad was right, she knew. She shouldn't throw things away, she should give them away to someone who needed them. That would be the best way to remember her husband.

Brad took the shirt from her and slipped it over his shoulders. "Thank you." She nodded while he buttoned up and slipped the shirttails into his jeans.

She lowered her eyes, trying to ignore the tight knot of fear in her throat. It was as if a noose were tightening around them. Something was going to happen. She was going to lose Brad—she could feel it in her blood. Then her life would be empty again, and it would be just as if this had never happened between them. No, Grandfather had told her that she would be richer for it.

She hoped that she could feel that way when he was actually gone.

Impetuously, she went up on her toes, and she kissed him again, tasting him, inhaling him. She did want to hang on to him, she didn't want to let him return to his real world.

It was wrong.

She broke away, turning around, reaching for the door. "You've got to call your boss, remember?"

"Yeah, I remember."

Half an hour later, they were back at the garage.

Brad went inside to call Purdy. Eric lingered beside the gas pumps, talking to Mac. Wendy hovered near the airboat, afraid that she wouldn't make much of a conversationalist that day.

The air was hot and sticky. Listening to the endless drone of a horde of mosquitoes, she absently lifted her hair from the back of her neck. She could see Brad through the glass enclosure. He looked so serious, almost like a stranger. She bit her lower lip. He was serious—very serious about his work. Unlike the man she loved, this Brad frightened her. He meant business.

She turned away, clenching and unclenching her fingers as she idly walked along the canal. She was so nervous that she didn't realize how far she had wandered. Nor did she notice the car that crept along the road, or the canoe that moved silently behind her, coming closer and closer.

She was so involved with her thoughts that she didn't begin to sense danger until it was almost upon her. And then, it was too late.

Behind her, a shadow loomed against the sun. Absently noticing the darkness, Wendy turned, frowning.

Two men stood before her. The first was tall and lean, with watery blue eyes and steel-gray hair. The second man was younger. He was huskily built, brawny. His eyes were brown, but they had the same chill glaze of ruthlessness.

Every nerve tensed as she sensed danger, cold, sharp, lethal. She opened her mouth to scream, but she was never able to issue a useful sound.

The brown-eyed man caught her by the neck and stuffed a cloth into her mouth. She thought she would choke to death, but she couldn't even cough properly, he held his hand so tightly against her. Desperate, she tried to lash out, but the smell of the cloth, sickeningly sweet, assailed her. She started to grow dizzy. The sun, the man, the sky, the world . . . everything swirled before her.

Dimly, she realized how foolish she had been. She had followed the canal around a curve. Eric wasn't really so far away, but he was talking to Mac beyond the rise of the grass. He couldn't see her, and she couldn't scream, so he couldn't hear her.

Her world was dimming so rapidly. She tried to struggle. She tried to free herself from that restricting hand, but it was like a steel band. The man's fingers bit into her flesh as he held her tighter and tighter. Barely, just barely, she managed to free her right arm and drag her curving fingers against his cheek.

He swore softly as her nails caught his face, drawing blood. He secured her hand again and hissed out a warning to her.

But he didn't lift the soaked rag from her face. The sticky sweetness created a buzz around her. Wendy never felt the cuff he gave her across the cheek. By the time he struck her, she was already falling. The world was spinning to blackness.

She was unconscious when he hoisted her into his arms and silently turned to follow the other man through the tall grasses to the waiting airboat.

Brad thoughtfully hung up the phone. It was basically over—if not the case, then at least his strange idyll out here. He was going to spend the day prowling through the swamp keeping an eye out for Jenkins or Michaelson. By tonight, he'd have a number of reinforcements out here: a few men to keep an eye on the shack, and more men to spread out, to wait for the drop that was scheduled. They didn't have Michaelson yet, but he wouldn't be looking for the man alone anymore. The noose was being tightened—and all they had to do was hope that they didn't scare their quarry away.

Purdy was determined to see Michaelson locked up. He was banking on Brad's eyewitness testimony against the man. And if they played it right, they could catch him red-handed with the drugs coming in from South America. The big machinery was moving. Brad realized that he was just a small part of it now, and he didn't know whether to feel relieved or deeply bereft.

Things wouldn't be the same. He wouldn't have a chance to be alone with Wendy again. Not as a pair of castaways in a strange paradise, isolated from the world. Today he would have to accept Eric's help, and he didn't want Wendy along with them. It was too dangerous. He had never known that Suarez had been watching him and Eric in the airboat the other day. Even if Suarez hadn't been able to come close enough to recognize him, he had seen Brad and Eric. To Brad, that was unnerving. He decided that Wendy should spend the day in the village with Willie and Mary. She should be safe with the family. Brad was certain that Willie knew how to protect his loved ones.

It was almost over. The realization hurt so much that he could hardly stand it. Hell, he'd known he had no right touching a woman like Wendy. They'd both said that they could take what came. They had both claimed to be adult, mature—willing to accept an affair for the time that they had together.

She had warned him not to care too deeply, just as he had warned her. And now here they were, at the end of it all....

And he felt like doubling over with pain, it hurt so damned much. Pain chewed at the walls of his stomach—and his heart.

She cared for him. He knew that. But he also knew that she didn't want a life with a man who lived in danger. She definitely didn't want a life with him. So that was that. There was a real world, and he had to return to it. He had a job, and he'd always known that it wasn't a job that was conducive to...

Marriage.

He wanted to marry her. He wanted her beside him when he woke up in the morning. She was a radiant angel, and he knew that she would be every bit as beautiful to him in fifty years. He wanted her all to himself for a while, and then he wanted to have that baby with her that she had once wanted and could surely want again.

But he had no right. His job was a necessary one, and he was good at it. He had no right to want her to suffer for him.

Maybe he owed them both the honesty of the depths of his feelings. She had told him this morning that nothing had changed in their life-styles. But the feelings between them had grown. She might have denied them a future with her words, but her kiss had said otherwise.

When he saw Eric smiling at him through the glass, Brad realized that he had been standing at the door for several long minutes.

This was idiotic. The idyll might be over, but Michaelson was still out there. And he had to be caught.

Swallowing hard, Brad impatiently turned to leave the office. Eric excused himself to Mac and came over to Brad, looking at him expectantly.

"There'll be some backup here tonight. We're still going to lie low, because we want to catch Michaelson with the goods. I want to keep my eyes open for Charlie Jenkins today—then I need to meet some men here tonight. They're sending a few to keep an eye on the shack, and—" He paused. "And a few to keep an eye on Wendy's place. Purdy agreed that we've put her into the path of danger. She needs some solid protection until this is really over." Brad didn't have to admit that he was too emotionally involved to be effective himself. Though he and Eric were a good pair, they'd be better off with some objective help around. "Would you mind taking a ride back out by the shack?"

Eric shook his head. "Not at all. What about Wendy? I take it you don't want her home alone, and I don't think she should be along with us."

"I thought we'd take her to Willie's." He grimaced. "She's not going to like it, but..." His voice trailed away and he shrugged. "We might as well get going."

Eric nodded, turning to look toward the canal. Suddenly, a frown compressed his features in hard lines. "I don't see her."

Brad's entire body seemed to constrict as he stared across the gas pumps toward the road. A car whooshed by, moving fast. He turned toward the canal. He had just seen her. He had been looking out the window while he had been talking to Purdy, and he had seen her standing there. Her hair had been loose on her shoulders, catching the sunshine. Her hands had been jammed into her pockets, her boot heels dug impatiently into the ground as she waited. She had been there, just moments ago.

He and Eric started to run at the same time. They reached the canal and the high grass together, sloshing their way into the water. His heart in his throat, Brad prayed that he would not find her. There'd be a bullet in her heart if Michaelson had found her. She'd be facedown in the swamp if she'd met with a cottonmouth or a diamondback. No, no, Wendy was too smart and too savvy to panic at a snakebite. She would have called for help. She would have known what she was doing. It had to have been Michaelson....

They didn't find her in the water. Brad tried to breathe, he told himself that he had to breathe. As Eric stared at him with his curious lime-green eyes, Brad noticed that behind the stonelike mask of the bronzed warrior, Eric was fighting a raw, clawing fear himself.

"Look at the road."

Brad did so. He saw where her boots had been dragged against the earth; he saw the scuffle of footprints.

"Michaelson," he swore in anguish.

"I don't think that he's killed her," Eric said tonelessly.

Brad shook his head, trying to clear it. "No, he wants her for something. Or else he would have—he would have killed her, quiet and quick, right here." He stared at Eric for a moment, then plunged through the shallow rim of grass and muck to the airboat. He looked about hastily, until he saw what he wanted. A stone held a note to the flooring by the motor. Brad tried to read the words, blinked furiously and made sense of the letters at last. He nodded at Eric.

"He's taken her to the shack."

"And he wants you to come?"

Brad nodded. "Both of us. Precisely—'bring the Indian along.' No one else, or he'll slit her throat."

"Why me?" Eric murmured.

Brad thought he understood. "I just got word that his plane came in—crashed in the swamp. Purdy thinks that it's out there buried in the muck somewhere, and Charlie Jenkins, the boy from the Okefenokee in Georgia, just isn't good enough in this maze. I'll wager that Michaelson wants you to find his stuff."

"And you?"

"He wants to kill me. I'm just a case of revenge."

Eric frowned. "And Wendy?"

"He'll keep her alive long enough to make you do what he wants." He paused, breathing deeply. "Hell, who knows. He—he might want more." He swore softly again.

Eric lowered his head, his fingers winding into impotent fists at his sides.

Brad realized that he was praying when he needed to be thinking—or maybe he needed to be doing both things. He braced himself and got a grip on his emotions.

"I'm calling Purdy back. He should know that Michaelson has Wendy. Maybe there's something he can do to help. Then we've got to get out to the shack. Is there any way to come around on that cabin from a different direction?"

"Go call. Let me try to see the terrain in my mind."

Brad hurried in to call Purdy. The boss was going to put his machinery into action sooner.

After he'd hung up, Brad gritted his teeth and explained the situation to Mac. Then he hurried down to the airboat to join Eric. The plan was risky, but it was their only chance. Otherwise, they were surely dead.

This way they had a chance. The odds were bad. Very bad.

But then, they were the only odds they had.

Brad leaped onto the airboat. Eric was already starting up the motor.

"I think we can approach from the back," he said. "I'll cut the motor and we'll paddle around the rear of the hammock. We'll have to wade through muck, and there might be quicksand. But we can come up around the back of the shack."

Brad closed his eyes and breathed a prayer of thanks. The odds were beginning to look a little bit better.

"Let's try it," he said. Eric nodded. They were tense and silent then as they wound their way back into the primitive depths of the swamp.

Wendy woke with a foul taste in her mouth, a taste similar to the sickening smell that had brought her to unconsciousness. She had a horrible headache and the world was still spinning so rapidly that she didn't know if she was sitting, standing or lying flat. Her arms ached, but not as badly as her head. For several long minutes, she was aware only of pain.

She opened her eyes and closed them again. She fought a wave of nausea and swallowed hard. Then she tried to open her eyes again.

She was able to focus this time. Above her were the boards of a bare and rotting roof. She was lying flat. Her arms hurt because her wrists were tied tightly together with rough rope. Her flesh was chapping and her shoulders were being wrenched by the miserable position.

"He's taking his sweet time."

At the sound of the voice, Wendy closed her eyes again. As heavy footsteps moved by her head, she slit her eyes open, feigning unconsciousness.

It was the man with the brutal hold, walking by her. The man with the brown eyes who had nabbed her and shoved the chloroform over her face.

"He'll come, Jenkins. Trust me. He'll come."

Another voice, very soft and somehow more menacing for it, answered. Wendy tried to let her head fall naturally to the side so that she could see the man.

It was the gray-haired man with the ice eyes. She didn't need to be told that this was Michaelson. Sitting at a crude table in the center of the small shack, he seemed entirely out of place. She could see that his shoes were expensive leather loafers. His suit looked to be fashionable linen. In the midst of the swamp, he was wearing a tie. He had spoken calmly, but he obviously didn't feel comfortable here.

"He'll come, yeah, but what about the Indian? What's the connection there?"

A third man spoke, a man with a definite accent. Wendy tried to survey the small cabin. She didn't dare open her eyes fully, and even the slightest movement was painful and difficult. It was the typical cabin of the weekend hunter, hastily built by non-professional labor. There were two windows, a bunk in one corner of the room, and a table in the center. A dark man, cradling some type of huge firearm, sat on one of the windowsills, dangling his legs. The brown-eyed man, Jenkins, kept pacing by Wendy's head. At least he was better dressed for the occasion, wearing military khakis. A rifle was slung over his shoulder.

She clenched her teeth, afraid that she was going to start shivering. These men meant to kill her, to kill them all. For a moment the horror of it was so great that a wave of icy fear washed over her, paralyzing her. She nearly screamed in sheer panic.

She fought it, clenching her teeth more tightly. She was a victim, just as Leif had been. But Leif had fought to the bitter end, and, dear God, she would fight, too. They were trying to trap Brad, but she was sure that he would realize that. And they were talking about Eric, too....

"We need the Indian," Jenkins said.

Michaelson let out a snort of derision. "Yes, we need the Indian. Because you have proved yourself worthless!"

Jenkins lunged over the table and slammed his fist against it. "You fool! Don't you understand! I'm good at tracking, damned good. You wouldn't have the girl if it wasn't for me. I'm the one who followed Suarez's trail to her house. I'm the one who knew about the girl, about McKenna's involvement with her—and even the damned Indian you want so badly now. But listen to me, and listen good. This mire out here is deadly, can't you comprehend that? Your plane went down in the middle of an area that's infested with snakes, and riddled with quicksand pits. Only a man who really knows this swamp can salvage the damned thing.''

Michaelson rose, his face rigid. He continued to speak softly. "Don't ever address me in that tone of voice, Jenkins. Ever.'' He strode over to the window and looked out. "If the Indian doesn't come, we'll have to rely on the girl.'' Wendy felt his gaze fall her way. "She lives out here. She'll know what she is doing.''

The dark-haired man with the accent let out a snickering sound. "I'm sure she knows what she is doing. I'm sure she does it very well.''

"Shut up, Pedro,'' Michaelson said. "Keep your mind on business and off the girl. When the plane is found, you can have her. Hell, you can have her any way you want her. But not until then, do you understand?''

"*¡Sí!*'' Pedro agreed sullenly.

Wendy felt the bile rise in her stomach again. She swallowed, fighting off another rise of panic.

"Hey!'' Jenkins said suddenly. The sound of his footsteps seemed to slam against Wendy's head, and then she did scream because he wrenched at her shoulders, dragging her up. "She's awake. The little bitch is awake. She's been listening to us.''

He jerked her to a sitting position and she nearly screamed again from the pain in her arms. Her eyes flew open, meeting his stare with a gaze of silvery fury. He laughed, watching her. "Pedro must be right. I'll bet she's a lot of fun.''

"Leave her alone," Michaelson said. "There's work to do."

"Hell, we've got to sit here and wait..." Jenkins said. He smiled. His face was so close to Wendy's that she could feel the foulness of his breath.

She spat at him and he howled in outrage, slapping her.

"I told you, leave the girl alone!" Michaelson's voice rose at last. He indicated the window. "You think that McKenna is a fool? I don't. I don't want him attacking us while you lie there with your pants down, you fool! Now, get away from her."

Jenkins shoved Wendy back down to the floor and wiped the spittle from his face. "Later, baby. I'll make it good. I promise."

"What's that?" the Latin man said suddenly.

Michaelson and Jenkins both moved toward the window.

Wendy heard a birdcall—soft and low, but clear and beautiful, slicing cleanly through the air.

"It's McKenna!" Jenkins said, startled. "It's McKenna, walking straight toward us."

Wendy tried to rise. She sat up, wincing against the hold of the rope on her wrists. Her heart began to leap and slam—and sink. What was he doing? Tears stung her eyes. He was coming for her! Well, of course he would. It was his job. Even if he had barely known her, he would have come for her. It was what he did for a living.

But he shouldn't have. Not that way. He shouldn't have just come to give up his life for hers. Didn't he know...?

"He's alone," Jenkins said harshly. "He took the damned airboat and came out here alone. We don't need him! We need the damned Indian."

Michaelson looked pensively at Wendy.

"We've still got the girl."

She forced herself to stare straight at him, trying to look calm. She had to stop panicking.

Brad was no fool. Nor was he alone. She had to proceed carefully.

Michaelson turned back to the window.

"When he comes close enough, shoot him," he told Jenkins.

"No!" Wendy screamed.

"Shoot him in the kneecap. Make it painful, make it slow. Make him see what happens to spies in my camp."

"No!" Wendy staggered to her feet. "No! So help me, you touch him, and I'll never help you find a thing. Your dope can rot out there with your pilot—"

"I can make her docile," Pedro interrupted. He glanced out the window, then sauntered toward Wendy and picked up a handful of her hair. "I can make her scream and cry and take you any damned place you want to go, boss."

Wendy jerked her head back, staring at the man defiantly. "Can you? You'll have to kill me first, and you won't get anywhere at all if I'm dead, too, will you?"

"Get away from the girl!" Michaelson ordered. "Leave her the hell alone until I say! Jenkins, you, too, ass!" Jenkins had turned to watch the Latin man. Michaelson scowled at them both, then turned to look out the window again. "Where is he?"

"What?" Jenkins demanded.

Michaelson seemed to explode. "He isn't there any more! McKenna has disappeared. Where the hell is he? I can't see him anymore!"

"He has to be out there!" Jenkins insisted.

"Yes, he's out there," Michaelson said. "He's out there, but it's a trick! It's some kind of a trick!"

There was silence as they all stared out the window. Then Michaelson cursed them all. Swerving around, he pulled an automatic from his breast pocket. Long strides brought him to Wendy.

He wrenched her in front of him, shoving the smooth steel of the gun against her cheek. "Let's go, sweetheart. I want McKenna dead almost as much as those jerks want you alive. The same kind of pleasure, you know, the same kind of high."

She tasted the steel. A small cry of pain escaped her as he prodded her with the gun. He threw open the door and pushed her out into the sunlight.

"McKenna! Show yourself." The nose of the gun pressed against Wendy's jaw. "Show yourself. Or else your girlfriend loses her face. You've got ten seconds. I'm counting. Do you hear me, McKenna? I'm counting."

Wendy winced, afraid to swallow. She heard the gun cock. She felt it, icy cold and hard against her skin. She closed her eyes, afraid to imagine the explosion of the flesh.

"I'm counting, McKenna. I'm counting!" Michaelson repeated in fury. "You've got until ten. One, McKenna. Two. Three, McKenna. Four. Five. Six..."

Chapter 13

"Stop!"

The metallic nose of the gun relaxed against Wendy's face at the cry. But it wasn't Brad who appeared this time; it was Eric.

He eased out from the tangle of foliage on the hammock and started walking toward them with long strides.

"I want McKenna, boy!" Michaelson called out. "You and your little girlfriend here can give us a few directions, and then go on your way. But I want McKenna. I have a score to settle with him."

Wendy thought that she would lose her mind with fear. Michaelson was still holding a gun on her, Eric could be shot and killed any second, and Brad had disappeared somewhere.

"McKenna took off on me, the stinking coward." Eric spit into the grass. "He's hiding here somewhere. Give me a chance—I can catch him."

Wendy winced as Michaelson raised the nose of the gun to her temple. "You'd better not be bluffing, boy."

"He's got to be back here. Help me. We'll get him."

Wendy sensed Michaelson's hesitation. Then he lowered the gun and aimed it against her spine. "Walk, girl. Walk straight toward your Indian friend." He turned back to the house. "Jenkins! Pedro! Come on—now!"

He pushed Wendy forward. She started walking. As she moved ahead the grass was growing thicker and the ground was beginning to give way. The shack stood on the high part of the hammock. This was treacherous ground below. Her boots sank in the mud.

As she came closer and closer to Eric, she stared into his eyes. Green and steady, they gave nothing away.

Where the hell was Brad? she wondered.

Michaelson was wondering the same thing. "This better not be a trap, Injun boy. If you make one false move, she's dead. I'll kill her slow. I'll crack her spine and shatter her tailbone."

Wendy shivered. She could still feel the cold steel barrel of the gun.

"No trap, I swear it," Eric reassured. "That slime just lit out of here. He was willing to let Wendy get killed in his place. If I find him, I want him. I know how to make people die slowly, too."

Michaelson grunted. Wendy stared at Eric, praying for courage.

The muck was growing deeper. Leif had taught her to avoid terrain like this. Too easily, the muck became quicksand. They shouldn't be walking here. Any step could be a false step.

"Come on, Wendy!" Eric called to her. "We've got to find that bastard! He split and ran out on us!"

"Eric . . . ?"

She looked at him, begging for an answer. Ignoring her fear, he led her farther away.

Michaelson shoved her in the back with the gun. "You heard him! Move. I want that G-man dead."

"Move, Wendy!" Eric persisted. She kept coming.

Then she realized that there were no sounds coming from behind them. Michaelson had ordered Jenkins and Pedro to come along behind him. They hadn't done so.

Michaelson muttered something. As Wendy felt the suck and pull against her boots, she remembered that Michaelson was wearing fancy leather loafers.

Struggling to lift her foot, she took another step. She stumbled, barely recovering before falling forward. She tried to pull her foot up again, but the suction was too strong. She sank deeper.

Michaelson crashed into her and his gun slipped from his fingers. Beneath them, the ground gurgled. Wendy looked down, watching as Michaelson's weapon was swallowed into the muck.

He began to swear again. Even as the words came out of his mouth, the muck rose around them.

It wasn't rising, Wendy thought hysterically. They were sinking together.

"Bastard!" Michaelson screamed out. Wendy realized that he was screaming at Eric, who continued to stare at him.

The ground held on to them, tightly. Wendy realized that she'd sunk up to her thighs in the grasping muck. A scream rose in her throat.

Just as she cried out, a terrible sound of agony exploded on the air. Michaelson twisted. Wendy realized that the bellow came from behind them, from the cabin.

Michaelson wrapped his arms around her tightly. "She goes down with me! Bastards! She goes down with me!"

Wendy cried out in pain and panic. His arms were choking her. He was bearing her down, down deeper and deeper into the relentless hold of the earth. He no longer held the gun, but he held her. And there was no escape.

She cast back her head and screamed.

Inside the cabin, Brad heard Wendy's scream.

So far, things had gone like clockwork, smooth as ice. He and Eric had carefully pondered the plan, and though it hadn't been foolproof, it had been the best they could do.

But it had gone well. He had managed to walk straight toward the cabin, then disappear flat against a side wall. If Michaelson, Jenkins or Pedro had looked around, he would have been finished before he had ever begun.

But they hadn't.

And Michaelson's temper had snapped, just as Brad had gambled that it would. Michaelson had dragged Wendy out. Then it had been hard to concentrate. Brad had reminded himself that their lives depended on his action during the next few minutes. Pressed flat against the cabin, he told himself that he was trained for this, that he needed to be cool and calculating.

It was probably the hardest thing he would ever do. Watching Michaelson slam the gun against Wendy's cheek, he'd turned and darted around the building, entering the cabin the very way that Michaelson had just exited it.

Pedro and Jenkins had been standing at the window, staring out.

Jenkins hadn't realized that Brad was in the cabin until he'd already knocked Pedro out with the rifle butt.

Jenkins was good with terrain, but he was too heavy to be a good fighter. He couldn't move quickly enough. Brad grimly took him with a knee jab to his gut and a swing of the rifle butt against his chin.

Pedro would be out for a long, long time. Although Brad was pretty sure that Jenkins had a broken jaw, he used his belt to tie up the man's arms. Jenkins was dangerous, more dangerous when he was wounded. Just like an animal. Hell, they were animals.

Brad was just finishing with Jenkins when he heard Wendy's scream.

His heart soaring to his throat, he burst out of the cabin and raced around the side.

He could see Eric running. He was a burst of speed, racing toward the quicksand pool.

And Brad saw why.

Wendy had played it like a trouper. Eric had worried that she would sense the quicksand and panic. But she had played the stoic and kept walking. Michaelson had become disarmed, which was even better than they had hoped. They had figured they would have to bargain for the gun.

But now they were going to have to bargain for Wendy's life.

Michaelson had her in as tight a grasp as the sucking earth. He was moving frantically, and with each movement, the two of them were sinking deeper.

"Let her go!" Brad hardly recognized his own voice, nor could he feel his feet against the ground. "Let her go!" he screamed again. He needed to be logical; he needed to talk, to tell Michaelson to calm down, to stay still. "Let her go!" he thundered out the command again.

Eric had already reached the black pool. He laid his body flat, reaching for Wendy's hands.

Brad thrashed into the mud. Instantly, he felt the pull of the muck, slithering over him, grabbing on to him. It was like an evil, living creature.

He ignored it. Wendy was before him, but Michaelson's arms were around her neck. The muck was up to her breasts.

"Brad!" she whispered his name. She was white as ash, filthy and trembling. Michaelson's hands were around her throat, bearing down on her. And still her eyes were beautifully silver. She was slipping away from the world, and still, her eyes were telling Brad that she loved him.

He let out a yell, a sound that he'd never heard before. It was a cry of the wild, as harsh and merciless as the land.

He caught on to Michaelson's hands, wrenching them from their choking hold on Wendy.

Michaelson wasn't beat. "Bastard!" he hissed at Brad. "Fed bastard, you'll go down with me."

Brad got off one good punch. Michaelson staggered in the muck, trying to aim back at him. Brad turned to shove Wendy toward Eric. She was slipping farther and farther. The pool of black mud was rising to her chin. "Give me your hand!" he called to her, reaching into the endless blackness. His fingers curled around hers.

He screamed out a curse and a prayer. With a horrible sound, the muck relinquished Wendy's hand.

Eric reached her; Brad was afraid that he would not be able to hold her, that the muck would be too slick and slippery.

Eric's fingers were a vise around Wendy's wrists. He had her.

Just in time. With peripheral vision, Brad saw Michaelson locking his fists to pound them down on him. He leaned to the side and Michaelson's blow just grazed him. Brad was sinking deeper, he realized. The muck really did seem to be alive. Like a breathing, black demon, it swarmed over his body, caressing his flesh with a sure promise of death.

"You're going with me, cop," Michaelson said. He started to laugh. Brad decided that the man was insane, but then, anyone who had ice in his veins instead of blood, the way Michaelson did, could not be completely sane.

"I'm not a cop," Brad said. "I'm DEA." Unfortunately, Brad realized, it was a moot point under these circumstances.

"Brad!" Wendy screamed his name. Twisting around, he could see that Eric had pulled her free. She was covered in the black muck, but she was free.

And he was nearly up to his throat.

"Brad! Take my hand!" Wendy cried. Those beautiful silver eyes of hers were on him. Her hair was covered in muck, but her eyes were pure.

"No, Wendy—"

"Take her hand!" Eric yelled. Brad realized the grip that Eric had around Wendy's legs. His heart pounded. *No,* he thought. *Wendy, go. Wendy, you're safe. Run out of here, I dragged you into this.*

"Brad!" she screeched.

"Dammit! I know what I'm doing!" Eric said.

Brad realized that he was suddenly exhausted. He could barely lift his arms. It required a supreme effort to move.

"Brad!"

Her cry gave him strength. He reached out, and her fingers curled around him. He could feel the tremendous effort that she and Eric put forth. He closed his eyes. He was the rope in a tug-of-war. The earth wanted him.

Then it began to give. Staring at Wendy's mud-covered fingers on his arms, he realized slowly that they were overcoming the pull of the muck. He was easing out of it.

There was a long, mournful sound. The muck seemed to cry out.

Then it bubbled and gurgled, and suddenly, he was free.

He landed on top of Wendy and Eric. Although they were all covered in mud, they began to laugh.

"Bastard! You lousy bas—"

Michaelson never finished the last word. His head disappeared with a sickening whoosh of suction.

It was almost me, Brad thought. It had almost been Wendy.

"Oh, God!" Wendy whispered.

He kissed her. She tasted like mud. When he released her, she was still laughing.

Then his spine tingled with awareness. A strange shadow had fallen over them.

Wendy's eyes widened as she felt the sudden constriction in Brad's muscles. She looked up and saw a stranger staring down at the three of them. Tall and lean with silver hair, he was a striking man. His eyes were blue, and they looked as if they could be hard. But there was warmth in them now—warmth and amusement.

"Purdy!" Brad said, astonished. "Sir!"

L. Davis Purdy stared down at the three of them, his hands on his hips. "McKenna, I run my ass ragged, I drag that distinguished older gentleman—" he paused, backing away slightly. Wendy saw that Willie was just behind him "—around the swamp, and what do I find? You—mud wrestling with his granddaughter."

"McKenna, you do get the hard assignments." A younger man stood at Purdy's side. He was shorter than Purdy, but lean and rip-cord hard. He had red hair and freckles, and he grinned at Brad and winked at Wendy.

"Gary," Brad said.

"What is this?" Eric demanded.

"Eric, Wendy—meet Mr. L. Davis Purdy. And Gary Henshaw."

Wendy automatically reached out a hand, then realized that she was covered in mud and still lying on the ground.

Purdy laughed, clutched her hand and helped her to her feet. "Mrs. Hawk, it's a pleasure to meet you. And Eric." Eric jumped to his feet by his own power then. Wendy offered Purdy a wavery smile, then she turned and ran to Willie, who hugged her fiercely.

"How did you get here?" Brad began, then he gazed at Willie, and the old Indian nodded to him gravely.

"Your friend from the garage, Mac, got us out to Mrs. Hawk's home, where we found the senior Mr. Hawk. He brought us out here." Purdy's pleasant smile faded for a moment. He inclined his head toward the quicksand pool. "Michaelson?"

Brad nodded to his boss.

"Maybe it's just as well," Purdy murmured. Then a smile curved the corners of his mouth. "You are a mess."

"Yeah? Well, where were you when we were becoming a mess?"

Gary laughed. "We checked out the shack. It looks like Pedro is waking up, but I don't think he's going anywhere."

"Oh?" Brad said.

"There was this great big cat standing over him. I was ready to shoot the thing, but Mr. Hawk assured me that the panther was a trusted and loyal pet."

"Baby!" Brad said.

"Honestly." Purdy looked at Gary and shook his head. "Leave the boy alone in the woods for a week, and he goes right to hell. Mud wrestling. And he thinks a hundred-and-fifty-pound panther is a pussycat. Hell. What's this man coming to?"

Brad glanced at Eric, and both men laughed. Purdy started walking back toward the shack. "We've got a few things to pick up at the shack. McKenna, you need a bath. Let's get moving here, shall we?"

He wasn't going to get any time alone with Wendy, Brad saw that quickly. From that moment on, they weren't even together.

Purdy ordered Gary to stay with the Hawks and help them in any way possible. He wanted Wendy and Eric to come back with them for statements, but he intended to let them go home first to bathe and change.

He wanted Brad to come with him immediately. It seemed there would be an informal interrogation with Charlie Jenkins and Pedro.

Before they parted, Brad noticed Wendy watching him. He saw the silver light in her eyes, glistening like tears, a shadow of sadness.

His heart plummeted and hammered. She considered it over, he realized. Right then and there, it was over.

He wanted to scream out her name, to push everyone aside and race to her. If he could hold her tightly enough, he could tell her that they were stronger than life's obstacles, that they could make it together.

He never had the chance to say a word. She stared at him a final second, and then she turned away.

"Brad, let's go," Purdy admonished him impatiently.

From then on, the day became a blur of rapid-fire activity. Purdy conducted questioning in the shack. Neither Pedro nor Jenkins put up much of a fight. Purdy wanted to know about the plane, and they were willing to answer questions, not that they could provide much help. Michaelson knew that the small cargo plane carrying his shipment had crashed somewhere in the vast swampland almost two days ago. They assumed the pilot was dead—there'd been no radio contact. Jenkins drew pictures on the ground, showing them where he thought the plane was. Then he begged for a doctor to set his jaw.

Purdy nodded to one of his men, a medic. The young man came over to Jenkins, gave him a pain pill and wrapped his jaw tightly. "There will be a chopper out here soon to rush you down to Jackson," Purdy assured Jenkins.

Purdy had barely spoken before the helicopter could be heard hovering above them. Since it couldn't land in the swamp, Jenkins was sent up first in a basket rigging, then Pedro followed. Brad stood on the ground and watched them go, rising into the sky. They would both heal. They would probably get stiff prison terms. Along with whatever else the D.A.'s office charged them with, kidnapping was sure to be a part of the prosecution.

Purdy set up a task force to search the swamp for the plane. He radioed in for air assistance, then he surveyed Brad from head to toe. Taking in the drying muck, he smiled.

"Well, it's over for you, McKenna."

Over, God, he hated that word. It couldn't be over. Even if she had turned away from him, it couldn't be over.

"Let's go back in," Purdy said. "I told you, you need a bath. Badly."

"Sir, I've come to know something about this place. I might be helpful in searching for the downed plane."

"Brad! It's over. You've done your job. And I need you back at the office to file reports and give your statements to the D.A. Let's move."

Brad exhaled and started walking. "I don't even have a lousy home to go to for a bath! My clothes are gone . . . my record collection is gone. I'm just damned grateful that I didn't have a German shepherd!"

Purdy slapped him on the back. "I rented an apartment for you—right on the water. The boys and I put together for a few outfits, and if I'm not mistaken, your insurance check is on the kitchen counter. But I need those statements and paperwork from you this week, so come on."

* * *

There wasn't anything wrong with the apartment Purdy had rented for him. And Purdy and Gary and some of the others had gone out and bought him some things, so he was able to take a shower and dress in a clean suit. There was even some stoneware in the cabinets, a few groceries and a kettle, so he was able to brew himself some instant coffee before heading into the office to start the endless paperwork.

There was nothing wrong with any of it. He had to admit that the apartment was even nicer than the one that Michaelson had blasted. The guys knew his taste fairly well, so the clothes were fine.

But the apartment seemed empty—empty as hell.

It wasn't his apartment that was lacking, it was his life.

He sat back on the sofa and closed his eyes. What would he be doing now, he wondered, if he had come back to his life exactly as it had been?

He'd have played one of his discs while he showered and dressed, for one. And what else? Well, he'd have gone back into the office, and when he was done, he'd have gone out with the guys to celebrate the fact that the job was done. It was over. They'd have gone to a nightclub on the beach for a few drinks.

And there might have been a woman. Someone career-minded, pretty, flashy. Someone out to have a good time, with no strings. They'd have liked each other, sure. They'd have had a good time. They might have made breakfast in the morning. They might even have remembered each other's names.

But Brad wasn't going out that night—not even for a few beers with the guys. He was going to file his paperwork, and he was going to try to see Wendy.

Unfortunately, his plan was thwarted. When Brad reached his office, he discovered that Wendy was being questioned by the district attorney. When he reached the D.A.'s office, he found out that Wendy had already gone.

Amazed, Brad asked Gary, "That's it? She's gone?"

"Oh, well, they may need to call her in again before the trial. The attorneys will want to talk to her again, I'm sure—"

"No, no. I mean, she left? Just like that? Did she—" He hesitated, his pride tripping him up. "Did she leave me a message?"

Gary shook his head. Brad stared at him a long moment.

When Brad was interviewed by the D.A., he answered every question in a tired monotone. When he was done, he headed back to his office, initiated the extensive paperwork, and later returned to his empty apartment.

He drank a beer, then drank another beer. He picked up the phone, and then he remembered that Wendy didn't have a phone.

She hadn't left him a message. She hadn't even said goodbye. Hell, they were worth more than that.

He had another beer. And another. Around 3:00 a.m. he finally fell asleep whispering her name. He didn't know if it was a curse or an anguished plea.

There was one nice thing about living alone, Wendy thought: privacy.

For two days, she'd been able to mope around the house. She'd been able to indulge in ridiculous crying sprees and talk out loud, cursing Brad and railing against him. She'd spent long, pensive hours staring at the blank television screen, reminding herself that she did not want him anyway.

She couldn't live with his job, and she knew that it would be wrong to ask him to change it. Even if she did, he would eventually resent her for it. It just couldn't work.

And the wretched man hadn't even come to see her when she had spent all those miserable hours with the D.A.! She'd answered a million questions then they'd somberly reminded her how much they would need her testimony to put away Jenkins and Pedro. The district attorney had seemed concerned over her volatile emotional state. She couldn't explain that her unbidden tears had nothing to do with the case—but with the DEA investigator. Fortunately, Eric had accompanied her. He had assured them all that Wendy was far stronger than she appeared.

And so she waited. For the first few days, she waited. She was convinced that he would come to her. She dreamed that she would wake up to find him there, standing in the doorway, dressed in old jeans. He would walk across the room, bend down to her and take her in his arms. In her dreams, their clothing would miraculously disappear, and she would feel the hot fire of his flesh next to hers.

But then she would wake up—alone. Or else it would be worse—Baby would be sprawled out on the bed, and she would growl and hiss in annoyance when Wendy threw her out.

Wendy returned to work at Eric's, but she couldn't concentrate on her work. She didn't know that she was absolutely worthless until Eric came in one afternoon, pulled the book she was reading out of her hand and turned it right side up.

Eric sat across from her, folding his fingers in contemplative fashion, studying her for several moments. "Why don't you go in to Lauderdale and see him?" he suggested at last.

She shook her head. "If he wanted to see me, he would come here."

"That seems logical to you. What if he's thinking the same thing? That you'd come see him if you wanted to?"

"I was there and he wasn't!"

"He probably had a million things to do, Wendy. Be reasonable. I'll tell you what. I've got a dinner date with some old friends on Las Olas next Friday night. I'll drop you by Brad's, and if you're unhappy there, you can just come and join me."

"No."

"Why not?"

"It's not right. I mean, what for, anyway? He likes his life the way that it is. I can't really be a part of it."

He grinned at her and leaned forward, taking her hands. "Wendy, people change. They fall in love, and their priorities change."

"Who says he's in love?" she whispered.

Eric shrugged. "I do. As Willie says, life is a river. To live it, you must follow your heart."

"I'll let you know," she told him softly.

By the time Friday rolled around, she had summoned up some courage. She had spent the day in a tub of bubble bath, washed her hair, given herself a manicure and a pedicure and laid out a silk cocktail dress.

At four in the afternoon, she was practically whitewashed. But her hair was still soaking wet and she was pacing around in a worn, floor-length terry robe, trying not to chew her nails while she thought it over.

She was confused about her purpose. What was she going to say? Can we hop into bed one more time, Brad, for old time's sake? Hi, Brad, I was in the neighborhood, so I just stopped over?

What if he had a woman there?

Her courage was beginning to fade when she heard the sound of a motor. She was surprised to see that it was Eric. They weren't due to leave for the evening until about seven, and he was supposed to be driving over. She opened the front door and saw her brother-in-law walking toward her with a packet of mail. "I picked this up at the post office," he said, handing her the mail. "And I just wanted to check on tonight. We still on?"

"I don't know, Eric—" Wendy began.

"I'll be back in a couple of hours." He waved to her and hurried away. She thought about calling him back to tell him that it was definitely off.

She didn't. Maybe she would just go to dinner with Eric and his friends. It might be good to get out.

Wandering into the bathroom, she examined her pale face and wet hair and decided that for a woman who had spent the entire day trying to look and smell delicious, she'd failed miserably.

Then she wandered back into the kitchen, idly leafing through the mail. She found the usual assortment of bills and junk mail, then her heart began to pound when she saw that one of the letters addressed to her was from Brad's office.

The bills fell to the floor as she ripped open the official-looking letter.

After she had opened it, she read it over and over. Then she felt as if she were a kettle, that heat was rising inside of her and she was fast approaching a boiling point.

It was a thank-you from the department. An official thank-you for her part in accommodating the agent.

It was meant from the heart, she was sure. But it was all so formal, so final.

"There are definite advantages to living alone!" she screamed in fury, throwing the letter down and stamping on it. Still, she didn't feel any better.

"That son of a bitch!" she swore, pacing up and down the hallway. She stormed into her bedroom, threw herself on her bed and slammed her fist against her pillow.

Then she realized, very slowly, that she wasn't alone. She swung around.

He was there, just as he had been in her dreams. Well, he was dressed in a blue business suit, but he was standing in the doorway, staring at her.

He looked good—damned good. He was handsome in navy. His white shirt was tailored and crisp, and he even had good taste in ties. His hair was combed back. His eyes appeared a little more haggard, his face a bit leaner.

But he was standing in front of her.

Automatically, her fingers moved to her wet hair. She'd planned this out so well! She'd meant to come to him in complete control, svelte and sophisticated, armed and armored against any vulnerability.

But he had come to her when she looked about as sophisticated as Tinkerbell. Her temper soared again. Wendy sprang to her knees, and then to her feet.

"You bastard!" she hissed.

"I—uh—I did knock. You didn't hear me."

"I didn't hear you?" She began to advance on him. "I let you in, I turn my home, my life, inside out. I get kidnapped by dope dealers. And do I get anything from you? Like maybe, goodbye, Wendy, thanks, it's been sweet? No!" She slammed both her fists against his chest. "No! I get a thank-you from the department for accommodating you!"

"Wendy—"

"I hate you! I absolutely despise you. You're a ruthless ingrate!" She took a swing at him. He ducked and caught her arms, imprisoning her against his body.

"Wendy—"

She struggled against him in a frenzy. "You weren't even there! I came into that office and I was a wonderful, model citizen, and you weren't even there!"

"Wendy—"

"You can go and rot in hell, Brad McKenna!"

He scooped her off the floor. Automatically, she looped her arms around his neck and stared into his eyes.

He started walking toward the bed. "I tried to see you," Brad said.

Her heart seemed aflame, her flesh seemed aflame. He was touching her, holding her again. He was walking straight toward the bed.

He laid her down. Gently tugging on the cord to her robe, he watched as it fell open. He caught his breath at the naked length of her. She saw the pulse start up against the bronze flesh at his throat. He laid his face against her and kissed her belly. She slipped her fingers into his hair.

"I was coming to see you tonight. I had it all planned out. I was going to wear silk. I was going to be beautiful."

"You are beautiful," he whispered huskily against her flesh. "Beautiful."

"You are a horrible, inconsiderate bastard, and I hate you," Wendy breathed. She could feel his lips, just grazing her skin.

He straightened and looked into her eyes. "Will you marry me, Wendy?"

Her eyes widened. "What?"

He loosened his tie. "I've thought about it. I know the way that you feel, but I think that we can come to some compromises. Life means much more to me now. I never knew how much it could mean until I found out what it was like to share. I love you, Wendy. I can't change what I am, my convictions, or the way that I feel, but I love you. I think that you love me, too. I've sat home these weeks staring at empty walls. I wanted you so badly. I thought that maybe you could forgive me for what I was. I thought that you would call me—"

"You didn't call me!" Wendy protested.

"You don't have a phone," Brad reminded her. "That's one thing that we're going to fix."

"What?" she said carefully. "We're going to live—here?"

"Well, it will take me at least an hour to get to work in the morning. But I figured that when I was working in Manhattan, my commute on the trains took me an hour, too. I'll still be with the DEA, but I'm through with the fieldwork. I want to come home at night—to come home here, to spend every night with you. We'll live here. With a phone."

"With a phone," Wendy repeated.

Brad's tie fell to the floor. His jacket, vest and shirt followed, but Wendy was still just staring at him, dumbfounded.

When he kicked off his shoes and trousers, she trembled and shuddered, alive with anticipation from head to toe. He stretched out over her and took her lips, kissing her slowly, savoring her lower lip, playing with her tongue. His left hand caressed the fullness of her curves, dallying over her breasts and between her legs. She was breathless when he pulled away from her, seeking her eyes. "Well?" he whispered.

"What?" Her mind wandered. What was he talking about? She returned his kiss so ardently and touched him with such fervor. He couldn't begin to think that she would deny him—not at this point.

Slow down, she warned herself. She smiled sweetly, trying to ignore the spiraling need inside of her. She drew her fingers down his chest and tightened them evocatively about the aroused shaft of his desire.

"Well? What's the verdict?" He kissed her lips, nuzzling his clean-shaven cheek against her throat. Then he met her eyes again. "Will you marry me?"

"Yes! Yes, I will!"

"Good." Brad smiled complacently. Then he lowered his weight upon her and thrust deeply inside of her. Deeper, and deeper, and then he held still. "I missed you so much," he whispered. "I can't leave you again. I really can't."

Wendy wound her arms around him. "I love you." She swallowed, savoring the feel of him. "I love you, and I don't think that I could ever let you go again."

Brad murmured something else, but she couldn't decipher his words. As he began to stroke her, hard and fast, the words just didn't matter anymore....

* * *

They were still lying there, drowsy and half-asleep—
having made love several times to make up for lost
time—when Wendy heard the motor of the airboat.

"Oh, dear!" She tried to leap up; some weight
stopped her. Baby! The cat had come in when they had
drifted off and made herself very comfortable, despite
the two humans in the bed. "Baby, get off!"

"Out!" Brad commanded. Baby growled at him. He
gave her a shove. "Off, I said!"

Baby obeyed. Wendy laughed, struggling back into
her robe. "That's Eric," she told Brad. He arched a
curious brow, lacing his fingers behind his head and
stretching out comfortably. "Hey!" She shoved him.
"You get up, too!"

He laughed and stepped into his trousers. "He's
going to know exactly what we've been doing," Wendy
wailed.

Brad laughed. "And what did he think he was
bringing you into the city to do?"

"To go respectably out to dinner!" Wendy lied indignantly. Brad just laughed and walked into the living room. By the time Wendy belted her robe, she
could hear the two men talking to one another. Guilt-
ily straightening her tousled hair, she joined them. Brad
swept her into the circle of his arm.

"He says that he'd be honored to be an usher at our
wedding. He's sure that Willie will be delighted to give
you away, and that maybe he'll break down and get a
phone when we do, too."

Wendy burst out laughing. Eric laughed and kissed
her.

"I told you, Wendy," he whispered, "we are all
fated to follow our hearts." He gave her a squeeze.
"Hey, have you got any champagne in here?"

Wendy did. It was warm, but they plopped a few ice cubes into it, and Eric toasted them.

Two months later, in the Church of the Little Flower, Willie did give her away. She wore a dress of soft gray, which highlighted the silver in her eyes.

Later, Brad told her that she was the most beautiful bride he had ever seen.

"Really?" she asked him. He had just been telling her how much he loved her gown, but that didn't seem to stop him from being overly anxious to remove it.

"Really."

"I'm so glad we were married."

"So am I," Brad said absently. There were a million little tiny hooks on the gown, and she wasn't helping him one bit.

"'Cause I think we're going to have a beautiful little newcomer," Wendy said demurely.

"That's nice," Brad murmured, annoyed by the maze of hooks on the damned dress.

Suddenly his fingers went still as he turned her toward him. "What?"

"Well, it could be a tawny-haired little visitor with golden eyes." Her voice trembled suddenly. "Do you mind?"

"Do I mind?" He could barely whisper. "I—I—no!"

He couldn't seem to find the proper words to tell her that he loved her, and that he was thrilled and awed by the prospect of a child—their child.

So he leaned over and kissed her, and showed her instead.

* * * * *

COMING
NEXT MONTH

#249 FROM GLOWING EMBERS—Emilie Richards

Years ago Julianna had been a poor girl from the wrong side of the
tracks who had loved—and married—Gray Sheridan, the richest kid
in town. Their life together hadn't worked, but when they met again
they were different people except for one thing—the love they
shared.

#250 THE SILVER SWAN—Andrea Parnell

Regina Lawton needed a holiday. Too many strange people had
been appearing in her life recently: prowlers, detectives and a
mysterious man named Pierce Buchannan. But once she got to her
vacation paradise, she found Pierce waiting for her—posing a very
potent danger to her heart.

#251 SUSPICIOUS MINDS—Paula Detmer Riggs

Naval investigator Roarke McKinley had trusted a woman once,
and it had almost cost him his life. Never again, he vowed—and
then he met Juliet Prentice. Though she was a suspected spy, his
resolve weakened. How could he serve his country if it meant
betraying the woman he loved?

#252 BETTER THAN EVER—
Marion Smith Collins

Ryan O'Hara had never brought Bree Fleming anything but trouble.
It was just too frightening to fall in love with a cop. This time it
wasn't love that brought them together, it was business, but Bree
found herself losing her heart all over again.

AVAILABLE THIS MONTH:

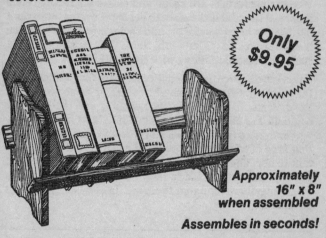

Silhouette Intimate Moments

At Dodd Memorial Hospital, Love is the Best Medicine

When temperatures are rising and pulses are racing, Dodd Memorial Hospital is the place to be. Every doctor, nurse and patient is a heart specialist, and their favorite prescription is a little romance. This month, finish Lucy Hamilton's Dodd Memorial Hospital Trilogy with HEARTBEATS, IM #245.

Nurse Vanessa Rice thought police sergeant Clay Williams was the most annoying man she knew. Then he showed up at Dodd Memorial with a gunshot wound, and the least she could do was be friends with him—if he'd let her. But Clay was interested in something more, and Vanessa didn't want that kind of commitment. She had a career that was important to her, and there was no room in her life for any man. But Clay was determined to show her that they could have a future together—and that there are times when the patient knows best.
